# HOPE
# NAVARRE

—

## A Ranch for His Family

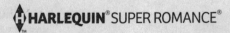

HARLEQUIN® SUPER ROMANCE®

Recycling programs
for this product may
not exist in your area.

ISBN-13: 978-0-373-60821-8

A RANCH FOR HIS FAMILY

Copyright © 2014 by Patricia MacDonald

**Printed in U.S.A.**

# "Underneath that bad haircut, I was the same girl."

Robyn paused and eyed him thoughtfully. "And underneath that eye patch, you are the same man."

Neal was silent for a long time as he stared at the green canopy overhead. The branches swayed and dipped in the hot, dry breeze. A single leaf fluttered down, and his gaze followed it as it landed like a tiny boat on the surface of the pond. "I wonder if that's true," he said at last.

Robyn cupped his cheek with her hand and turned his face toward her. "I know it's true," she insisted gently.

She was so close. He could feel the warmth of her beside him. The wind lifted the ends of her drying hair and let it curl softly at the edge of her face. God, he had missed her. Only she could make him feel whole again.

He captured the hand on his cheek and pressed a kiss against her soft palm. She didn't pull away. He saw her eyes widen and her lips part with surprise. He pulled her toward him until those lips touched his.

Dear Reader,

I hope you enjoy *A Ranch for His Family*. Neal Bryant, the hero of this book, is the only character that has popped full-blown and whole into my head while I was writing. Granted, he showed up when I was trying to write his brother's story, but Neal has a way of making women do what he wants without really trying, so the story became Neal's story. What can I say? I'm a pushover for a sexy cowboy.

Robyn, the only woman who can manage Neal, was much harder to create. She had to be tough, and she had to be able to put him in his place when he needed it, but she also had to understand what made him tick. I think I have succeeded in making a well-matched hero and heroine, but you get to be the judge of that.

The setting for this book was a no-brainer. I grew up on the western edge of the beautiful Flint Hills of Kansas and I have been in love with that grassy, windswept prairie since before I was old enough to know that cowboys are sexy. I hope my love of the people and the land comes through in these pages. It's a special place. With a lot of sexy cowboys!

Enjoy the story and feel free to let me know what you thought of it. You can visit me on the web at www.hopenavarre.com.

All the best,

Hope Navarre

# ABOUT THE AUTHOR

Hope Navarre grew up surrounded by brothers, horses and cattle among the rolling hills of central Kansas. She fell in love with reading and with books at a young age. Cowboys have always been her favorite heroes. Westerns by Zane Grey and Louis L'Amour, as well as the adventures of girl detective Trixie Belden, filled the hours when Hope wasn't riding her horses, playing softball or fishing down at the creek.

The urge to write a story of her own first appeared when she was in high school. The star-crossed lovers of her first unfinished novel remain trapped forever in the crumbling ruins of a church in war-torn Europe, but at least they are together. College, a career in nursing, marriage and motherhood put Hope's dreams of one day writing a book on the back burner of her life until the late 1990s. With her family grown, she decided she had time to write a book. At that point, there was no holding her back. She became a member of a local writer's group, joined the national writing organization Romance Writers of America and set out to learn as much as she could about the business of writing.

Today, Hope enjoys setting her books in her beloved Kansas and the scenic Flint Hills, where cowboys, horses and cattle remain a part of everyday life. You can visit her on the web at www.hopenavarre.com.

This book is dedicated to my wonderful agent, Pam Hopkins.

Thanks for holding my hand all these years and for helping me find a home for my stories.

# *CHAPTER ONE*

"OH! THAT'S COMING off a bull the hard way, folks, and that'll mean no score for this young cowboy."

Neal Bryant paid scant attention to the rodeo announcer and none to the disappointed cowboy dusting himself off in front of the rodeo chutes. Instead, Neal scanned the packed bleachers rising behind the white pole fence hung with banners for Wranglers, Resistol Hats and Justin Boots, searching for one face in the milling, colorful crowd from his hometown. A face that haunted his dreams—the face of Robyn O'Connor.

It would be five years, and he still couldn't get her out of his mind. The ache of missing her, of knowing he'd thrown away the best thing in his life, never left him.

Would Robyn's dark hair still be short? Or would she have grown it long again? He liked it best when she had it long. He remembered the way it felt in his fingers. How he could wrap his hands in it and pull her close. He loved the way it would spill like silk across his chest when they made love.

He'd heard from his mother that Robyn had married not long after she'd left him, but that she was single again. He should be glad about that, but he wasn't. He wanted Robyn to be happy.

His mother and Robyn's mother were neighbors and best friends. He could've made a point of keeping track of her, but he'd chosen not to. On his infrequent visits home, her name was off-limits as far as he was concerned. Robyn's life was her own now. She'd made it plain that there was no place for him in it.

He gave up looking for Robyn in the crowd. It was a stupid move coming back. He hadn't been to a rodeo in Bluff Springs in years. He wasn't sure why he was here now.

Maybe she didn't come to the rodeos anymore. After rolling down the sleeves of his blue-and-white-striped shirt, he fastened the snaps and then drew on his rosin-darkened leather glove. One thing Neal knew for certain, she wouldn't come to this rodeo if she knew he was riding.

He gave his attention back to the rodeo. The smell of dust, livestock and popcorn filled the evening air as the carnival music from the midway spilled over the arena. Another bull and rider burst from the chute beside him and began their awesome dance across the churned dirt of the arena floor. The crowd cheered wildly when the horn sounded. One of his competitors had lasted the full eight.

The announcer's voice blared over the PA system again. "The judges' score is eighty-five. A great ride, ladies and gentlemen. And now we have a last-minute entry, but one I know you'll enjoy. In chute number three, a native son of these Flint Hills and currently number one in the national standings—let's hear it for Neal Bryant, looking for eight on board Dust Devil."

A roar of cheering and applause erupted. Tipping his hat to the crowd from the top rail of the bucking chute, Neal scanned the bleachers one last time. If she was out there, he didn't see her. Biting back his disappointment, he turned his attention to the bull coming through the stock gate.

The announcer's voice droned on. "A two-time runner-up at the National Finals Rodeo…"

Those words penetrated Neal's concentration, and his jaw clenched in annoyance. Two-time runner-up was just another way of saying two-time loser. He hated losing.

This year was going to be different. He knew it in his bones. This was his year. He'd given up everything to make it to the top of his sport. Failure wasn't an option.

As he glanced out over the stands once more, he relaxed. He'd ridden his first calf in this Bluff Springs, Kansas, arena when he was eight years old. He'd won that Little Britches go-round, and like his father before him, rodeo had gotten into his blood.

The people there were friends, neighbors and some of his biggest fans. They deserved to see a damn fine ride, and he was going to give them one.

Maybe, just maybe, the one person he wanted to see would be watching.

Neal handed his cowboy hat to one of the men working the chutes and pulled on his helmet with the attached face mask. He lowered himself into the chute. His rigging was quickly pulled tightly around the bull's massive torso, and then the bull rope was laid snugly over the palm of his buck-skin glove. Wrapping it once around the back of his hand, he laid it across his palm again and then pounded the fingers of his rosined glove down on the braided leather until he was satisfied with his grip.

The bull moved restlessly below him. The bell on the bottom of the rope clanged loudly when Dust Devil slammed his head against the gate. He was itching to get the rider off his back, and he knew which way was out.

"Old Devil here, he likes to spin to the left," the rodeo clown said from outside the gate.

Neal recognized the man's voice. It was Kent Daley, an experienced bullfighter. Kent had saved the hide of more than one unlucky rider, including Neal. They had traveled the same rodeo circuit for years.

"I see you're still playing with your wife's makeup, Kent. Aren't you getting a little long in the tooth for this business?"

"I'll give it up the day a bull's hot breath on my butt doesn't make me run fast."

"Just keep this one off mine, okay?"

"Devil likes to spin tight. When you come off, get out of his way. He loves to stomp on folks. He's got a mean streak a mile wide."

"What makes you think I'm gonna come off?"

"Cocky, ain't ya?"

"Getting bucked off is so undignified."

"Well, when you dismount, you should remove yourself from this bovine's vicinity with all haste."

"That's the plan. Thanks."

Neal adjusted his weight until he was satisfied with his seat. He knew this bull. He'd ridden him twice before, but he had only stayed on for the full eight seconds one time. He couldn't have hoped for a better draw, since both the bull and the rider were judged during the event. The harder a bull bucked, the higher the score his rider earned.

Dust Devil liked to take three or four big leaping bucks straight down the arena before he started into the tight spin that had earned him his name. The high jumps earned more points. A rider couldn't win with a lazy bull under him.

"Okay, boys." Neal was ready. He raised his hand and nodded. The gate flew open, and the massive gray bull exploded into the arena with a powerful lunge.

The bull leaped again, thrashing in midair as he tried to shake his rider. When he made a third lunge, Neal's lips drew back in a savage smile. He had this one.

Adrenaline pumped through his body. The roaring crowd was nothing but a colorful blur at the edge of his vision as he concentrated on the animal beneath him. Devil's massive head swung sharply to the left, and Neal shifted his weight when the bull started into his spin. He was going to ride him for sure this time. Suddenly, Dust Devil stumbled. The mammoth animal lost his footing and crashed to his knees.

Catapulted forward, Neal flew over his riding hand, twisting it tighter in the rope. Devil lurched to his feet with Neal dangling helplessly against his side.

Neal struggled to free his hand as the bull continued to buck and thrash, tossing him like a rag doll. Kent Daley darted in and began trying to loosen the bull rope. Kent's partner dodged back and forth in front of the bull, taunting the animal to keep him from turning back on Kent as he worked. At last, Neal's rigging slipped loose.

He fell into the dirt beneath Devil's hooves. He tried to roll aside. A crushing blow to his ribs forced the air from his lungs as one of Dust Devil's hooves drove up under the edge of his protective vest. Neal curled into a ball of agony. He couldn't breathe.

Kent dropped down beside him. "Are you hurt?"

"I can make it," Neal gasped. He pulled his helmet off to get more air. It didn't help.

Devil ran the second clown into the safety of the padded barrel. With a furious blow of his head, the bull sent the barrel flying. Then he turned back to the men crouched on the arena floor.

"Get me out of here," Neal managed through clenched teeth. Dagger-sharp pain lanced through his side. He tasted blood in his mouth. Grabbing his helmet lying in the dirt beside him, he suppressed a groan as Kent shouldered him to his feet and half dragged, half carried him toward the fence. Neal couldn't make his legs work right.

Safety loomed only a few steps away when Dust Devil bore down on them again. After letting go of Neal, Kent turned to lure the bull away. His brightly colored, baggy clothing made him a more inviting target. Neal staggered two more steps. With one hand on the fence, he glanced back to see Kent get hooked and tossed high into the air. He landed facedown in the dirt and lay still. Dust Devil whirled back for the fallen clown.

Other men and riders were racing toward them, but no one was as close as Neal was. He turned away from the fence and limped toward the crumpled figure on the arena floor. Neal drew the bull's attention by yelling and waving his arm. The massive animal hesitated for an instant, and then charged the fallen man.

Neal threw his helmet. It hit the bull square in the face. Enraged, Dust Devil changed direction and charged him.

Neal took a step backward, turned and tried for the fence. He stumbled and fell to his hands and knees. As he glanced over his shoulder, he had a split second to wonder if he was going to die, and if Robyn would care. Then the world exploded in a brilliant, bloodred flash of pain, followed mercifully by darkness.

ROBYN MORGAN CROSSED the nearly empty hospital parking lot and inserted her key in her car door. She paused and raised her head to listen. The distant sound of a siren broke the quiet of the balmy June night. She recognized the distinctive wail of the county ambulance.

*Drat!* If she'd only been a minute faster getting into her car, she wouldn't have heard it. Or, she admitted with a wry smile, if she hadn't spent the past twenty minutes pouring over the application form for a nurse-practitioner scholarship her supervisor had given her. Twenty minutes of pure wishful thinking.

She couldn't get over the shock of it. The accompanying letter stated that she had been recommended for a full private scholarship at the University of Colorado. The scholarships would be awarded to four candidates chosen from the names put forth by physicians practicing family medicine in Kansas, Colorado and Nebraska. The deadline for returning the application was September 1.

She had no idea who'd submitted her name, but it was flattering to know her expertise had been noted, especially since the school was one of the best in the country. But, like the carrot on a string in front of a donkey, the promise of a chance at professional advancement and a better salary dangled just out of her reach.

She couldn't go back to school now, not with the trouble she and her mother were having with the ranch. It was tough making ends meet, and the gap widened every month. Her mom couldn't do it alone. Robyn knew there would be expenses in going to school out of state that even a full scholarship wouldn't cover.

Yet it was an opportunity she might never have

again. There had to be some way she could make it work. She racked her tired brain for a solution but came up blank. No, she was only kidding herself. The offer was tempting in the extreme, but the timing couldn't have been worse.

Meanwhile, was she going to stay late and help with whatever the ambulance was bringing, or was she going home? She battled with her conscience as she stood in the parking lot. Her shift was over. She'd given report to the night nurse. She could go home. She should go home.

Biting her lip, she listened to the siren's wail growing louder.

Someone else could handle the crisis for once. She was tired. She didn't feel like rushing in to save the day.

But her mother would have put Chance to bed hours ago. He wouldn't know his mother hadn't come home on time. The night-shift nurse, Jane Rawlings, was a good nurse, but she was young and inexperienced. What if it was something Jane couldn't handle?

Robyn's shoulders slumped in defeat. Once again, her overblown sense of responsibility won out. After pulling her keys from the car door, she threw them in her purse and hurried back through the hospital door. The look of relief on Jane's face said she'd made the right decision.

"Thank goodness. I thought you'd gone."

Robyn dropped her purse in a drawer behind the emergency room desk. "I should have been. One of these days, I'm going to put my own life before this job. I swear I am."

"Right. That'll happen about twenty-four hours after you're dead." The skeptical comment came from Dr. Adam Cain as he strode in.

He rubbed the sleep from his eyes and then raked his fingers through his thick blond hair. "What's coming?"

Jane read from the notes she had taken when the call came in. "A bull rider has been injured over at the rodeo. The paramedics say the guy's in bad shape. They're suggesting we call for an airlift." She read off his vital signs, as well.

Dr. Cain nodded. "All right, alert Kansas City General's team that we are going to need them. It will take a little while to get the chopper ready."

Startled, Robyn asked, "You're going to call an air ambulance transfer without seeing the patient first?"

"I'm been moonlighting in this one-horse town long enough to know that your paramedics know their stuff. If they think this guy needs an airlift, I'm sure he does. Every second counts this far from a trauma center. If he looks like something we can handle, we'll cancel the transport."

Jane chuckled. "You'd better count again, Doc. We've got more than one horse in Bluff Springs."

He grinned. "I stand corrected. In this two-hundred-and-fifty-horse town."

Robyn smiled at him. "That's more like it. When you first came here, I had my doubts about you. But I think you'll make a decent country doctor after all."

"Coming from a nurse like you, that's high praise, indeed." Returning her smile, he pulled off his white lab coat and draped it over the desk.

A blush heated her cheeks. She quickly turned away. Now wasn't the time to let her growing attraction for this man get in the way. They worked well together. That was all. She shouldn't read anything into his friendliness. Every unmarried nurse in the hospital, and half of the married ones, had a crush on the handsome resident who worked weekends in their small town. She didn't intend to add herself to the list.

He glanced at the clock. "Does your husband mind you working late? Or is he used to it?"

"She isn't married," Jane piped up. Robyn shot her a quick frown, but Jane only grinned and winked. A newlywed herself, Jane made no secret of the fact she thought Robyn should be dating again.

"You're not married?" His tone was puzzled. He glanced at her hand. "You wear a ring."

"My husband passed away four years ago," Robyn said quietly.

"I'm sorry." His voice held true compassion. She liked that about him.

"Thank you." Even after so many years, she still found it difficult to talk about Colin.

She quickly moved the conversation back to the task at hand. "I'll check the IV supplies and make sure we have everything. Jane, you get started on the paperwork."

When the ambulance backed up to the doors, they were ready and waiting for it.

"What do we have, gentlemen?" Dr. Cain grabbed the foot of the gurney. He guided it inside the doors and into the nearest room. Thick, blood-soaked bandages covered most of the patient's face. A wide foam-and-plastic collar held his head and neck immobile. The front of his blue-and-white-striped shirt was covered with blood—a lot of blood. Robyn grasped his wrist to check his pulse.

The paramedic held an IV bag high in one hand. "White male, early thirties. He took a horn to the face. He has severe lacerations to the left cheek and eye. Looks bad for his eye, Doc. He was trampled, too. Labored breathing, concave left lower chest, no breath sounds on that side."

"Fractured ribs, probably a punctured lung. Stupidest sport ever invented." Dr. Cain snatched his stethoscope from around his neck, pulled back the patient's shirt and listened.

Looping his stethoscope over his neck again, he said tersely, "Jane, get me a chest-tube tray. Crank up his oxygen to 15 liters. Let me hear some vital signs, people."

Robyn was already gathering the information he wanted. She used the blood-pressure cuff the ambulance crew had wrapped around his arm. She took a reading and said, "BP is ninety over fifty. Pulse ninety, weak and thready, respiration's thirty-eight and labored."

Dr. Cain peeled back the dressings on the man's face and frowned. "You're right. I doubt we can save his eye. Keep a moist sterile dressing on this. We'll let the surgeons in Kansas City sort it out."

Jane wheeled a metal stand up beside them and pulled the wrappings off a sterile pack. "Here's the chest-tube tray."

"We need X-rays of his skull, neck, chest and abdomen." Dr. Cain snapped out orders. "Get lab and X-ray in here now! I want a blood gas, a complete blood count and I want him typed and cross matched for a blood transfusion. Do we have a name?"

The two paramedics didn't answer. Robyn raised the phone to her ear and punched in the number for X-ray, but she felt the men's gazes on her. She turned toward them.

"It's Neal Bryant," one of them said.

The room grew dark at the edges of Robyn's

vision and seemed to tilt. The phone fell from her nerveless fingers and clattered to the floor. She groped behind her for the wall.

*Dear God, it can't be!* She stared at the still, blood-soaked figure in stunned disbelief.

"Robyn? Robyn, who is he to you?" Dr. Cain's voice seemed to come from a long way away.

"Nobody," she whispered, wishing it were true.

"They were engaged once," Jane said, then picked up the phone and spoke quickly. "Portable X-ray in E.R., stat."

For a long, painful moment, Robyn's heart seemed to freeze. Then it began to pound wildly inside her chest. She couldn't get enough air. She drew in one deep breath, then another, and slowly her vision began to clear. "It was a long time ago."

"Well, he's going to be a dead nobody if we don't get this chest tube in. Help or get out of the way." Dr. Cain's voice was harsh as he began to swab Neal's chest with antiseptic.

"What?" She looked at him in confusion.

"You heard me. Help, or get out of here. I need a nurse, not a jilted sweetheart. Someone start another IV line, and get this shirt out of my way."

"Of course, I'm sorry." Robyn picked up a pair of scissors. Her hands trembled, but she managed to cut away the bloody fabric from Neal's chest.

Neal flinched and moaned when the chest tube went in, and she grabbed the hand he raised.

"Neal, can you hear me? You're in the hospital. You're going to be okay."

God she hoped that was true. His hand tightened on hers, and he tried to speak. She bent close to hear his voice, which was muffled by the oxygen mask. "Robyn?"

"Yes, Neal, it's me. You're going to be okay."

His grip tightened. "I'm sorry," he rasped. "Want you…to know…" His voice trailed away, and his hand fell limp.

"How soon on that Air-Life flight?" Dr. Cain's question spurred her back into action. She wrapped a tourniquet around Neal's muscular forearm and began to prep for another IV line.

"Twenty minutes," Jane said.

"Type and cross for two units. We've got a lot of blood coming out of this chest tube. Get a unit of O neg. in as fast as you can. Do you have that IV yet?"

"Yes." Robyn slid the needle into place and taped it.

"Start Ringer's lactate wide-open, and Robyn?"

"Yes?"

"Good job."

She nodded. "I'd better notify his family."

"Let Jane do it. I need you." He held out a gloved hand and said, "Suture."

Somehow Robyn managed to keep working, but she couldn't stop glancing at the clock. Time seemed to move in slow motion. Where was the transport crew? How much longer before they arrived? She listened to each rattling breath Neal took and prayed he would keep breathing. The nurse in her kept functioning, snipping sutures, checking vital signs, starting blood, while another part of her watched the whole scene with a sense of disbelief.

It was the nightmare scene she had always feared when they were together.

She wasn't surprised Neal had been seriously injured. He was a world-class bull rider. He risked injury, even death, a hundred times each year. That was part of the reason she'd walked away from him five years ago. A small part.

What did surprise her was how much she still cared.

At last the outside doors slid open and the transport crew rushed in. Dressed in blue-and-white jumpsuits and carrying large red-and-white cases, they set up on the scene with practiced ease. It was a relief to step out of the way and let them take over. Within minutes, Neal had been assessed and was loaded onto their stretcher. He was quickly wheeled out the door, across the parking lot and up to the waiting helicopter.

Neal's mother's white Buick Regal tore into the lot as he was being lifted aboard. Ellie Bryant jumped out of her car and raced toward the chopper. The crew let her in beside him as Dr. Cain and Robyn hurried toward her. Leaning in the chopper, Ellie spoke to her son and kissed him before the crew urged her aside.

Robyn took Ellie by the shoulders and pulled her away. Covering their faces with their arms, the two women huddled together as the chopper rose into the air and clung to each other until the sound of it faded away.

Ellie used both hands to wipe the tears from her cheeks. "I've always been afraid of this. At least he was close to home and not a thousand miles away."

Turning to Robyn, she asked, "Will he live?"

"He's getting the best care possible, but it is bad."

Dr. Cain came up and rested a hand on Ellie's shoulder as he spoke. "Do you have someone who can drive you to Kansas City tonight? I think you should go as quickly as possible."

"My oldest son and his wife are in Dallas. I'm fine to go by myself."

"I'll go with you," Robyn surprised herself by offering.

"Are you sure?" Ellie asked.

"Yes, I'm sure. You shouldn't drive all that way alone. Let me call Mom and make some arrangements for Chance."

Robyn rushed back inside to make the call. She

couldn't rest until she knew that Neal would live.
If he didn't, she'd never have the chance to tell
him he had a son.

## CHAPTER TWO

ROBYN AND ELLIE sat quietly beside Neal's bed in the ICU on their third day of vigil. He still hadn't roused. Sunshine poured through the window and painted a bright band of light across the white sheets. Outside, the blue sky promised another hot summer day.

His mother rose and closed the curtain against the brightness. She pressed both hands to the small of her back and stretched. Turning to Robyn, she said, "I'm going to step out and get a bite. Do you want anything?"

"No, thanks." She didn't have much of an appetite.

"I swear the smell in this hospital makes me sick. I think I'll run across the street to McDonald's."

Robyn smiled. She found the faint antiseptic smell comforting and familiar. "You don't fool me. You just like their French fries better than the ones in the cafeteria."

"I'm a sucker for a Big Mac, too. I won't be gone long."

"Take your time. His vital signs are stable. I know you could use the break."

"Is there any way to tell how much longer he'll be unconscious?"

"Not really." The doctors had placed him in a medical comma to monitor the swelling in his brain. They had stopped his sedation that morning. He should have been awake by now. Robyn didn't want to worry his mother any more than she had to.

Ellie stopped beside her and laid a hand on her shoulder. "Thanks for staying with me, honey. Jake and Connie are flying in tonight. They will be able to spell me so you can go home. I know you miss Chance."

"I do. I've never been away from him for this long."

"I used to think that you would be my daughter-in-law one day. I never gave up hoping my hard-headed youngest would realize his mistake and come settle down with you."

Robyn covered Ellie's hand with her own. She avoided looking at the older woman. "Neal and I were kids when we were head over heels for each other. We mistook infatuation for love. It wasn't meant to be."

While her statement wasn't a complete lie, it wasn't the truth, either. She had been deeply in love with Neal, but he hadn't loved her in return.

"Well, a body can still hope," Ellie declared and then left the room.

Neal moaned softly. Robyn leaned forward to brush back a dark brown curl and laid her hand lightly on his forehead. His skin was warm to the touch but not feverish. His color was sickly pale under his deep tan. A thick bandage covered the left side of his face.

She moved her hand and laid it over his where it rested on the bed at his side. A gentle smile touched her lips as she remembered a time when they had measured their hands against each other's. His fingers were long, straight and calloused. Her little finger curved outward, and he had laughed as he'd teased her about that.

They had laughed about so much when they were young. Her smile faded. Tears stung her eyes, but she refused to let them fall. She couldn't remember a time when she hadn't been in love with him.

In grade school, she had followed him around like a faithful puppy. Having grown up as neighbors, they were inseparable friends. It didn't matter to Neal that she was a girl. She could ride and rope as good as any boy.

In high school, they'd begun to rodeo together as a team roping pair. During Neal's senior year, their friendship had evolved into a tender teenage love affair. When he'd graduated the year before her, she'd worried constantly that he might meet someone else at college. It was during that time that he had given up roping and began riding bulls.

She'd hated it. She had known what could happen. Not long after that, he'd quit school and begun traveling the pro rodeo circuit. His father had been furious.

She had tried to wait patiently for Neal's infrequent visits home, but in the end, she'd simply had to follow him. She'd moved into his tiny camper and set up house. Being with him had been wonderful and terrifying at the same time. She had hated watching him put himself in danger. They'd had some fine arguments about it, but he wouldn't quit. She had tried not to let her fear and worry show. He'd loved riding, and she'd loved him. She'd been happy in spite of the rough life and hardships of being on the circuit because she'd known his heart belonged to her. All she could do was pray that he survived.

During the long months of traveling and living out of a secondhand camper, she'd dreamed of the day when they would leave the rodeo behind, settle down outside Bluff Springs and raise a family on the ranch where she'd grown up.

Then one day, she had learned a painful truth. No one woman owned his heart. Her dreams had withered and died in that instant.

Robyn sighed and let her head fall back against the chair cushion. That heartbreak belonged in the past. She had moved on with her life. A lot of things hadn't worked out the way she'd expected them to. The ranch she had grown up on was failing now that her father was gone. If something didn't change soon, they would have to sell. She hated the idea. She had dreamed that one day her son would raise his children there.

She had expected to marry her childhood sweetheart and live happily ever after, but Neal had broken her heart, and she'd left him. When she had discovered she had a reason to go back, her pride had kept her away and driven her to make a choice that had changed the course of her life and many others.

She gazed at Neal's pale, still face. He would never know what that decision had cost both of them.

The small voice of her conscience whispered that she was wrong to keep her secret. What if Neal had died without knowing he had a son? Could she live with that?

She glanced at the wedding band she wore on her left hand. She had promised her husband, as he lay dying in a hospital bed very much like this one, that she would never reveal Chance wasn't his child.

Closing her eyes, she whispered, "Were we wrong, Colin?"

She had been young, deeply hurt and bitter when she'd left Neal. She hadn't discovered until weeks later that she was pregnant. Neal had never wanted children. She had refused to use a child to force him back into a relationship that he clearly didn't want with her. She had let him have the freedom he craved. Not a day went by that she didn't question her choice.

There was no going back, no way to undo the past. Right or wrong, she'd kept her secret.

Weariness crept into her bones. She closed her eyes to rest them. She must have fallen asleep, because she jerked awake sometime later when a hoarse voice whispered, "Where am I?"

She sat up and brushed the hair out of her eyes. "Hey, cowboy. It's about time you woke up."

"Me? You're the one snoring." His voice was weak, but she was so glad to hear it.

She smiled softly. "How rude of me. Do you know where you are?"

"A torture chamber?"

"Close. A hospital in Kansas City. Would you like some water?"

"Yes," he croaked.

She picked up a white Styrofoam cup from the bedside table and held the bent straw to his lips.

He sipped slowly. When he turned his face away, she put the cup down. "How do you feel?"

"Like the bull rode me for the full eight." His voice was stronger when he answered her. His feeble joke triggered a new flood of relief. His doctors had been worried about possible brain damage.

"I think you threw him before the whistle," she answered.

"Kent," he said suddenly. "Kent Daley, is he okay? I saw the bull knock him down."

"He's fine," she assured him. "He was out cold for a few minutes, but that's all. The outriders managed to keep the bull off of him."

Neal relaxed. "That's good. He's a decent guy."

"He's been here twice to see you. He's very grateful for what you did."

"He did the same for me."

Neal focused on her face for a long moment. She waited until the silence became unbearable. She knew what was coming. "What?"

"How bad is it?" His voice wasn't quite steady.

Robyn bit her lip to stop its trembling. She searched for the courage to tell him the full extent of his injuries. She dreaded the news she was going to deliver. She thought for a second about going out and finding his doctor, but she decided against it. Neal wouldn't want an outsider with him for this.

His hand closed over hers, and he squeezed gently. "Come on, Tweety, give it to me straight. I know I can wiggle my toes, but it hurts to breathe, and my head's on fire."

Her heart wrenched at his use of her childhood nickname. They had been friends long before they had become lovers, long before he broke her heart. He would need a friend now.

In a calm voice, she began. "It's bad, Neal. You have three broken ribs. One of them punctured your lung. You lost a lot of blood. Your face hurts because you also have a fractured cheekbone, a shattered eye socket and..." Her voice trailed away. She couldn't do this.

His grip on her hand tightened. "And?"

"The bull hooked your face with his horn. The doctors couldn't save your left eye."

"Oh, God, no!" His anguished cry tore at her heart.

"I'm so sorry," she whispered.

NEAL KNEW HIS grip had to be crushing her small hand. It couldn't be true. He didn't want to believe her. The pain in his head intensified until he almost screamed.

Forcing himself to let go of her, he raised a trembling hand to grope at the bandages on his face. His eye was gone. He was half-blind. He wanted to tear the dressings off and prove it wasn't true.

"Is that the worst of it?" he managed to ask.

"Yes. You will have a scar on your face, but you'll be able to get a prosthesis as soon as it's healed."

"A glass eye, you mean?" Repugnance filled him. This was some kind of cruel joke. It couldn't be happening.

No, the real joke was that *she* was the one to see him like this.

She leaned close and took his hand. "I can't imagine what you're going through, but your family and friends will be here for you. You will get through this."

The pain in his head grew along with his need to lash out. He jerked away from her. "You should leave now. It's what you do best."

"I'm so sorry, Neal."

"I don't want your pity! Leave me alone."

"Anger is a very normal reaction to such terrible news."

How could she be so calm about the worst moment in his life? It infuriated him. It wasn't rational to blame her, but he couldn't help himself. "Don't tell me what's normal. Just get out!"

"Neal, please," she pleaded.

"Get out!" he shouted.

The pain was making him sick. He didn't want

her to see him puke his guts up. He closed his eye and gritted his teeth. Cold beads of sweat broke out across his forehead as his stomach roiled.

The room grew quiet. Had she gone?

A feeling of panic swelled in him. He didn't want her to go. He needed her. He had always needed her; he just didn't know how much until she was gone.

A hand touched his face and a cool cloth was laid on his brow. "Breathe through your mouth. Take slow, deep breaths," she said.

"I told you—"

"Shut up. I'm a nurse, and you'll do as I say. I have a basin here if you need it."

Damn her. She knew what he needed almost before he did.

Did she know he needed to feel her lips against his? That he wanted to hold her in his arms? Did she know that he still lay awake at night missing her warmth next to him?

No, she couldn't know, and he'd be damned if he would tell her now. *She* had left him.

He heard the door open as someone came into the room, but he couldn't see who it was. The door was on his blind side.

His blind side! Just thinking the words made him feel sicker. This couldn't be happening. It had to be a nightmare. Any second he would wake up.

Robyn moved away and spoke quietly to someone. The door opened and closed again. He wanted to call her back. He didn't want to be alone. He wanted her by his side. He raised his hand, groping for her.

She moved back into his line of sight and his feeling of panic began to lessen. He heard the door again, and a woman's voice said, "This will help."

A cold sensation snaked up his arm from the IV in the back of his hand. After a few minutes, the pain and nausea began to recede.

Robyn held his other hand. "The nurse has given you something for the pain. Is that better?"

"Yes," he admitted weakly. He grew strangely weightless. The pain slipped away, leaving him weary. There was so much he wanted to say to Robyn, only he had no idea where to start.

Her fingers caressed his face. "Sleep now. Your mother will be back soon."

"Don't go." He wanted her to stay. Foolish as he knew that wish was, he didn't want her to go.

"You're going to be okay, Neal."

"I'm sorry I yelled at you." He tried to hold on to the feeling of her hand touching his face, to the scent like spring flowers she always wore, but everything began to fade. He couldn't sleep. He fought against the drug. "Tell me why," he begged.

"Why, what?"

"Why you left me."

"Because you didn't love me."

She was wrong, so wrong, but he couldn't form the words to tell her as the darkness closed over him.

The drugged sleep brought him no peace. Instead, it carried him into a world of foggy, half-formed nightmares where an enormous bull with bloody horns pursued him relentlessly. He awoke in near darkness with pain pounding in his head again and the taste of fear in his mouth.

He turned to search for Robyn, craving the gentleness of her touch. His hopes soared for an instant until he recognized his mother asleep in the chair beside him.

Robyn was gone. The pain he felt then had nothing to do with his injury. It was an old, familiar pain. One he knew he deserved.

Raising his hand slowly, he touched the gauze bandage on his face. He hadn't dreamed this. His eye was gone. He would be scarred for life.

Why him? What kind of life would he have as a one-eyed freak? A sudden thought sent a new chill of fear through him.

What if he couldn't ride again? What would he do? He couldn't lose that. Not that.

He was Neal Bryant, soon to be a world-champion bull rider. Not a runner-up. Not a loser. He'd given up everything to make it this far. Everything, including Robyn.

His hands clenched into fists on the sheets. He would ride again. He had to.

## CHAPTER THREE

"MOM, ARE YOU sure you want to go through with this?" Robyn sat behind the wheel of her battered green Ford pickup and struggled not to cry as she gazed at her mother's face. Martha O'Connor was pale but composed as she buttoned the top button of her blue cotton blouse.

She took a deep breath and nodded once. "I don't want to do it, but I have to. I have no other choice. The ranch is too much for me to handle now that your dad is gone. There are too many decisions to make, too much work that needs doing. This is the only way."

"I could help more," Robyn offered one last time. It didn't seem right to sell the ranch that had been in their family for generations. Who would love it as much as her family had? Her great-great-grandparents had come from Ireland and settled in the green treeless hills so unlike their native land. They were hearty people. They had survived in spite of drought, prairie fires and floods and built a ranch to be proud of. She would make them proud by keeping her head up.

Her mother said, "You can't help more. You work five and six days a week as it is. If we move into town, you'll be able to spend more time with Chance. You won't be driving thirty miles twice a day to get to work and back. I should have put the place up for sale two years ago when we started losing money, but I thought— Well, it doesn't matter what I thought. This drought has finished us."

She turned pleading eyes toward Robyn. "You can make a decent living as a nurse. You don't need to worry about outguessing the weather or gambling everything on the cattle market. You don't need to watch your dreams wither and dry into dust. I want a stable, secure life for you and my grandson. Can you understand that?"

"Are you doing this because you think Chance won't be able to run the ranch?"

"I'm doing this because I can't run the ranch. This is my decision. You know it hasn't been an easy one. To tell the truth, if we don't sell now, we'll lose the place anyway. I've borrowed as much as I can against it. If we spruce the place up and get top dollar for it, we can pay off the mortgage and afford the special schooling Chance will need."

"That will take a lot of sprucing, Mom."

"We'll have to hire some help, but it can be done. I know how much you want to become a nurse practitioner. This might make that possible, or at least not as difficult. If the place brings what it is worth, you can go to school and I can have a comfortable retirement."

Robyn reached to grip her mother's hand. "You deserve that. I understand, honest I do. Only, can't I feel a little sad that my childhood home is going up for sale?"

"Yes, of course you can. Just don't start crying. If you do, I'll never be able to go through with it."

"I won't cry in front of you. I promise."

Her mother squeezed Robyn's hand. "Good. I'll be back in half an hour."

"Are you sure you don't want me to come in with you?"

Martha stepped out of the truck. "I need to do this alone. I only hope your father would understand."

"Dad always put the family first, Mom. He'd understand. I'm sure of it. He would say it's just a big piece of dirt. The people we love are what's important."

"You're right—bless you for that." Martha closed the truck door, smoothed the front of her navy blue skirt and squared her shoulders. Then she crossed the street and walked into the Flint Hills Real Estate office with her head up.

Robyn watched with a sinking heart as her mother entered the building. She had hoped the ranch would pass into the hands of her children one day. So much for another girlhood dream. They seemed to have all fallen by the wayside.

She pushed her short dark curls off her forehead as a trickle of sweat slipped down her temple in the rising, late-June heat. The trouble with letting go of the dreams she'd once cherished was finding something to replace them.

A white sedan pulled up to the curb two spaces down from her truck in front of the drugstore. She recognized Ellie Bryant's car and watched Neal swing his long legs out of the passenger side. Fighting down the compulsion to rush over and help him, she studied him closely.

Weeks had passed since the accident, but he still moved stiffly. His mother came around beside him. He pointedly ignored her offered hand. Robyn was glad she hadn't jumped out to help.

As he stood beside the car, she saw he was still pale beneath his tan, but his color was better than the last time she'd seen him. The bandages were gone, and she got her first look at the scar he would bear for the rest of his life. A crooked red line ran up from the center of his left cheek and disappeared beneath the black eye patch he wore.

She wanted to feel pity, but she couldn't deny the truth. It wasn't pity that sent her pulse racing. It was the sweet rush of desire he always triggered in her.

As the familiar longing swept over her, she

closed her eyes to fight it. She wouldn't fall for him again. She had more pride than that. He didn't love her. He'd proved it beyond a shadow of a doubt five years ago.

When she had a grip on her emotions, she opened her eyes and saw a pair of teenage girls walking past the front of her truck. Their gazes were pinned on Neal and looks of admiration sprang onto their young faces. Their walks slowed and turned into prowling saunters.

He tipped his hat as they strolled past him, but something struck Robyn as odd about his move. She'd seen him do that a thousand times. What was different this time?

Then she knew. He'd used his left hand to touch the brim of his hat. Was he trying to cover the scarred side of his face?

A quick pang of compassion pushed a lump into her throat. His appearance had been drastically altered. It would be hard for anyone, but it had to be especially hard for someone as proud as Neal was.

He had always been a handsome man. Women had flocked around him. He was above-average height and lean, with a cowboy's natural swagger. He wore his brown hair slightly long, and it curled at his shirt collar. She'd always thought his hazel eyes were his best feature, but it was his impish sense of humor she had adored.

She watched the two girls glance back at him before they turned the corner. Neal might not realize it, but the eye patch made him look dangerous and exotic. He would be the object of some teenage fantasies for many nights to come judging by the girls' reactions. Who could blame them? He was a sexy hunk.

He started to step up on the curb, but he didn't step high enough and stumbled. He regained his balance quickly, but he pressed his arm to his side. Had he hurt himself?

His mother rushed around the car to help as he leaned against the hood, but he shook her off. Robyn found herself out of the truck and standing beside him before she realized what she was doing. "Are you okay?"

His head snapped up at the sound of her voice, and his lips pressed into a tight line. "Sure. One too many beers, I guess."

She frowned as she studied his face. "Don't be a smart aleck. You're having trouble judging distance because of your altered depth perception."

"They tell me I'll get used to it."

"Did you hurt your ribs?" his mother asked.

"I jarred them, that's all. I'm fine. Go and do your shopping, Mom. I don't need a babysitter."

Surprised by the sharp sarcasm in his voice, Robyn glanced at his mother. A look of hurt flashed across Ellie's face, but it disappeared quickly as she pasted a smile on. She stepped away from him and let her arms fall to her sides.

"Okay. I won't be long." Turning away, she hurried into the drugstore. The bell over the door clanged as it closed behind her.

"I see your manners haven't improved," Robyn snapped.

He frowned at her. "What's that supposed to mean?"

"Your mother is only trying to help."

"I see you haven't changed, either," he drawled, leaning against the car hood.

She refused to rise to his bait and kept her mouth shut. She'd said too much already.

He looked her up and down. "You still butt into other people's business. I didn't like you trying to tell me what to do years ago, and I don't like it now."

What on earth had possessed her to think he needed her help? Robyn didn't know if she was more furious with him or with herself. "Someone needs to tell you what to do, you slow-witted stubborn oaf. You were plain mean to your mother."

He scowled at her but didn't reply.

Maybe it was none of her business, but he was going to get an earful. His mother didn't deserve that kind of treatment. "Your mother watched helplessly as they loaded you on a chopper and then drove for two hundred miles, praying you would still be alive when she got to the hospital. While they were putting you back together, Humpty Dumpty, she paced the waiting room for hours, worried sick with fear. When she finally heard you would live, they told her you might have brain damage. I could barely get her to leave your bedside. She didn't sleep for two nights straight."

Robyn poked a finger into the top button of his shirt. "So cut her a little slack if she's overprotective, and be kind to her. She's been through a lot."

Robyn wouldn't tell him all those fears and sleepless nights were hers, as well. He wouldn't care.

His face could have been carved from granite. "Are you finished?"

She folded her arms across her chest and clamped her jaw closed on all the other things she wanted to shout at him. "Yes."

From behind her, she heard someone speak. "Mr. Bryant, can I have your autograph, please?"

She turned around and saw three high-school-age boys standing on the sidewalk, looking eager but uncertain.

Neal's face softened. "Sure, I'd be glad to."

"We saw your last ride," the lanky one said in a rush. He wore a cowboy hat pushed back on his blond hair.

"That was so brave the way you drew the bull

away from the clown when he was down." Awe filled the second boy's voice.

"Yeah, we could see you were hurt," the third boy interjected. His eyes brimmed with admiration. "You could have made it to the fence, but you ran back to help him."

"I sure hope you'll be able to keep on riding," the first boy added, holding out a pen and a slip of paper.

Neal took the pen and scrawled his signature on the paper. "I've got to give these ribs a chance to heal, but I intend to be in the National Finals come December."

"Thank you, sir." The boy took the paper back and stared at it in awe as they walked away. "I told you havin' one eye wouldn't keep him from riding," the blond boy insisted proudly.

Robyn stared at Neal in disbelief. "You don't mean that, do you?"

He looked at her. "What?"

"That you'll go back to riding bulls."

He stiffened and stood away from the car. "You bet I mean it."

"I guess the doctors were right. You are brain damaged!" She spun on her heels and stalked off.

NEAL FELT HIS resentment fade. A reluctant smile tugged at the corners of his mouth. She didn't pull any punches when it came to telling him what she thought. She hadn't changed a bit.

He tilted his head slightly as he studied her retreating form. Well, maybe a little, but it was all for the better.

Her boyish figure was gone. She'd put on some weight, but it only made her curves more generous. The hips filling out her Wranglers now were anything but boyish.

He pressed his lips back into a thin line. Okay, he still found her attractive; too bad for him. She'd dropped him like a hot rock and moved on with her life. He was glad she had. She deserved better. There was no point standing in the hot sun and wishing things had turned out differently.

He glanced toward the drugstore. Much as he hated to admit it, she was right about one thing. He'd been taking his frustrations and his anger out on anyone who came within range, including his mother. Everyone in his family had suffered his bouts of temper in silence, as if they were afraid to say anything. Only Robyn seemed able to treat him the way she had before the accident.

He wanted that. He wanted people to stop treating him like an invalid, to stop treating him differently.

Rubbing his hand across his jaw, he admitted the cold hard truth. He was different. The brash and reckless cowboy he'd once been was gone.

A quaking coward now stood in his boots. Neal hated the man he had become.

Every time he closed his eye, he saw the huge, gray bull bearing down on him. Even in his sleep, he could feel Dust Devil's hot breath on his neck. He'd jerk awake with his heart pounding in his chest so hard he couldn't draw a breath.

Sometimes, he woke in the darkness afraid he had gone completely blind. He'd taken to sleeping with a night-light on like some frightened toddler.

Robyn might think he was crazy, but until he could ride again, he knew his fear would only grow. Getting back on a bull was the only way to fight it. As soon as he was healed, he would climb on a bull if it killed him. He had to. He couldn't live knowing he'd lost his nerve.

But right now, he had another mission. As Robyn had so gently pointed out, he needed to apologize to his mother.

The bell jangled overhead as he entered the long, narrow building from the late 1800s. He moved carefully past the display cases filled with ceramic and glass figurines and local souvenirs. The smells of potpourri and scented candles surrounded him with their sweet fragrances. He crossed to the pharmacy through a wide archway and paused. Little had changed here since his boyhood days.

Above his head, globe lights and a wooden fan

hung on pipes suspended from the high, pressed-tin ceiling. The blades of the fan hummed faintly over the sounds of Tim McGraw coming from a radio on the back counter. His mother stood in front of a tall counter, talking to the pharmacist behind it.

Neal turned his gaze to the unique, old-fashioned soda fountain that occupied the far corner. Five chrome bar stools covered in green vinyl lined up in front of a bar decorated with distinctive brown, rust and orange Mexican tiles. A wide brown marble counter topped the bar. Fluted glasses and silver tumblers sat in neat rows on the oak shelves that framed a large mirror behind the counter.

He sat down on the first stool. The mirror reflected a man in a black hat and eye patch. It took a second before Neal recognized himself. He tore his gaze away from the scarred cowboy and forced a smile to his lips when his mother joined him. "Remember when you used to bring us kids here for ice cream?"

"Of course I do. You loved coming here."

"Every time we had to go to the dentist, you would bring us here afterwards. Something about that never made sense, dentist then ice cream."

She smiled. "It was the only way I could get both of you to behave. I had to bribe you."

"Maybe it will still work."

Her grin widened. "Now, why didn't I think of that? The promise of a chocolate malt used to turn you into an angel for at least an hour."

"I've been pretty hard to live with lately, haven't I?" he asked quietly.

Her eyes narrowed in speculation. "Now that you mention it, yes, you have."

"I'm sorry, Mom."

"I know, dear. I try not to take it personally. You've been through a lot."

He pushed the brim of his hat up. "Well, since you know what it takes to bribe me into being good, why don't you tell me what you'd like?"

She rubbed her hands together like a gleeful child. "I'd love a hot-fudge sundae with extra whipped cream, extra nuts and extra cherries."

Leaning back, he eyed her petite figure. "I had no idea you indulged in the hard stuff."

"It's the whipped cream that gets me. It brings back such fond memories of your father."

He held up a hand. "I don't think I'm old enough to hear this."

She gave him a playful slap on his arm. "Don't be sassy. Your father used to bring me here when we were courting. We always ordered a double hot-fudge sundae with extra whipped cream to share."

"Whew. That's a relief. I was imagining all kinds of kinky things."

Her mouth dropped open. "If you weren't so old, I'd turn you across my knee."

"Hey, I'm an injured man, remember?"

They gave their order to the smiling young woman behind the counter and waited while she prepared it. Neal took his malt and sipped the smooth chocolate ice cream slowly. He watched with an indulgent smile while his mother savored her treat.

Setting his drink down, he stared at the metal tumbler for a moment and then scraped the thin coat of frost on the outside of it with his thumbnail. "You and Robyn seem to have remained pretty close."

"Her mother and I are dear friends—you know that. We go way back. Did you know I was dating Frank before Martha stole him away from me?"

He looked at her in surprise. "And you're still friends?"

"It was the best thing that ever happened to me."

"Because you met Dad?"

She nodded. "I went out with your father to try to make Frank jealous. I'd like to believe I would have discovered what a wonderful man your father was anyway, but somehow I don't think that's true. I think I would have settled for Frank, and I would have never known what real love was.

Thankfully, Martha and I both ended up with the right man."

She eyed him intently for a long moment. "Can I ask you a personal question?"

"Shoot."

"Why did you and Robyn break up?"

Neal stabbed his straw up and down in the thick malt. "She hated my riding bulls. We fought about it all the time. We were on the circuit in North Dakota when she got the call from her mother."

"When Frank suffered a stroke?"

"Yeah. Robyn flew home and she never came back."

"Did you try to contact her?"

"She was a big girl. She made up her own mind. I wasn't going to beg her to come back."

"Neal, you know that I love you. The Bryant men have very few faults, but their pride is one of them."

Anger stirred in him. "What should I have done? Dragged her back by the hair?"

"You should have come to see her and demanded to know what was wrong."

He couldn't help the sarcasm that slipped out. "She sure didn't miss me much. I heard she got married a couple months later. Did she leave him, too?"

"No, Colin Morgan died six months after the wedding."

That bit of news stunned him. He shook his head slowly. "I didn't know. Why didn't you tell me?"

"If I remember correctly, you told me point-blank that you never wanted to talk about her again. So I didn't."

Foolish pride could do that to a man. "That must have been rough for her."

"It was so sad, but, thankfully, they had a beautiful little boy named Chance. I know that having Chance has helped her deal with her grief. Children give us hope."

Robyn had a kid? He didn't know that, either. Apparently, there was a lot about Robyn O'Connor Morgan he didn't know.

His mother toyed with her spoon a moment before she said, "Robyn's single now, and her mother says she's not seeing anyone. Maybe you two could patch things up."

He shook his head. "Not much chance of that. Besides, I'll be leaving soon."

"What?" Her eyes widened in surprise.

"I'll be leaving as soon as the doctor gives me the okay. Another four weeks at most. I've got a lot of catching up to do if I'm going to make it into the National Finals."

"You're going back to riding bulls? I don't believe it." Tears welled up in her eyes as she stared at him.

"Mom, what did you think I was going to do?"

"I don't know, but I never considered you'd be foolish enough to risk your life again. I've spent every day since I got that phone call giving thanks to God that you're alive. I'm sorry you lost an eye. I'm sorry that your face is scarred, but it could have been so much worse. I thought this would be the end of your bull riding."

"You don't understand. I can't quit like this."

She stood and wiped away her tears. "I can't bear it if you go back! I've already buried a husband—I don't want to bury one of my children, too." She turned away, then hurried out the door.

Neal stared after her, feeling ashamed and confused. Why didn't anyone understand? He was a bull rider, for heaven's sake. It was who he was as much as what he did. He'd been among the best of the best. If he couldn't ride, then there wasn't anything left for him. His gaze was drawn to the stranger in the mirror wearing his clothes.

Hell, who did he think he was kidding? The thought of trying to ride again turned his insides to jelly. He was afraid, plain and simple. And that fact scared him worse than anything. He'd never been afraid in his whole life.

He needed to ride again, needed to prove he was still the same man he'd always been and not the coward who cringed like a child in the darkness. Life like this wasn't worth living.

# CHAPTER FOUR

ROBYN SAW ELLIE Bryant was crying as she hurried out of the drugstore, and her annoyance at Neal grew by leaps and bounds. Apparently, nothing she'd said had gotten through his thick head. He followed his mother out of the store a few moments later, and they drove away.

The truck door opened and Robyn's mother stuck her head in. "All done. What shall we do next?" Her mother's chipper voice rang hollow.

"Are you okay, Mom?"

"I can't believe what a relief it is to have finally done this."

"I'm glad." She would try to be supportive for her mother's sake.

"I need to run into the drugstore for a minute. Then I'll be ready to go."

"I've got the whole day off, so take your time. Tell you what, let's have lunch at the Hayward House, my treat."

"Sounds great."

Her mother entered the store, and Robyn turned up the radio to listen to her favorite country song and hum along. A few minutes later, her cell phone rang. Frowning, she pulled her phone from her purse. She'd taken Chance to a sitter today, something she didn't normally do. She hated leaving him with anyone but her mother. She'd given the sitter this number.

Her feeling of alarm vanished as soon as she saw the caller ID. She recognized the voice on the other end. It was the hospital operator.

"I'm glad I got you, Robyn. Dr. Cain needs you to come in right away."

On her day off? What could be so important? "What's going on?"

"It's Mildred Eldrich, one of our deaf patients. She's had a stroke. We need your help to communicate with her."

Robyn saw her mother walk out of the drugstore. "All right, I'll be there in a few minutes." She snapped the phone closed as her mother climbed into the truck.

"Who was that?" Martha asked.

"The hospital. Something has come up and they need me."

Martha scowled. "Can't they get along without you for one day? I declare, that place will suck the life out of you if you let it."

"They need someone who can sign for a deaf patient."

"Oh, well, that's different. If it's not too much

trouble, can we run by the Bryant ranch on our way home?"

She shot her mother a suspicious look. "Why?"

"The pharmacist said Ellie came in to get a prescription refilled, but then she left without it. It's for her high blood pressure. He's afraid she'll run out. I told him we could drop it off on our way home. I left a message on her machine so she doesn't turn around and drive back in."

Robyn had seen Ellie in tears as she'd left the store. It wasn't surprising that she'd forgotten her medicine. Having Neal Bryant for a son would be more than enough to raise any sane woman's blood pressure.

"Sure. We can drop it off after lunch."

"Well, if you're going to the hospital, I'm going shopping. The dress store is having a sale. Give me a call when you're done at the hospital and I'll meet you at the restaurant." She opened the truck door and hopped out.

"See you then."

A few minutes later, Robyn entered the Hill County Hospital through the front doors. After checking to find which room Mrs. Eldrich was in, Robyn made her way down the hall, pushed open the door of 106 and entered quietly.

Dr. Cain sat beside the bed of the small, elderly woman and wrote on a pad with a blue marker. He held the message up for her to read, but she pushed it away with her left hand and moaned softly. He bowed his head a moment, and then he reached out and laid his hand gently over hers. "That's okay, Mrs. Eldrich, we can try again later."

Robyn said, "Hello. What can I do to help?"

He glanced up and smiled as she moved to stand beside him. "Am I glad to see you."

"Tell me what's going on."

"Mrs. Eldrich has suffered a stroke that has paralyzed her right side. She won't answer any of my questions and I can't tell why. The nurse from the care home says she hasn't had any trouble reading lips or writing until this morning."

"Has she tried writing with her left hand?"

"She's tried, but I can't make out any of it."

Robyn sat on the bed and touched the woman's shoulder.

Mrs. Eldrich opened her eyes, but she seemed to have trouble focusing. Robyn began to sign, but the woman closed her eyes and tossed restlessly in the bed. Her left hand twisted the covers into a tight wad and then slowly she began shaping letters.

"What is she saying?" he asked.

"She says, 'See half.'"

"See half of what?"

Robyn glanced at his perplexed face. "I think she means she can only see half of everything."

Comprehension dawned on his face. "Hemiopia. No wonder she can't read lips or my writing. She has vision only in the left half of each eye. Why didn't I think of that? Ask her if she's in pain. Man, I'm glad you showed up."

They spent the next hour assessing Mrs. Eldrich. Robyn spelled the questions slowly on the woman's hand, letting her feel each letter, and waited as she spelled her answers slowly with her left hand in return. Finally, Dr. Cain called a halt.

"Tell her to rest now. I'll have the nurse bring her something to help her sleep."

Together, they left the room. Out in the hall, he paused. "Thanks for coming in. I don't know how I would have managed without you."

"No problem. I was already in town. I have an idea how the rest of the staff can communicate with Mrs. Eldrich."

"How?"

"We could use a raised alphabet board. We have one for the children to play with in the lobby. Mrs. Eldrich could feel the letters to spell words for the staff, and the staff could guide her hand to each letter to spell a reply. It wouldn't be perfect, but it might work."

He smiled and started down the hall. "That sounds like a great idea. You amaze me. Did they teach you to be this creative in nursing school?"

She fell into step beside him. "Sure. Don't

doctors have to take Make Do with What You've Got 101?"

He shook his head. "I don't remember it. I may have cut class that day."

She grinned. "You must have missed it when you were in Basic Bad Handwriting."

"Hey, my handwriting isn't that bad. Is it?"

"For a doctor or for a preschooler?"

"Ouch! I don't think I deserved that."

"Maybe not," she conceded.

He stopped beside the nursing station and faced her. His expression grew serious. "My handwriting may be bad, but my eyesight's not. I know a good nurse when I see one."

Surprised, she said, "Thank you."

"You're welcome. Have you ever thought about going on with your training, maybe into advanced practice, like a family-medicine nurse practitioner?"

"Sure, someday I'd love to, but I can't afford to go back to school anytime soon."

The additional years of education to become a family-medicine nurse practitioner would allow her to diagnose and treat patients without the constant supervision of a physician. She would be able to perform prenatal, well-child, and adult checkups, even diagnose and manage minor traumas like suturing cuts and splinting broken bones, things she wasn't allowed by law to do as a registered nurse. Her ability to make treatment decisions, order tests and write prescriptions would free up the physicians to concentrate on more complex diseases and conditions. An NP would be a welcome asset to a rural hospital already struggling with a shortage of doctors, but education costs money.

"Didn't you get the application for the NP scholarships I gave to the nursing supervisor?"

"You did that?" she asked in amazement. She'd only worked with him for a few short months.

"Yes. Did you fill it out?"

She hadn't, but she hadn't thrown it away, either. It lay in the top drawer of her desk, tempting her with its possibilities, even though she knew she couldn't send it. Not now, not with her family losing the ranch.

Now more than ever, they'd need a steady income until the ranch sold, and who knew how long that would take? But she wasn't about to discuss her financial problems with him. "I like what I'm doing, and I'm needed here."

"Think about it. You have a gift for medicine, and I'd hate to see it go to waste."

"Thank you, but I hardly think my talent is going to waste here. You needed me today."

He flipped open the chart. "Indeed I did. I'll just scribble a few illegible orders here."

She grinned. "Sorry about the handwriting crack."

"You can make it up to me."

"And how would I do that?"

He closed the chart and smiled at her. "Have dinner with me tonight."

His request caught her totally off guard. Quickly, she glanced around to see who might have overheard his offer, but the nursing station was deserted. She stared at his friendly, handsome face and blurted out, "I don't know what to say."

His bright blue eyes sparkled with amusement. "How about, 'Yes, Adam, I'd love to have dinner with you. I thought you would never ask.'"

She clasped her arms across her middle and stared at the floor. "I can't."

"Tomorrow night?" he asked hopefully.

"I don't think it would be a good idea. I'm sorry."

"No, I'm the one who's sorry. I didn't mean to upset you."

He was silent a long moment. When she glanced at him, his kind smile made her regret her hasty decision. "You didn't upset me. You just surprised me."

"You realize you are condemning me to another night of cafeteria food, don't you?"

Her smile returned. "If that is a bid for sympathy, you'll have to do better. The food here is excellent."

He chuckled and put the chart back into the wire rack. "Yes, it is. The coconut-cream pie is the main reason I moonlight here. So why won't you have dinner with me? Do you avoid doctors in general, or are you involved with someone?"

"I don't think it would be a good idea since we have to work together. It might create a problem."

"I see. I thought maybe you and your bull rider were trying to work things out."

"Neal?" she asked in surprise. "What gave you that idea?"

"I saw your face when they brought him in. I'd say there are still some pretty strong feelings on your part."

"Well, you would be wrong. That was over a long time ago," she snapped. She refused to accept there was anything left of her former feelings for Neal except the remnants of an adolescent fantasy.

Adam held up both hands. "Whoa. I'm sorry I said anything."

Her protest had been too sharp. She forced a smile to her stiff lips. "You need to understand that his mother and mine are best friends. They've been our neighbors all my life. I can't tell you how often I've heard the phrase, 'You and Neal should get back together.' It's kind of a sore subject with me."

He nodded solemnly. "Gabriella Prichard."

She frowned. "Who?"

"Gabriella Prichard. That's the woman my mother wants me to marry. I call her Crabby Gabby. Not to her face, of course. She feels the same about me. Our mothers are the best of friends. They throw us together at every opportunity. Neither of them will accept the idea that Gabby and I aren't right for each other."

Robyn had to laugh at his glum expression. "I know how hard that can be."

He brightened and flashed an impish grin. "It seems you and I have quite a bit in common."

"Maybe," she admitted cautiously.

"If you won't go out with me because we work together, I can always stop working here. Say the word."

"That's blackmail. You know we need you."

He crossed his arms over his chest. "Yes, but is it effective blackmail?"

"Maybe," she admitted. It had been a long time since a man had showed interest in her as a woman. It gave her ego a much-needed boost. She didn't believe for a minute that it was anything more than Adam's boredom at being stuck in a small town. So what would it hurt to go out and have a little fun? Besides, it might take her mind off a certain irritating cowboy.

"I'll think about it," she conceded.

NEAL STEPPED OUT of the car as soon as his mother pulled to a stop in the drive, but he made no move toward the house. Restlessness rippled through him. He didn't want to go inside. He'd spent too much time indoors. He was going stir-crazy.

"Are you coming?" his mother asked, heading to the front door.

"I think I'll take a walk down to the barns."

She nodded and disappeared inside the house.

She was probably glad to get him out from underfoot. He hadn't been the best of company. He had managed to apologize for upsetting her on the way home, but she was still dead set against his returning to the rodeo.

After crossing the ranch yard to the first of two large red barns, he stepped into the welcoming dimness. The smell of animals, hay and oiled leather mingled with the faint scent of dust. He smiled. Now he really felt like he was home. He and his brother, Jake, had practically lived in the barns.

Together, they had raised and trained some pretty good cow ponies. While Neal had drifted away to the rodeo, Jake had continued breeding quarter horses and training them for roping and cutting. His nearby ranch, the Flying JB, was renowned for producing quality stock horses.

Down the wide front aisle of the barn, four horses looked over their stalls and whinnied. Neal's mother maintained an expansive cattle ranch with the help of a few hired men. Like nearly all Flint Hills ranchers, she still used horses to work cattle. ATVs were useful, but they couldn't learn to read which way a calf was going to break from the herd the way a good cow pony could.

Neal stopped at the first stall. He drew a hand down the horse's silky neck. "Think I came in here to feed you? No such luck, honey. You must be one of Jake's."

The sorrel mare nodded her head as if in agreement.

Neal grinned. "I thought so. He's not the only one that can spot a good horse."

He moved past them to where his saddle and his rigging rested on worn sawhorses at the end of the aisle. They had been cleaned and oiled by his brother, no doubt.

He checked over his bull-riding rig carefully, as much from habit as anything else, and slipped his hand into the handle. Suddenly he was trapped in the rope, dangling from the bull's side. The room tilted as sweat broke out on his forehead.

He yanked his hand away. Taking a step back, he sucked in a heavy breath to slow his racing heart. As much as he wanted to believe it had been a moment of dizziness caused by his headache, he knew it wasn't. It was pure and simple fear.

One of the horses whinnied again. Neal focused on the animal. Maybe a horseback ride was what he needed.

Sure. Once he got back in the saddle, a ride would blow the cobwebs from his mind.

If he could even stay upright on a horse. Sometimes he had trouble just standing.

He looked around. He was alone. Now was as good a time as any to find out if he could do it. When there wouldn't be any witnesses if he fell off.

He saddled the mare and led her outside. Dizziness made him sway when he swung up into the saddle, but he stayed on. Once his head stopped reeling, he sat up straight. It felt good to be back on a horse, even if it did make his ribs ache.

Without a word to anyone, he turned his mount and rode out into the wide, rolling grasslands of the Flint Hills with one special destination in mind.

ROBYN MULLED OVER Adam's surprising offer as she and her mother ate lunch at the Hayward House restaurant, but she didn't mention it. Later, as she drove the familiar miles back to the ranch, her mother sat beside her and rambled about the things that needed doing around the ranch before it could be sold. Her monologue didn't require a reply, so Robyn was free to let her mind drift.

If nothing else, Adam had given her self-esteem a nice lift. He not only wanted to take her out, but he was the one who'd submitted her name for the scholarship. It was nice to have her skills noticed and appreciated. He thought she was a good nurse. Well, she was, and she'd be a fine nurse practitioner, too. Someday.

At the thought, her happy mood faded. Even if she wanted to, she couldn't go after her NP now. That dream would have to wait, but she refused to accept that she wouldn't reach it. One of her dreams had to come true.

Adam's flattery aside, the real question remained. Should she go out with him? The prospect was tempting. He was fun to be around, very good-looking and nice...for a doctor.

She glanced at her mother. Maybe going out with Adam would prove to some people once and for all that she wasn't waiting for Neal to drift back into her life and sweep her away.

She could do better than a bacon-brained, two-timing, stubborn, ill-tempered rodeo cowboy.

"Robyn, you missed the turnoff! We were going to stop and give Ellie her prescription, remember?" Her mother's voice snapped Robyn back to the present.

"I'm sorry, Mom, I forgot."

Turning the truck around on the narrow highway, she drove back and turned into the Bryants' half-mile-long gravel lane. As they pulled into the ranch yard, she saw Ellie beside the corral, trying to catch a loose horse. The sorrel mare paced wide-eyed with her head high and trailing the reins. Her chest was bathed in lathered sweat and flecks of foam. Ellie gave up trying to catch her and hurried to the truck.

"Oh, thank goodness. You have to help me find him."

Robyn stepped out of the truck. "Find who? What's wrong?"

"It's Neal. He rode out hours ago, and his horse just came in without him."

# CHAPTER FIVE

AN HOUR LATER, Robyn reined her borrowed horse to a stop and studied the ground closely. The prairie grass was dry and brittle, and the dirt was hard as brick. If Neal had ridden this way, there wasn't any sign that she could detect. She wiped another trickle of sweat from her brow with the back of her hand. What the hell had he been he thinking?

It had to be close to a hundred degrees today. This summer had been the hottest and the driest she could remember. The relentless heat was sucking the life out of the countryside, and it would suck the life out of anyone foolish enough to venture into it without plenty of water.

She bit her lip as her worry intensified. Neal's empty canteen had still been on his saddle. Unless he had another, he was without water.

*The idiot!* Why would he go riding in this heat when he wasn't used to it? He'd only been out of the hospital a few short weeks. The man was in for the tongue-lashing of his life when she found him. If she found him. Half a dozen riders were spread out across the enormous ranch because no one had an idea where Neal might have gone. She had a suspicion, but it was a long shot.

She pushed the wide brim of one of Ellie's cowboy hats back, lifted her canteen and took a quick drink, then poured some on her hand and rubbed it on her face and neck. It helped a little, but her back and shoulders were so hot it felt like someone was trying to iron her shirt with her still in it. She screwed the lid back on her canteen. She wouldn't waste any more water trying to get cool. She might need it all.

The strong, hot breeze quickly dried the dampness on her face as it stirred the tall, drooping sunflowers beside the trail and hissed through the long brown grass around her.

Nudging the pinto forward, she rode toward a deep draw that cut a zigzag course across the prairie. She let the horse pick his way carefully down the steep trail. Decades of cattle going down to water had trod a narrow cut in the high bank. Her stirrups scraped the sides as they descended.

She turned suddenly and looked behind her. A second set of scrape marks lined the dirt just below hers. Another rider had come this way. She had guessed right. She knew now where Neal had been heading.

At the bottom of the draw, a tiny trickle of water strung together muddy puddles and filled the deep hoofprints left by thirsty cattle. Four

Black Angus steers watched her warily from downstream, where they stood knee deep in the mud. Their tails swung constantly to keep away the flies that hovered over their backs. A fresh set of prints from a horse led upstream. Robyn turned to follow them. She couldn't believe Neal was foolish enough to try to make such a long ride in his shape. He could barely walk. What would possess him to go all the way to Little Bowl Springs Canyon?

Even as the thought crossed her mind, she knew the answer. It had been their special place when they were young. It was where he'd first made love to her.

NEAL TRIPPED AND fell face-first onto the prairie. After a long moment, he opened his eye, and a forest of bluestem grass settled into view in front of him. Lifting his head off the ground, he spat out the dirt caked at the corner of his mouth.

Carefully, he pushed himself to his hands and knees. Agony pounded inside his skull and his ribs ached. The urge to lie back down was overwhelming.

Slowly, he sat back on his heels and forced himself to study his surroundings. He got his bearings again as he squinted at the rolling grassland broken by deep, narrow gullies and rocky canyons. He hadn't made much progress.

This part of the ranch was virtually inaccessible except on horseback or on foot. And he was still on foot. His horse was nowhere in sight. *Jake didn't train 'em like he used to.*

What had Robyn called him that morning? A stupid, stubborn oaf? He closed his eye against the bright light. She had the stupid part right. He'd ridden out without telling anyone where he was headed, and now he was going to pay for it. By his best guess, he had four more miles to stagger or crawl before he got near the ranch house. Since his horse wasn't standing nearby, he could only hope the mare had gone back to the barn. If she hadn't, it could be dark before anyone became worried enough to start a search.

He forced himself to stand. After a moment, the dizziness receded. He held on to his aching ribs with one arm and braced the other on his thigh. His hat lay a few feet away. He moved toward it with unsteady steps. Painfully, he bent to retrieve it and settled it on his head.

The shade it provided his scorched face was a relief he knew would be short-lived. He held up a hand to block the glare as he judged the time by the position of the sun. It was still high in the afternoon sky, which meant it would be three or four more hours before the temperature began to drop.

He had no water, no shade and little strength after spending much of the past month in bed. All in all, he was in a pretty tight spot. His biggest danger now was the risk of heatstroke.

He started walking in the direction of home. A small canyon cut a meandering course through the prairie a half mile away. Its high walls would provide him with some shade, and there was water at the bottom of it. The stagnant pools wouldn't be drinkable, but they would help to cool him.

The source of the small stream lay a mile in the other direction, in a small gorge where a spring bubbled out of a rocky ledge. There, the water would be cold and clear as it tumbled out of the earth and fell into a series of small pools carved out of the limestone slabs. But that spring lay in the opposite direction of the ranch house.

He'd been headed there before his ignoble dismount. The spring held a special place in his heart. A place from his childhood and his youth, but he'd been a fool to try to ride that far his first time out.

He looked back across the grassy plateau behind him. To try to reach the spring now would add hours to his hike home later. He sighed and began to walk toward the canyon wall and the ranch beyond it.

He cursed the sweltering heat, his worthless horse and the rough ground littered with rocks that hid in the long dry grass and tried to trip him as he made his way toward the canyon and the promise of relief from the relentless sun. He was almost to the rim when he stumbled and fell to his hands and knees.

A grunt of agony escaped him. Pain lanced through his ribs, and he struggled to catch his breath. When he did, he let loose a string of swearwords that would have singed the ears off a sailor.

In the silence that followed, he heard hoofbeats. A moment later, a horse and rider clambered up out of the canyon in front of him.

"From the sounds of it, I'd say you aren't dead, at least."

Neal hung his head. Thankfully, someone had found him, but why did it have to be Robyn?

"Just what do you think you're doing?" she demanded, reining her horse to a stop beside him.

He stared at the ground between his hands and wished with all his heart that she had discovered him while he was still on his feet.

"Would you believe I lost a contact?" He pushed up and sat back on his heels with his hands braced on his thighs. "I guess it doesn't matter, it was the left one."

He peered at her face. His brother's gaze would have slid away from his eye patch. His mother would have grown tight-lipped and told him not to joke about it. But not Robyn. She struggled to keep a smile off her face and lost as she shook her head.

"Oh, honestly!" she declared, dismounting.

He felt his own face relax when she dropped to her knees in front of him. "Honestly? I was trying to decide whether I should jump to my feet and shout for joy that someone found me before I wound up as a set of bleached bones or to pound the ground in frustration because it was you."

"I could ride off and pretend I never saw you."

He studied her face so close to his own. Lord, how he loved the sparkle that shimmered in her eyes, the way the sun turned her skin a warm honey-brown, the way her lips curved when she smiled. She was still so beautiful, and he had let her slip through his fingers. He really was a fool.

"No. My pride isn't what it used to be," he conceded. That was the truth. He leaned forward and braced one hand on the ground as he pressed his left arm against his ribs.

"Are you hurt?" Her smile vanished, and he missed it instantly.

"No, but I hope you have some water."

"Of course." She jumped up, grabbed the canteen off her saddle and handed it to him. He took it gratefully and raised it to his lips.

"What happened? What on earth possessed you to try to ride all this way on a day as hot as Hades? Your mother was worried sick when your horse came in without you. She, my mother and half a dozen men are out scouring the ranch for you. You never even told anyone where you were headed. You used to have better sense."

Neal drank his fill, then pulled off his hat and poured the water over his head and neck. "God, that feels wonderful."

"Well, don't waste it. It's a long ride home," she scolded.

He eased his hat back and handed her the canteen. "It will be a long ride if you keep harping at me. My skull hurts enough without you beating me over the head with how stupid I've been. Believe it or not, it did dawn on me that I overestimated my ability."

He was oddly pleased to see the look of concern that filled her eyes.

"Are you sure you aren't hurt?" she asked.

"Nothing except a large bruise on my pride and a headache. My ribs are sore, but I don't think there's any new damage."

She curled her fingers lightly around his wrist. His gaze was drawn to her hand. It felt cool against his hot skin, soft yet capable. Her touch had always been magic. He wanted to take her in his arms and kiss her breathless.

After a moment, she seemed to notice his gaze, and she jerked her hand away. "Have you been out in the sun all this time?" she asked quickly.

"Yes," he admitted. Maybe that was what was wrong with him. He'd been in the sun too long. Or maybe he'd hit his head harder than he thought. Why else would he be thinking about making love to her under the wide-open sky, to a woman who had left him and married another man?

*She wouldn't have married him if you had married her first.*

The thought filled him with regret. His idea of a life without strings had made it easy for her to leave him.

Had it been easy?

He rubbed his forehead as the pain came pounding back. Here he was again, going over what-ifs in the hot sun. "I don't suppose you have any aspirin?"

"I think there's some in the first-aid kit. Let me check." She stood and began to rummage in her bulging saddlebags.

"You've got a first-aid kit?" he asked in surprise.

"What can I say? I think like a nurse," she snapped. "I tried to pack everything I thought I might need, but the ambulance wouldn't fit. Do you want to tell me what happened?"

She knelt down and handed him two aspirin. He swallowed them with another long swig from the canteen and wiped his mouth on his sleeve. "I thought a ride might do me some good, help loosen up my muscles, take my mind off of things."

He studied her face. Softly, he said, "I was going up to Little Bowl Springs."

Her gaze slid away from his. It seemed that she hadn't forgotten their special place. "I guessed as much. How'd you lose your horse?"

"No story there," he said bitterly. "She stumbled in a gopher hole, and I fell off."

He closed his eye and sighed. "Can we discuss this on the way home?" The cool water had helped briefly, but his headache was back with a vengeance. He wavered on his knees. The heat seemed to be smothering him, making it hard to breathe.

ROBYN BIT HER lip as she studied Neal's pale face. Relief at having found him made her almost giddy. Thank God he was safe. It took every ounce of self-control she could muster not to throw her arms around him in a heartfelt hug. It was only because she was glad he wasn't hurt, she told herself. Not because she wanted to hold him close one more time.

She dismissed that disturbing thought. He'd been out in the sun for hours. She could plainly see he wasn't in any shape to spend another few hours in it riding home. Little Bowl Springs was only a mile away. There was shade and plenty of water; they could rest up and ride home in the cool of the evening.

It made sense, except she had never expected to go back there again. Especially with him.

She stood up and pulled her cell phone from her pocket. Ellie answered on the second ring.

"I found him," Robyn said.

"Thank heavens!" Relief filled Ellie's voice. "Is he all right?"

"He's had a fall and too much sun, but he seems okay."

"Where are you?"

"About a mile south of Little Bowl Springs."

"We're by the windmill in Section Three. I don't think we can get a truck all the way up to the springs, but we can get one as far as the south side of the creek about three miles from you."

Robyn stood aside as Neal climbed to his feet and leaned against her horse. He grabbed the saddle horn with both hands and tried to put his foot in the stirrup, but he missed. He hung on to the horn and rested his head on the tooled leather. She made up her mind.

"Look, we're going to head up to the spring and wait until evening to start back. I need to get him out of the sun. I'll call you before we leave there, and you can meet us at the creek crossing."

"Are you sure?"

"Yes. I'm not used to this heat, either, and there's no rush to get him home. Is Mom with you?"

"No. She's gone to pick up Chance. She said to tell you she'll wait for you at home."

"Good." That was one less worry for now. She said goodbye, folded the phone closed and stuffed it into her pocket. She gathered the reins and grabbed Neal's arm. He tried to shrug off her hand.

"I can make it," he growled.

"Yes, you can. If I let go, you'll make it right back to the ground." She paid no attention to his objections as she held his booted foot and placed it in the stirrup. Then she got behind him and shoved as he pulled himself up into the saddle.

"You never could keep your hands off my butt," he said through gritted teeth.

"Oh, shut up and get behind the saddle. I'm driving," she snapped in irritation.

"You're the boss." He eased behind the saddle and spoke gently to the horse that shifted uneasily at the maneuver.

"Lean back so I can get on, or you'll end up with my boot in your ear." The mental image helped soothe her irritation. She swung up into the saddle, and the horse sidestepped at the extra weight. "Easy, fella," she murmured.

Immediately, she regretted her decision to have Neal ride behind her. His arms circled her as he leaned forward and held on. His broad chest pressed against her back, and the feeling brought a quick flash of memories. Memories of the nights when he'd held her like this in the dark and made her feel so loved and cherished.

"You smell wonderful—like spring flowers," he murmured against her hair.

She didn't answer. She didn't dare. Her emotions were a wild jumble of anger, guilt, longing and regret. She nudged the horse forward. A mile farther on, they descended into the winding canyon again and followed the floor of it until they rounded a sharp bend and rode into paradise.

Tall cottonwood trees filled the small box canyon. Their leaves flashed silver and green in the faint breeze that penetrated the narrow white limestone walls. A spring burst from halfway up the wall at the back of the canyon and fell softly onto stone steps. Over the centuries, the water had carved out a hollow in the stone and created a bowl where the water pooled, and then it slipped over the rim to fall into the next bowl, and then the next, until it splashed into a large pond at the foot of the cottonwoods.

Little Bowl Springs. It was a special place that belonged to a distant, happy past. It lay almost exactly the same distance from her home as from Neal's. It had made the perfect spot for them to meet as kids and while away the long summer days. Later, when they were older, it became their special romantic rendezvous.

She drew the horse to a stop beneath the trees. "You can let go now," she said tartly. He did and slid off over the horse's rump. Perversely, she missed the feelings of his arms around her as soon as he let go.

Chiding herself for the fool she was, she swung her leg over the horse's neck and dropped to the ground. After leading the pinto to the top of the canyon, she tethered him where he could crop grass and reach the water without difficulty. She began to unsaddle him. She unbuckled the girth, but before she could lift the saddle, Neal brushed her hands aside and lifted it easily.

"I can get it," she protested.

"I don't mind being rescued by a woman, but I draw the line at watching one work while I rest in the shade."

His lips were pressed into a tight line; she knew it must hurt his ribs to lift the heavy rig, but she kept quiet. He carried the saddle to the foot of a tall cottonwood and propped it up as a backrest.

Pointing at it, he said, "Sit."

She did as she was told. For now. Pulling up several handfuls of dry grass, he began to rub down the horse. Against her better judgment, she leaned back and let him do the job. He moved slowly, and his hand strayed several times to rub his brow, but he managed well enough. When he finished, he walked back to her.

She handed him the canteen, and he took a long drink. When he was finished, he sat down beside her. Neither of them said a word as they rested in the shade and let the peace of the little canyon steal over them.

At last, Neal stood and said, "I think you should strip."

"What?" Startled, she glared at him.

He began to unbutton his shirt. "Unless you intend to swim with your clothes on."

"I don't intend to swim at all," she answered primly.

"Suit yourself." He sat down and pulled off his boots.

Then he stood, shed his shirt and hung it on a limb near his head. "I'm hot, and I'm going to get cool."

Her gaze was drawn to his muscular body and the thick, corded muscles of his arms and shoulders as they flexed. The small scar from the chest tube was almost invisible in the sprinkling of dark hair that covered his broad chest and glinted with beads of sweat.

She watched a single droplet slip free of a curl. She followed its path as it slid over the sculpted firmness of his belly. Mesmerized, she watched as it paused for an instant at his navel and then raced down to disappear behind his hand as he slowly unbuckled the belt that rode low on his hips.

She licked her dry lips. The tiny clink of the metal snap popping open broke the spell. Her gaze flew to his face. He was watching her. The black eye patch made his expression hard to read, but she recognized the dangerous smile that barely curved his sensual mouth.

She raised her chin. "You shouldn't get your wound wet."

"It's healed. My doctor gave me the okay to shower and to swim. He said I could resume… other activities, too." His grin widened as he began slowly unzipping his jeans.

Bolting to her feet, she rushed past him. "I— I'm going to get a drink from the spring," she managed to stutter.

"There's still water in the canteen."

"I want a cold drink."

"Watch out for snakes in those rocks," he called after her.

She paused and stared at the hillside in front of her. She hated snakes. She didn't remember seeing any there when she was a kid. Was he trying to scare her? She glanced back at him, but he had turned to face the water.

With one easy movement, he shed his jeans, and she had a perfect view of his taut, strong legs and buttocks clad only in a pair of navy briefs. She started to call out a warning, but she pressed her lips closed and let him dive into the pool. His head and torso shot out of the water, and his whoop of surprise echoed off the high walls.

"Whooee, it's cold!"

A smug smile of satisfaction curved her lips as she turned away. She did remember how chilly the spring-fed pool stayed, even in the heat of summer.

Listening to his shouts and splashing behind her, she climbed the rocky slope to the source of the spring. When she reached it, she scrubbed her hands vigorously under the stream of cold, clear water and then cupped them to drink. The water was as sweet and refreshing as she remembered.

She drank her fill and wiped a trickle from her chin with the hem of her shirt. Then she sat back on the stone and surveyed the oasis below her.

The horse was busy tearing up mouthfuls of green grass that grew down to the water's edge. Neal was wading toward the deep end of the pool and splashing water at a dragonfly that hovered close to the surface beside him. The sound of the water falling over the rocks and splashing into the pool below began to soothe her frayed nerves. She closed her eyes and relaxed.

The peace of the place stole over her once more. Had it been like this when she was a kid, or had she been too busy having fun to notice? If only she could slip back in time and become that carefree child again. A rattle of stones clattered off to her right, and her eyes snapped open. Maybe he hadn't been kidding about the snakes.

Quickly she stood and brushed off her jeans as she looked around carefully. She glanced down at the pool. The horse continued to crop grass and dragonflies skimmed the still surface of the pond, but there was no sign of Neal.

She waited a long moment for him to reappear. Where was he?

"Neal?" she called.

The horse looked up at her briefly before he dropped his head and began to graze again. She picked her way down the broken rocks surrounding the spring and surveyed the pool. Where was Neal? He couldn't hold his breath this long, could he?

"This isn't funny, Neal," she yelled as she began to walk along the edge of the pond, searching its opaque depths. He had been rubbing his head earlier—what if he'd passed out in the water?

"You come out right now. I'm not coming in after you. Do you hear me?"

Still no answer. "If this is your idea of a joke, I'm going to tear you up worse than that old bull did. You answer me this minute!" she shouted.

Only silence greeted her. She sat down on the bank and quickly pulled off her boots. Then she stood and shed her jeans. A large limb from the cottonwood tree stretched out parallel to the sur-

face of the pond. She stepped out onto it, hoping
to see better. The moment she did, a hand shot out
of the water, grabbed her ankle and yanked. She
toppled into the water.

She came up coughing, sputtering and furious.
As she pushed her bangs and some unidentified
weed aside, she heard the sound of loud, familiar laughter. The same laughter that had echoed
throughout her childhood. Laughter that had been
missing from her life for a long time.

NEAL COULDN'T HELP but laugh, even though it hurt
his ribs. He watched Robyn brush the water out
of her eyes and pull a long strand of green pondweed out of her hair. Her eyes were as green as
the stray weed, and they brimmed with loathing
as she rose to her feet. Her wet cotton shirt held
another strand of the green stuff, draped over one
shoulder like a banner, and he began to laugh
again.

"I can't believe you fell for that same old trick."
His healing ribs rebelled, and he pressed his hand
against them.

"I was twelve the last time you tried it. For
some unknown reason, I assumed you had grown
up since then." She discovered the weeds cling-
ing to her clothes, tore them off and threw them
at him.

The wet weeds splattered in a gooey mess against his chest. "Yuck."

"What possessed you to do this?" she demanded through clenched teeth.

"You weren't going to come in and swim," he answered defensively as he realized his little joke had gone over badly.

"No, I wasn't." She began to slog toward the shore.

"I'm sorry," he called after her.

"You are such a lamebrain. Ouch— Oh!" She fell backward into the water with a grimace of pain and grabbed her leg.

He moved toward her. "What's wrong?"

"Cramp!" she bit out through clenched teeth, floundering into deeper water.

"Hold on—let me help. Don't struggle." His joke had really blown up in his face. He quickly reached her side.

"Okay, I won't!" She surged out of the water and pushed his head under with both hands.

It was his turn to come up sputtering.

Her lilting laughter echoed across the water. "I can't believe you fell for the old 'I've got a cramp' trick."

"You little she-devil. You're going to pay for that." He squinted at her as he wiped his face.

"Have to catch me first," she taunted, then dived in and stroked for the far bank.

He couldn't catch her even when his ribs didn't hurt. She'd always been the better swimmer. He was only halfway across when she pulled herself out of the water on the far bank. When his hand touched the edge, she dived over his head and surfaced in the middle of the pool.

"I'm still faster than you," she shouted.

He swam to her side with leisurely strokes. "That may be, but I bet I can still hold my breath longer."

"Ha! Just try."

They moved to the shallow end for their age-old contest.

"We'll go on the count of three. Agreed?" she asked.

"Agreed." He bobbed beside her as she began to count.

"One, two, three!" She held her nose and dived under the water. A second later, her legs shot up into the air.

He stood beside her and admired the view of her shapely legs as she struggled to stay upside down. He'd always loved her legs. Come to think of it, there wasn't much about her body that he didn't like. A minute passed before her feet came down. He sank under the water and came up gasping for air a few seconds after her.

She frowned at him. "Okay, you still do that one better, but not by much."

He grinned as he slicked back his hair. "No, not by much."

A quick arch of her hand sent a spray of water over him. When he opened his eye, she was paddling away. He followed her slowly. Together they swam, splashed and floated in the pool for the next half hour.

Finally, Robyn called a halt. He followed as she pulled herself out of the water. She turned away quickly when he began to climb out. After sluicing off as much water as he could, he pulled his jeans on over his wet legs. The air was hot even in the shade of the trees. He knew it wouldn't take long to dry off.

He lay down, stretched out in the soft grass and raised himself up on one elbow to watch her. She twisted the water from the front of her T-shirt as she frowned at the baggy material. God, he wanted to make love to her right that second.

"Oh, well, I guess I'll drip-dry," she muttered.

"Why don't you put on my shirt and hang yours up? I won't peek," he added.

"I'll bet you won't," she replied drily, but she grabbed his shirt from the limb. He craned his neck to watch her, but she stepped behind a willow clump and foiled his view.

When she came back into sight, his chambray shirt came to the middle of her thighs, but it rode higher as she stretched to hang her wet clothes on a limb.

Sitting up, he shifted his position. If this kept up, he was going to need another dip in the cold water. Did she have any idea how sexy she looked?

She glanced his way. "Is something wrong?"

He scratched his side. "Too bad we don't have a blanket. The grass is making me itch."

"Ask and you shall receive," she quipped. She crossed to the saddlebags and bent to rummage in one. She held up a folded pad of material. After shaking it open, she spread a white sheet on the grass.

"A sheet? Why would you bring a sheet?"

"In case I needed to cover your dead body."

He arched one eyebrow. "There's a fun thought."

"A sheet can be torn into strips for bandages or splints."

"You're quite the little Girl Scout, aren't you?" Always prepared. That was Robyn.

"Disaster nurse, actually." She anchored the corners of the sheet with stones, then stood and brushed off her hands. She surveyed him for a long moment. "I'd say you qualify as a disaster."

"Ha-ha! I don't suppose you packed anything really useful, like a hamper filled with fried chicken and potato salad?"

He hated to let on that her ingenuity impressed him as he moved onto the smooth cotton material.

The thick grass underneath made a comfortable bed. He stretched out and folded his arms behind his head.

She went back to the saddlebag, then tossed a small red foil packet onto his stomach. "Sorry, all I have are a couple of granola bars. I didn't have time to go grocery shopping before I rode to your rescue."

She dropped cross-legged onto the sheet beside him and began to unwrap hers. He rolled onto his side and propped his head on his hand. For a long moment, he studied her face. "I don't believe I've thanked you for that."

She looked away. "No need."

He touched his eye patch. "Thanks, Tweety. Not just for today, but for that night, too. It helped knowing you were there."

She continued to stare at the wrapper in her hand.

"Does it bother you?" he asked.

She shot him a puzzled look. "What?"

"You know—my face." He lay back, crossed his arms behind his head again and waited tensely for her reply.

"Yes and no."

"Oh, that was helpful," he scoffed.

She stretched out beside him. "You didn't let me finish. Do you remember when my hair was really long?"

He glanced at her. How could he forget? "It was down to your waist, and you wore it pulled back in a ponytail or a braid most of the time, but you looked stunning when you wore it loose."

"Thanks. Do you remember the first time I had it cut?"

He smiled. "You looked like a French poodle. I never knew it was so curly."

She nodded and turned to face him. "I swear, for the first two weeks, every time I caught a glimpse of myself in a mirror, I didn't recognize me. It was like looking at a stranger."

Neal sobered as he gazed into her green eyes. They were filled with sympathy and understanding. Or maybe it was pity.

He lay back and stared at the branches overhead. *Please, don't let it be pity.*

"You look different, Neal, but I'm getting used to it."

"This ain't exactly a bad haircut." He tried to control the bitterness in his voice.

"No, it's not," she said quietly. "But underneath that bad haircut, I was the same girl, and underneath that eye patch, you are the same man."

He was silent for a long time as he stared at the green canopy overhead. The branches swayed and dipped in the hot, dry breeze. A single leaf fluttered down, and his gaze followed it as it landed like a tiny boat on the surface of the pond. "I wonder if that's true," he said at last.

She cupped his cheek with her hand and turned his face toward her. "I know it's true," she insisted gently.

She was so close. He could feel the warmth of her beside him. The wind lifted the ends of her drying hair and let it curl softly at the edge of her face. God, he had missed her. Only she could make him feel whole again.

He captured the hand on his cheek and pressed a kiss against her soft palm. She didn't pull away. He saw her eyes widen and her lips part with surprise. He pulled her toward him until those lips touched his.

ROBYN FELT THE world spin out of focus as Neal's mouth closed over hers. All the pent-up emotions of the day—worry, fear, the memory of the closeness they'd once shared—they all tumbled through her mind, leaving her incredibly vulnerable. Did she still love him? How was that possible?

She couldn't seem to draw away. His arms encircled her and pulled her closer. It felt so right to lie against him. She remembered this: the taste of him and the feel of him. It had been so long.

His mouth left hers to nuzzle her neck. He nipped her earlobe gently and soothed the tiny bite with his tongue. She shuddered with pleasure.

"Oh, girl, I've missed you. Why did I ever let you go?" His voice, husky and deep, sent shivers down her spine as his hold on her tightened. His mouth closed over hers once more in a hard kiss that silenced any reply she could have uttered.

The long kiss ended at last, leaving them both breathless and panting. He pressed his lips to her temple and whispered, "I don't know what went wrong between us, but give me another chance, honey. We can work it out—I know we can."

*Another chance?* The words doused her passion like a bucket of ice water.

What was she doing? Had she completely lost her mind?

"Stop," she muttered weakly. She began to struggle in his embrace.

# CHAPTER SIX

"LET GO OF ME!" Robyn shoved against Neal's chest.

"Honey, what's wrong?" His hold slackened, but he didn't release her.

"I can't do this."

"I don't understand."

She heard the confusion in his voice, and she knew it was her fault. How could she have let things get so far out of hand?

"Tell me what's the matter," he pleaded.

For an instant, she was tempted, so tempted, but she couldn't. She called up every ounce of anger she once felt toward him and struggled harder. "I said, let go of me!"

"Not until you tell me what I did that upset you. Talk to me."

"You don't want to talk," she spat. "You just want to get laid."

He let go of her, and she tumbled backward. "Well, excuse me for the misunderstanding. Two seconds ago, you were climbing on top of me and sticking your tongue down my throat. What was I supposed to think you wanted?"

She clasped trembling arms across her middle as she rose to her feet and backed away from him. "I'm sorry. It was a mistake."

He raked his hands through his hair, took a deep breath and let it out slowly. "I don't believe what's happening here is a mistake," he said calmly. "There's still something good between us. You feel it, too."

She turned away without answering.

He rose and caught her by the shoulders. "I know what a mistake is, Robyn. I've made plenty of them. The biggest one was letting you go after you walked out on me years ago. Why did you leave me?"

Jerking free of his hold, she spun to face him. Her anger surged to a boil. "Don't pretend you don't know."

"I don't. Tell me."

"Do I have to spell it out?"

"Yes, I think it's time you did."

"I left because you were sleeping with Meredith Owens."

The bitter truth came out in a rush. She held her breath as she waited for him to deny it. Somewhere, inside her heart, she still carried the faint hope that it hadn't been true. She had loved him so much.

He stepped back. His arms fell to his sides. "Who told you that?"

He didn't deny it. She closed her eyes against the pain. How could it still hurt so much?

"Meredith did," she answered at last. She opened her eyes and faced him. "How could you? I thought you loved me."

"You knew? All this time you knew and you never said anything?"

"What was there to say? You made your choice, and so did I. If you had given me the least inkling that you loved me, maybe we could have worked it out. Who knows? But I never heard a word from you. Not one word. What was I supposed to think? Was I supposed to crawl back to you?"

"I'm sorry." He looked so stunned.

Even now, she wanted to reach out and ease his pain. Why couldn't she get over him?

She hardened her heart. "Sorry you cheated on me or sorry I found out?"

He stiffened. "Does it matter?"

"Not really. I never thought much of women who went back to men who betrayed them."

His expression turned hard. "Really? I always thought you were one who believed to err is human, to forgive is divine."

"And I thought you were an honorable guy. Guess we were both wrong. I had to make some tough decisions on my own after I left."

"Tough as in whether or not to marry the first guy you met? It didn't take you long to find someone else. Two months?"

Her fury came back in full force. "And that was as bad as what you did? You jerk. You don't get another chance. You don't deserve the one you have. The best thing I ever did was keep him away from you."

Robyn slapped a hand to her mouth as she realized what she'd said. *Oh, God.* What had she done?

A strange look came over Neal's face. "What are you saying?"

"That I'm through talking to you." She started to turn away, but he grabbed her arm.

"We're not through. What did you mean? What are you trying to hide?"

Her anger evaporated. Maybe she had blurted it out because she was so very tired of hiding the truth. "You have a son. His name is Chance."

The color drained from Neal's face. He took a step back. "Are you serious? We took precautions."

"No birth control is one hundred percent effective except abstinence. We didn't use that method. I knew you didn't want kids. You knew I did."

He held up both hands. "Wait. Are you telling me that your kid is my biological son?"

"Yes."

He stood silent for the longest time. What was he thinking? Finally, he asked, "Does he know?"

"He's three years old. Of course he doesn't know."

"Did your husband know?" He was getting angry. She expected that.

She stared at the ground. "Colin and I didn't have any secrets from each other."

Neal came to stand directly in front of her. His eyes blazed with fury. "Why tell me now?"

*Because I want to hurt you the way you hurt me. Because I want to kill these feelings I still have for you.*

She couldn't, wouldn't admit those things to him.

"I don't know. You made me angry acting like nothing had changed. A quick romp in the grass has consequences, but you didn't even think of that, did you?"

He stepped closer. His face was only inches away. "I don't buy that. You never were a good liar."

"Okay." She spun away from him. "Maybe I told you because when I thought you were going to die, I knew what I did was wrong."

"No kidding! And now you want me to tell you it was okay. You want me to say that I don't care that you kept this from me. I'm supposed to be fine with the idea that people believe some other man is my son's father!" His voice rose until he was shouting.

She shouted back. "Yes! You are going to be okay with all of it."

"The hell I am!"

"My son and I have a life that does not—*and never has*—included you. Until five minutes ago, you didn't know and didn't care that he existed. You never wanted kids, so don't pretend that you've suddenly developed a parental streak."

His anger faded before her eyes. She was right and he knew it. "You should have told me, Robyn."

"We can stand here all day and argue about who should have and shouldn't have done this or that. It won't change anything."

"I didn't love her. I want you to know that."

"Frankly, that doesn't help."

"It's not like we were married."

She opened her mouth in shock, then snapped it shut. "We were together!"

He took a step back and held up both hands. "I know. That was a really stupid thing to say. I didn't mean it. I'm sorry. The whole thing was my fault. My mistake. There's no excuse for what I did."

She heard the sincerity in his voice and she believed him. "Very few men can put their foot in their mouth as well as you can, Neal."

He managed a wry smile and shoved both hands in his front pockets. "It's a gift."

He looked so much like Chance did when he was being scolded that she had to turn away. She pushed her hair back with one hand. "We've both made mistakes that can't be undone. We were great friends when we were young. When we grew up, we grew apart. Let's leave it at that."

"Do you want child support? I can do that much for you, can't I?"

She closed her eyes. *Don't start being nice, Neal. I can't stay angry with you if you're going to be nice.*

"I don't want child support. That would hardly be fair since I don't want you in his life at all."

"What about my family? Doesn't my mother have the right to know her grandson?"

"Your mother and my mother are best friends. She sees Chance all the time. She spends almost as much time with him as she does with Jake's kids. I can't make it right for everyone. If I say he's your son, then Colin's parents will have to know he isn't their grandchild. Colin was their only son. They cherish Chance. I won't do that to them. They have lost so much already."

The pinto gave a loud whinny and they both turned, startled by the sound. An answering whinny came from beyond the canyon entrance. A moment later, a rider came into view. Robyn recognized Neal's brother, Jake. He rode a stocky bay and led an Appaloosa behind him.

Robyn poked her finger into Neal's chest. "If you tell anyone about this, I'll deny it and make your life a living hell."

She turned away from him, scooped up her boots and jeans and snatched her still-damp shirt from the branch as she headed for the willow clump. Thank God Jake was here. At least she didn't have to spend one more minute alone with Neal.

She stopped behind the willows and yanked his shirt off over her head without undoing the buttons, but she paused for an instant and held the sun-warmed cotton against her cheek. It held his scent. Tears stung her eyes. Why did he still have the power to hurt her?

Why had she told him the truth? Was she nuts?

Dropping his shirt, she began to pull on her own as she chided herself for her stupidity. How could she have fallen back into his arms so easily? She struggled to tug down the damp pink material. What an idiot she was!

She glanced at his shirt lying on the ground, and she stomped on it. Crossing her arms, she willed the tears back and stared out at the quiet blue water. How could she have forgotten even for a minute what he had done to her?

At least now he knew what she had done in

return. Would he keep her secret, or would he make trouble for her?

It was a little late to be thinking about that. Why hadn't she kept her mouth shut?

Why had she let him kiss her?

The leaves of the cottonwoods fluttered overhead and the willow's long strands swayed in the gentle breeze; their tips tapped circles on the calm surface of the pond. It was this place. Something here made it easy to slip back into the past, to pretend their lives had never changed, that she and Neal had never changed.

She grabbed a willow stem and stripped it to the end. Opening her hand, she let the dainty leaves fall onto the water, watching as they slowly drifted apart.

This place might seem unchanged, but it was only an illusion. She was not the same wide-eyed adolescent who used to play here, and Neal wasn't her perfect hero. She'd spent a lifetime adoring him, and he had turned that adoration into dust.

Spinning away from the water, she stepped into her jeans, then sat down and pulled on one boot. She had been so sure she was over him, but after one kiss, she had literally flung herself at him. She needed to get away, to put some distance between them, to get her head back on straight. Her anger swelled again.

This wasn't love. It was a simple case of lust.

She jerked on her other boot. Maybe it had been a long time since she'd had sex, but she wasn't about to give Neal Bryant a quick tumble because he didn't have some adoring Buckle Bunny handy. She had more self-respect than that.

She stood, dusted her hands together and picked up his shirt. Okay, she didn't care for the picture of herself as a sex-starved widow, but it was better than being the kind of weak-willed woman who went back to the man who had cheated on her.

She wasn't that kind of woman. She didn't need a man. Certainly not some rodeo bum who was here today and gone tomorrow.

She had made a good life for herself and for Chance, a stable life, and she wasn't about to let Neal mess it up.

THE BUSHES SWAYED where Robyn had disappeared behind them. She had known all along. He had a hard time absorbing that fact. It changed everything—and yet it changed nothing. No wonder she had stayed away.

God, how could he have been so stupid? If he'd gone after her and begged her to forgive him all those years ago, would things be different now?

That was a no-brainer. He'd be a father with a kid following him around.

As much as he hated to admit it, Robyn might have made the best decision for both of them.

She was right. He'd never wanted kids. They tied a man down. He wasn't ready for that. He might never be.

He could mess up his own life, but he didn't want to be responsible for messing up another human being. He only had to look at his own relationship with his emotionally distant father to know how deep that kind of hurt could go.

How many times had he tried to win his dad's affection or at least get noticed? More times than he cared to think about. Now that his father was gone, he'd never have the chance to change that.

A hail from behind him drew his attention. He turned away and stepped out to meet his brother. Jake rode up, reined to a halt and leaned an arm on the saddle horn. His gaze slid from the wildly swaying willows to Neal's face. He arched one eyebrow. "Did I come at a bad time?"

"Yes. Go away."

"Now that's gratitude for you." He swung down from his mount and handed Neal the reins of the second horse. "I come all this way to save your butt a ride home behind a saddle and this is the thanks I get?"

"Sorry." Neal combed his hair back with both hands and glanced toward the willows. He didn't like the way things had ended between him and Robyn. He might not have wanted the responsibility of children, but it didn't feel right to pretend the boy wasn't his now that he knew the truth.

This wasn't something they could discuss in front of Jake. Neal would have to find time alone with her. From the looks of things, that was going to be hard to do.

He turned to his brother. "Thanks for bringing me a horse."

"Don't mention it," Jake replied with a lopsided grin. "I love taking long, dusty rides on scorching-hot days."

Robyn emerged from the willow clump. "Yes, thanks for coming, Jake."

She threw Neal his shirt. It struck the middle of his chest. He caught it with one hand. "You saved me a long, boring trip back to your mother's place. I'll ride home from here. If you gentlemen will excuse me, I've wasted enough of my day." With that, she turned on her heels, picked up the saddle and started for her horse.

Neal began to pull on his shirt and button it. Jake frowned at him. He handed Neal the reins of his horse and started after her. "Let me do that for you."

"No need." She smoothed the blanket on the pinto's back and lifted the heavy saddle.

Jake reached her and laid a hand over hers. "Let me help."

She jerked the saddle away from him. "I said I

can get it." She threw the saddle up, hooked the stirrup over the horn and reached for the girth. Jake glanced at Neal with a puzzled expression.

Neal shrugged. "Sometimes it's best to let her have her own way."

The pinto grunted in surprise as she yanked the cinch tight. She dropped the stirrup and turned to Jake. "I'll get the horse back to your mother tomorrow, if that's all right."

"Don't worry about it. I'll send one of the hands to pick him up in the morning."

"Suit yourself." She mounted and headed out of the canyon without a backward glance. At the mouth, she turned north toward her home and rode out of sight.

Jake walked back to Neal. "I was worried you might get heatstroke out here, but I'd say you were in more danger from frostbite. What did you do?"

Neal handed him the reins of the bay and mounted the Appaloosa. "Very funny. Has anyone ever told you to mind your own business?"

"My wife tells me that all the time." Jake swung up into the saddle.

"You should listen to her," Neal snapped. He wheeled his horse and kicked him into a trot.

"She tells me that, too," Jake yelled, trailing after his brother.

The creak of saddle leather and the clatter of hooves over stone were the only sounds as the men rode single file down the canyon floor. The heat was oppressive away from the shade. Overhead, a pair of hawks glided in large, lazy circles against the hard blue sky.

After a mile, the trail cut to the top of the canyon wall. Both horses scrambled up the steep slope and emerged onto the wide, grassy plateau where Neal had been thrown. Jake nudged his mount up beside Neal's, and they started across the prairie side by side.

"It might help to talk about it," Jake suggested.

"Talk about what?" Neal snarled.

Jake reached out and grabbed the reins, pulling the Appaloosa to a stop. "About whatever it is that's eating your guts out, little brother. And don't tell me to mind my own business. My family is my business. Like it or not, you're family."

Neal stared hard at his brother's hand. Jake let go of his reins and sat back. "I'm not saying you haven't had cause to act like a bear with a sore head, but we are all wondering when it's going to stop."

Neal looked up and found his brother watching him intently. "Did you ever wish you could go back in time? I do. I wish I could go back and change the one thing that screwed up my life."

"You could have gotten hurt on any bull you rode in the past ten years."

Neal touched the black patch on his face. "I'm not talking about this. I'm talking about Robyn."

He nudged his horse into a walk, and Jake's mount fell into step alongside. "Mom asked me this morning why Robyn left me, and I told her I didn't know. She asked me why I didn't go after her and demand an explanation. The truth is I was ashamed."

"Ashamed? Of what?"

"You don't know what it's like on the rodeo circuit. There are women who idolize you, trail after you, beg and scheme to sleep with you. They don't care who you are. All they see is that you ride bulls. They think that must make you fantastic in bed. I tell you, it's hard to resist."

"I imagine it would be," Jake said quietly. "Is that what happened?"

"I had been on the circuit for a year before Robyn joined me. She was like a breath of fresh air from home. She knew me. She cared about me. Me. Not some fantasy. We had a good thing together, but I was too young or maybe just too stupid to realize how much I loved her. She'd always been part of my life. I took it for granted she always would be."

Neal stared into the distance. The rolling hills shimmered and wavered, an illusion created by heat waves rising from the prairie in the late afternoon. It was just as hard for him to bring into focus what had gone wrong between Robyn and him.

"After our first year together, she started talking about quitting the circuit, settling down and having a family. Hell, I wasn't ready to settle down. I was moving up in the standings, and I didn't want anything to get in my way."

"Did she know how you felt?"

"Sure she did. We had plenty of fights about it. She wanted me to give up bull riding. For me, that meant giving up my dream. I wasn't willing to quit."

"So you split up because you both wanted different things out of life?"

"I tried to believe that. We'd hit a rough spot in our relationship. It seemed like we were always fighting about something. She wanted to get married. Everyone was expecting us to—her parents, our parents, my friends. I felt like I had a noose tightening around my neck."

"I thought you wanted to marry her."

"I suppose I did, but just the thought of being responsible for a family was enough to blow my mind. You know how I am. You've always been the responsible one, and I've—"

"Always been the wild one," Jake finished for him.

"Yeah, and damned good at it. Dad used to say

responsibility stuck to you like glue and rolled off me like rain off a tin roof."

Jake shook his head. "Dad was hard on you, but it was because the two of you were so alike. He didn't want you to make the same mistakes he made."

Their father had been on the pro rodeo circuit during their early childhood. When he'd come home to ranch for good, he did everything he could to discourage Neal from following in his footsteps. His disapproval only spurred Neal's drive to become the better rider. He became determined to outdo his father's record. Win more. Earn more. Bring home the world-championship buckle that had eluded his father. Then his father would have to take notice. Only it hadn't happened that way. His father had passed away before Neal could throw his success in his face.

"Nothing I did was ever good enough for our old man."

"Neal, that's not true."

"That's how I remember it."

"We'll agree to disagree on the topic, but aren't you changing the subject? I thought we were talking about you and Robyn."

Jake was right. Jake was always right. Neal drew a deep breath and blew it out. "I'm not sure how things got so messed up between us. Money was tight. The camper we lived in was too old and too small. Being on the road constantly was a grind. I do know I didn't help matters. I started staying out late with the boys instead of going home. It gave her one more thing to harp at me about."

Neal paused. It was hard to admit he had been in the wrong, especially to Jake. How could he tell his big brother what a jerk he'd been?

"There has to be more to it than that," Jake coaxed.

Neal nodded. "Yeah, there was. One night I went drinking with a buddy of mine, Ned Owens. We stayed out until the bars closed, and Ned got totally wasted. He passed out, and I drove him back to his trailer. His wife was waiting up. She said to let him sleep it off out in the car. She invited me in for a nightcap."

"You went?"

"I wasn't in any hurry to get the tongue-lashing I knew Robyn was going to give me, so I said yes. One thing led to another, and we ended up having sex on her sofa."

He glanced at Jake to gauge his reaction. His expression was noncommittal.

Neal bowed his head. "Jeez, even now I can't believe I had sex with my friend's wife while he was passed out in my car. I haven't lived the life of a saint, but that was the lowest thing I've ever done."

"I see," Jake said slowly. "It sounds to me like she was a willing participant."

"Oh, yeah, she was very willing. For weeks, Meredith made my life miserable trying for a repeat performance. I told her as nicely as I could that it had been a mistake. She didn't want to hear it. I found out she's the one who told Robyn about us."

"You know what they say about a woman scorned. Old sayings hang around for a reason."

"So I've noticed. That night, I crawled back to our trailer like a whipped dog. I felt like scum. Hell, I was scum. Robyn was asleep. I got into bed, trying not to wake her. She rolled over and slid her arm across my chest. She was so innocent, so sweet."

The shame of that night still burned in his chest. "Robyn was more than the girl I was living with. She was my friend, my best friend, and I betrayed her. For what? I realized that night how much I loved Robyn."

"So you told her what happened?"

Neal almost laughed. "Are you kidding? I didn't have the kind of courage it took to tell the woman I loved that I had made the biggest mistake of my life."

He shook his head. "I tried to pretend nothing had happened. I thought she'd never find out. A few days later, Robyn got the call that her father had had a stroke and she flew home. I waited for her to come back, to call or something, but she didn't. After a few weeks, I realized it was over. I got exactly what I deserved."

"So you let her go?"

"Yeah. When I heard she got married soon after, I was actually glad. Somehow it made what I had done seem like less of a betrayal if she hadn't really loved me. I honestly wanted her to be happy. I knew I wasn't the man for the job."

"I take it you learned today that she found out about your indiscretion?"

"Yes." He'd learned that and a whole lot more. He had a son. It was hard to get his head around that bit of information.

"Okay, answer me one question. Are you still in love with her?"

"I don't know. Maybe."

"Fair enough, little brother. What are you going to do about it?"

## CHAPTER SEVEN

NEAL SHOT JAKE a puzzled look. "What do you mean what do I intend to do about it? What can I do?"

"I'm asking if you intend to tell her you were a fool and that you still love her."

If only that would be enough. "Get real. You saw how it was. She hates my guts."

They rode in silence for a while, and then Jake said, "You know, I don't think she does."

Neal looked at him sharply. "What makes you say that?"

"Actions speak louder than words. She drove Mom to Kansas City the night you were hurt. She stayed with you until you were out of danger. Today, she grabbed a horse and rode out to find you before anyone else did. Call me crazy, but that doesn't sound like a woman who hates your guts. I think she still cares about you."

"Maybe, but she doesn't trust me. How can I expect her to?"

"I don't know the answer to that one, but I expect it will involve a lot of groveling. Before you can gain her forgiveness, Neal, you are going to have to forgive yourself."

Neal mulled over his brother's words as they rode. He'd never forgiven himself for that one mistake a foolish and much younger man had made. Maybe it was time to let that go.

They topped a low rise and rode past a large herd of cattle. The steers raised their heads to watch them. Two red Herefords turned and trotted away. The rest of the herd moved to follow them. Neal found himself studying them carefully, looking for signs of illness or injury, and he smiled. Once a cowhand, always a cowhand.

But it felt good to be out riding the range. He'd missed this, too, this feeling of belonging to the wide earth, of being part of something bigger than himself.

He reined to a stop and called to Jake. "That small, black bald-faced calf is limping on his right front leg."

"I see him." Jake reached down and pulled loose his lariat. "Do you feel like earning your keep, little brother?" he asked, shaking out a loop.

Neal hesitated. "Jake, I don't know...."

"What? You afraid you might miss?"

"Yeah," he managed to croak, although it almost killed him to admit it. There were a lot of things he couldn't do.

Jake reached over, tugged Neal's rope free and

slapped the coils against Neal's chest. "Hell, when you had two good eyes you missed most of the time. I can rope better than you with both eyes closed. Head or heels?"

Neal's tension eased, and he gave his brother a look of gratitude. He took the rope and began to shake out a loop. "Okay, hotshot, you take the heels."

Jake chuckled. "You want the head because it's a bigger target."

Neal nudged the Appaloosa toward the herd. "I'm being easy on you. I've seen you rope. This way all you have to do is put your loop on the ground and let him step in it."

"I've got five bucks that says the only thing you'll get a rope around is your horse's ears."

"Big brother, you're on."

They rode into the herd and cut the limping steer away from the others. It took three tries before Neal's loop fell over the calf's head, and he felt like shouting when it finally landed. Jake threw his rope on the back legs and they stretched the calf until it fell onto its side.

Both cow ponies knew what to do, and they kept the ropes taut as Neal dismounted and moved down the rope to the bawling animal. He saw that a small strand of broken wire had become wrapped around the hoof. He carefully worked the rusted piece loose.

The men freed the steer and coiled their ropes as they watched him run after the rest of the herd. Neal knew he was grinning like an idiot, but he didn't care. He patted the horse's neck. "This is a nice cow pony you've got here."

"He's the start of an Appaloosa line that I want to breed. Good job with the rope, by the way. I guess this proves you can do anything if you put your mind to it," Jake said quietly.

Neal shot a look at his brother's smiling face and his own grin faded. Anything he wanted? No, roping a calf was a far cry from riding a bull. His stomach lurched at the thought of lowering himself into a chute again.

He forced the fear back down inside and tried to laugh it off. "Hell, I thought it proved I'll do anything for money. You owe me five bucks."

"What?"

"Five bucks. Pay up."

"It took you a dozen tries. The rope fell on him by accident."

"Five bucks." Neal held out his hand.

"It wasn't a real bet. We didn't shake on it."

"Five bucks now, and stop trying to weasel out of it," Neal said as he mounted his horse. Their banter continued as they rode home, but Neal's thoughts continually returned to Robyn and her stunning announcement.

He was a father. To a kid he'd never met.

If he had come after Robyn when she'd left, what would their lives be like now? She wasn't indifferent to him. Her kisses proved that. There was just as much sizzle as always between them, but good sex hadn't been enough to keep their relationship together. That took trust.

He had destroyed that trust before he'd realized what they had together, what she meant to him.

The old saying "you don't know what you've got till it's gone" should be tattooed on his forehead.

The question now was, did he want to rekindle a romance with her? Was it even possible? Any relationship would have to include her son. Was he ready for that?

Not wanting kids was a whole lot different than finding out he already had one. If nothing else, Robyn owed him the chance to get to know his son.

She didn't trust him. He got that part of it. He was actually surprised that she had told him the truth. He could blow her big secret, but he wouldn't. Proving to her that she could trust him would be tough. Was it worth the effort?

He thought again of the way she had felt in his arms today. She made him feel like a whole man. Like the man he used to be. Hell, yes. She was worth the effort. But where did he start?

"THANKS, MR. MYERS," Robyn called over her shoulder as she stepped out of the grocery store. She turned around and bumped into a broad, denim-clad chest. "Oh, excuse me."

She looked up into Neal's tan face. Her traitorous heart lurched into double-time. It had been a week since that day at the spring, and his face had been haunting her dreams every night.

Willing her voice to stay steady, she said, "Oh, it's you." She tried to shoulder past him, but he stopped her by grabbing one of the overflowing grocery bags she carried.

"Let me help you with that." He pulled the bag out of her arm.

"I can manage," she protested.

"No trouble." He walked to her truck and stood beside it. She had no choice but to follow him. She opened the pickup door and he set the bag on the seat. He took the second bag from her and set it beside the first. He turned and faced her, and he didn't move out of her way.

Unwilling to meet his gaze, she muttered, "Thank you."

"You're welcome." He still didn't move.

"I need to get going. I'm in a hurry." She couldn't believe how much she wanted to stay. Why couldn't he leave her alone?

"Seems like you're always in a hurry these

days. Can't return my calls, can't make time to see me."

"That's because I'm busy. Please move."

"No."

She glared at him then. "What do you want?"

"I'm not going anywhere until I tell you how sorry I am."

She held up one hand. "Please, I don't want to hear this."

"Well, too bad, because I need to say it."

After pulling off his hat, he ran his fingers through his hair and then gripped the brim of his hat with both hands. "I never meant to hurt you, but I did. I'm so sorry. I was a fool. There isn't any excuse for what I did. Maybe you thought I didn't come after you because I didn't want you anymore. That wasn't true. I didn't come after you because I knew you deserved a better man than I was."

There was so much pain on his face. She didn't want to forgive him, but she wavered, wanting to salvage something of their past. They'd shared something incredibly special once. "Thank you for being honest."

"You're welcome. You deserve someone who can give you the life you want. You're a fine and beautiful woman, Tweety. Don't let anyone tell you different."

He glanced from the hat he was turning slowly

in his hands to her face. "I know you don't want me in the picture, but it doesn't feel right knowing I have a son and doing nothing for him. I've set up a trust that he will get access to when he turns twenty-one. There will be money to pay for college, or whatever. No strings attached."

"I can't let you do that."

"Too bad. It's done."

"Then on his behalf, I thank you."

"No thanks needed. Robyn, I'd really like to meet him. I'd like to get to know him."

She shook her head. Why had she opened her foolish mouth in the first place? "No."

"Just meet him, nothing else. You said it yourself our families are friends and neighbors. I'm bound to run into him someday."

"Someday, but not now." Not when her emotions were so raw. Not when she was questioning the wisdom of what she had done.

"All right. I just wanted you to know I'm sorry for what I did to you. More than anything else, I have missed your friendship. Maybe someday we can be friends again."

He settled his hat on his head, touched the brim in a brief salute and then walked away without waiting for her reply.

When he was out of sight, she climbed slowly into her truck. She sat and stared at the wedding band on her left hand where it rested on the steering wheel. The ring was a symbol of a promise she had made in haste to a young man who was dying. A promise made for all the wrong reasons, and one she had regretted every single day since she had given it.

She dropped her head into her hands in misery and whispered, "I miss your friendship, too, Neal. How did we end up like this?"

After a moment, she raised her head and stared at the gold band once more. "I made a promise, and I have to keep it."

There was no use wondering how things would have turned out if she had made a different choice. She had to live with what she had done. With a tired sigh, she put the truck in gear and started for home.

Seeing Neal had stirred up feelings she wasn't ready to face. Stepping on the gas, she tried to get ahead of her confusion. She was over him.

The town's only stoplight turned red in front of her. She slammed on the brakes just in time. An elderly woman, waiting to cross the street with her dog, shot Robyn a sour look. Robyn raised a hand in apology.

Okay, so she wasn't over Neal. Now what?

Their relationship had ended in limbo, with no clear closure for either of them. It was past time to put that chapter of her life away for good. If she accepted that her attraction to him was a leftover part of that chapter, she could move on.

Only, how?

"Oh, Colin, I wish you were here to help me." They had met in the coffee shop at the hospital where her father had been a patient. Colin's kindness and gentle nature had allowed Robyn to reveal all that she was going through in those first weeks after she'd left Neal. Colin's unconditional support had allowed her to face a future without Neal. It was only later that she'd learned how ill Colin was.

She sat up straight. Her grip on the steering wheel tightened. Colin was gone, but the people he'd wanted so badly to help weren't. She would call his parents and ask them to come for an extended visit. With Colin's parents at the ranch, she would have a reminder every waking minute of the promise she had made and the reason for it. If they could stay until Neal was gone, that was all she needed.

Two days later, Robyn was nailing a new picket on the fence to replace a broken one when a familiar black Lexus pulled up in front of the two-story stone-and-timber ranch house. Her father-in-law flashed a dazzling smile and waved as he stepped out of the car.

Tall and handsome still, Edward Morgan wore his seventy-odd years with distinction. His face was lined with a gentle humor that continually amazed her. Colin had been so much like him. Life had not been kind to Edward, yet somehow he managed to find the strength to bear it. How could she do less?

"Edward, how wonderful to see you." She reached his side and gave him a big hug.

He planted a kiss on her cheek. "I've been missing my favorite daughter-in-law. Why didn't we think of this sooner?"

Guilt blossomed in her. Since Neal had dropped back into her life, she couldn't seem to think of anything, or anyone, else. "I'm sorry. There has been so much to do since we decided to sell the ranch. I've barely had a moment to myself. We're going to have the auction in three weeks."

"I can't believe you want us to stay when you're so busy. Are you sure we won't be in the way?"

"Oh, not at all. You know you're always welcome here. I know how much you love the country. I wanted you to enjoy this place one last time. Before it's gone for good."

"Edward? Edward, where are you?" a halting and worried voice called from inside the car.

"I'm right here, dear." Edward removed a wheelchair from the back of the car and unfolded it. After opening the passenger side door, he bent and lifted his tiny, fragile wife from the front seat.

Sorrow touched Robyn's heart as she watched

Edward gently place Clara in the wheelchair. The once vivacious woman seemed to fade more each time Robyn saw her. Her white hair was drawn back into an elegant chignon. She was as neat as a pin in a simple blue dress with a wide white collar and full skirt, but her blue eyes that had once sparkled and snapped with humor and wit had become dull and lifeless.

"Do you think it's going to snow? Colin didn't take his coat today." Clara began to pleat the material of her dress into small, neat folds.

Edward smoothed her hair gently. He knelt in front of her and stilled her hands by gathering them in his. "It's not going to snow, Clara. It's summer. Feel the heat?"

Robyn knelt at her mother-in-law's side. Her professional training allowed her to hide the shock that rocked her. "Hello, Clara, it's nice to see you again."

"Hello." Clara's eyes showed no sign of recognition as she gazed at Robyn. "Have you come to tune my piano?"

Robyn glanced sharply at Edward. He shook his head and spoke in a firm voice. "Darling, you remember Colin's wife. We're here to visit her and little Chance."

Her eyes brightened for a moment. "Colin's baby?"

"That's right, Colin's baby."

She nodded and smiled as she began to hum softly. She pulled her hands away from his and began to pleat her dress once more.

Robyn motioned to Edward with a tilt of her head and they moved away. She laid a hand on his arm, wishing she could offer this brave man more comfort than a simple touch.

Colin's mother had doted on her only child, but she had never been a strong woman. A car accident had confined her to a wheelchair when Colin was ten. She'd suffered two mild heart attacks before he was out of high school. When his condition had worsened, he'd feared his death would kill his mother, as well. He'd desperately wanted to give her a reason to live, something to hang on to. He'd wanted to give her a grandchild.

Clara had survived her son's death, and Colin had been right. It was because of the baby. But now her mind had begun to slip away. For a brief moment, Robyn was glad Colin hadn't lived to see his mother come to this.

"She's worse, isn't she?" Robyn asked Edward softly.

Patting her hand where it rested on his arm, he nodded. "She has good days and bad days. She's a tad confused now, but she'll be right as rain after she's had a little rest."

"I'm so sorry. Maybe this wasn't a good idea."

"She's much better when Chance is around. I'm glad you invited us."

Robyn scanned his face. "You look exhausted."

His smile widened. "Still tactful as always, aren't you? I'm doing all right. I never thought having Clara in a wheelchair would be a blessing, but at least she can't wander off."

"I'm sorry, Edward. I should help more."

"Now, girl, as you so often pointed out to me when Clara and I wanted you to stay with us after Colin died, you have your own life to live."

"That was different."

"I don't see how."

"Back then, I needed to prove I could stand on my own two feet."

He grinned, shaking his head. "Is that why you spent two years in that god-awful basement apartment while you finished your training instead of letting us help by paying for a nice place to live? If I recall, you couldn't stand on your own two feet in that place without smacking your head on the ceiling."

"It wasn't that bad. Besides, you know it was never about the money. Your emotional support and your love were what Chance and I needed, and you gave us plenty of that."

"You should have let us help pay your way through school. We can still afford to help," he said gruffly.

"Stop. You lost that argument many years ago."

The sound of the screen door slamming pulled their attention to the front porch as a little blond streak flew down the steps and ran straight to Clara. At almost four, Chance was still small for his age, but he was agile, and he didn't hesitate as he flung himself at his grandmother.

Clara looked momentarily startled as the boy threw his arms around her knees, dropped his head onto her lap and hugged her. She patted his head. "Colin, are you home already?"

Chance lifted his head and smiled. She blinked several times, and then cupped his face with her hands. "Oh, how silly of me. I called you Colin, didn't I?" She helped him climb onto her lap. "Ooh! My goodness, you've grown. Edward, come and see how big our grandson has gotten."

Robyn felt the tenseness drain out of her father-in-law's body. "I knew it would do her good to see him. After Colin died, I thought it would be the end of her, but when Chance was born, it was like the sun came back into her life."

He dropped an arm around Robyn's shoulders and gave her a quick hug. "Thank you for giving us back part of our son."

She saw the happiness shining in his eyes as he watched his wife and grandson, and she knew she could never do anything that would destroy it. A promise was a promise. Even if she regretted making it, she would keep it.

She laid a hand on Edward's arm. "I'm so glad you could come. Now I'll have some help getting this place in shape."

"I don't know what I can do. I don't know the first thing about ranching. I doubt you have a need for a retired science professor. We'll only be in the way."

"No, you won't. Besides, Chance needs to spend time with both of you."

As long as Edward and Clara were there, Robyn knew she could find the strength she needed to avoid Neal. Once his doctor gave him the okay, he would be off to the rodeo circuit again and out of their lives. And the memory of his kisses would fade in time. Wouldn't they?

## CHAPTER EIGHT

"I DON'T KNOW if this is such a good idea, Martha. Wait a minute." Ellie Bryant pulled the phone away from her ear and leaned around the kitchen counter to check the stairwell. It was empty.

She raised the receiver again. "I thought I heard Neal coming down, but he's not up yet. He's been trying to do too much. He's been out riding every day. He sure inherited his stubborn streak from his father."

"Ellie, you know our children are never going to get together without a push," Martha insisted.

"Maybe." Ellie hesitated to agree with her long-time friend even if she believed Martha was right. There was more to Robyn and Neal's split than either of them let on.

"Robyn is acting like a dog that's lost the last bone on earth. She hasn't moped this much since he went away to college and she was still in high school."

"She's not in high school anymore. Your daughter is old enough to make up her own mind. She's a mother. She has more to think about than who she wants to date. Leave her be. She won't thank you for meddling."

"She still loves Neal—I know it. Tell me you think Neal doesn't feel the same way."

Ellie couldn't lie. She saw the sadness in Neal, and she knew his feelings for Robyn were the cause. "Even if he does, I don't like to interfere in the lives of my children."

"Oh, phooey! Save that rubbish for someone who will buy it. I won't. I know you, Ellie, and you love to interfere as much as I do. Maybe more."

Ellie grinned as she gripped the phone. "Not quite as much as you do. And only when it's in their best interest. Which is always my top priority."

"Our kids don't realize that their mothers still know best. Besides, it's not like we are doing anything illegal. All we're trying to do is to get them to spend some time together. Nature will take its course if we can get them alone."

"And you think this scheme of yours will do that?" Ellie asked in disbelief.

"It's not a scheme. I do need the help." Martha's voice quivered.

"Why haven't you said something? You know I would do anything for you."

"I didn't say anything because I've got some pride. Or I did have. Ever since I lost Frank, this ranch has been going downhill. We were never as well-off as you were, and I'm not ashamed of it. We made do. But now I need to get a good price for this place. It's all I've got left. Please, Ellie, I'm asking for your help now."

Sympathy for Martha forced Ellie to reconsider. They had been friends since their grade-school days, but the loss of the men they loved within a year of each other had pushed them into a special closeness. If Jacob's death had been as lingering and as costly as Frank's, Ellie might have found herself in the same position Martha was in now.

She loved Robyn like a daughter, and she adored little Chance as much as her own grandchildren, with good reason if her suspicions were correct, but meddling in their lives didn't seem right. This wasn't a case of a simple lovers' quarrel. She could see that much for herself.

"I honestly don't know if I can get Neal to agree to work for you," Ellie said at last.

"You can do it. Tell him you know I desperately need the help, but I can't afford to pay the kind of wage a top hand would get. That's true. Tell him you want him out from under your feet. Tell him I'll feed him as part of his pay. Oh, tell him anything. Just get him to spend the next few weeks here. All he and Robyn need is a little time together. They love each other. They'll see that. Wouldn't you like them to get back together?"

"I'm just not sure." Ellie knew Neal needed something to focus on besides his injury, but was Robyn the answer?

"What's the worst thing that could happen?" Martha demanded.

"They could find out what we're up to and hate us for it."

"No," Martha answered with a sad sigh. "The worst thing that could happen is that they would go on just like they are. Miserable without each other."

"I need to think this over."

"You know, Ellie, Robyn will never take Chance on the rodeo circuit. I think she would insist that Neal quit the rodeo for good."

Ellie glanced up the stairwell once more. It was something she hadn't considered. Her grip tightened on the phone. She dreaded the thought of Neal returning to his deadly sport. Was she foolish to hope Robyn might convince him to give it up and settle down?

Well, it wouldn't be the first foolish thing she'd wished for in her life. She took a deep breath and thrust her misgivings aside. "All right, Martha, I'll do it. What's the plan? When do we start?"

"We start tomorrow. Get him to come and apply for a job with me."

"And if he says no?"

"You're his mother. You know how to turn up the guilt as well as I do. You'll think of something."

NEAL DREW HIS horse to a stop beside the white picket fence surrounding the O'Connor ranch house and scanned the yard. It was a hive of activity in the late afternoon. A white-haired man he didn't recognize was using a pressure washer to clean the rows of farm machinery beside the barn. A tractor with a bale fork drove past and pushed the long steel spear into the first of three large round hay bales on a flatbed truck.

Martha O'Connor was adding a fresh coat of paint to the pickets at the far corner of the fence. A small boy with curly blond hair was busy bouncing a large red, white and blue ball on the sidewalk that led from the front gate to the wide porch steps.

Neal studied the child and frowned slightly. Was this his son? Somehow, he'd pictured a small, dark-haired version of Robyn. This boy took after Neal's dad's side of the family, that was for sure. Most of the Bryants were Nordic types, tall with curly blond hair and sky blue eyes. Neal, with dark hair and dark eyes like his mother, was an exception.

What had Colin Morgan looked like, Neal wondered. A sudden feeling of resentment caught him by surprise. Robyn had left him and married a man he'd never even met. The fact that the man was dead didn't lessen the feeling of jealousy that crawled over Neal. Everyone believed this boy belonged to her husband. Would he ever be able to reveal the truth?

It was hard to picture Robyn as a mother. In Neal's mind, she had stayed the same since the day she'd left him. The reality of just how much her life had changed was playing in front of him. He wasn't at all sure of how he felt about that. Or about pretending this child wasn't his son.

The boy gave the ball a high toss, but his small hands missed when it came down. It bounced over the gate and out into the yard. He pushed open the gate. The bell on it jangled, and a sudden loud beeping that signaled the tractor backing up swallowed the sound.

The child caught sight of Neal and stopped. He glanced at his ball a dozen feet away and then stared at Neal with wary eyes. The sight of the golden-haired boy standing in front of the picket fence triggered a vague memory in Neal's mind. Had he seen the kid before? It didn't seem likely.

He forced a smile to his lips. "Hi, there. You must be Chance. Is your mother home?"

The boy didn't answer. He kept his eyes on Neal

as he edged toward his ball. He was moving right into the path of the backing tractor.

Neal's smile vanished. "Hey, watch out."

The large red machine with wide dual tires continued backing up as the driver lifted the huge round bale of hay away from the truck. The driver in the cab glanced back once, but Neal realized he didn't see the child moving into his path. Robyn's son seemed unaware of his danger as he kept his gaze glued to Neal. He took one more step backward, then turned and darted after his toy.

"Look out!" Neal shouted.

The boy froze when he saw the tractor looming over him.

Neal dug his spurs into his horse. The startled animal leaped forward. Neal reached down and snatched the child up a second before the huge tires flattened the brightly colored ball.

The kid began screaming and kicking almost at once. Neal struggled to hold on to the boy and bring the frightened horse under control. "Hold still. You're going to get us both thrown," he snapped.

People began running toward them. Neal caught a glimpse of Robyn's white face as she raced down the porch steps and flew out the gate. She reached Neal's side first. After pulling her son from his arm, she dropped to her knees, clutching him close.

"Oh, my God! Oh, my God!" she muttered in a trembling voice, her face the color of chalk.

The boy stopped screaming the moment his mother grabbed him. He stared up at Neal with wide eyes. He never said a word.

"You could have been killed," Neal bit out as he swung down and held on to the still-skittish horse. "Didn't you hear me yell? Are you deaf?"

He knew he sounded harsh, but his own heart was just beginning to beat again. The kid has scared him witless.

Robyn looked up. "Yes, he is."

"What?" Neal stared, dumbfounded.

"He is deaf." She watched him with a strange look in her eyes, waiting for him to say something.

His mind reeled as her words sank in. Why hadn't someone told him Robyn's child was handicapped? Why hadn't she told him?

What else didn't he know? She was watching him closely as he digested the news.

Somehow, he sensed that what he said next would be very important to her. Only he didn't have a clue what it should be. Before he could frame a reply, the others surrounded them.

Martha reached them next. "Is he all right? I'm so sorry. I was watching him, and the next instant, when I looked up, he was gone."

The elderly man beside her turned the boy's face toward his own. His hands flew in sign language as he scolded him. "You have got to be more careful, Chance. You could have been hurt."

He let his hand rest for a moment on the child's head as he closed his eyes. Then he turned to Neal. "I can't thank you enough for your quick action, young man."

"Yes, thank you, Neal." Martha threw her arms around him. She was trembling with shock.

She released him and turned to the obviously shaken teenage boy who had stepped down from the tractor. "Danny, what were you thinking? You know you have to be careful when Chance is around."

"I'm sorry, Mrs. O'Connor. I didn't see him— honest I didn't." He twisted the brim of his hat between his hands. "Is he okay?"

Robyn stood with Chance in her arms. "He's just scared like the rest of us."

"It wasn't Danny's fault. The boy ran right in his path." Neal made an effort to defend the young driver. The kid wasn't to blame and everything had turned out okay.

"I'll take Chance up to the house." Robyn walked away, still holding her son tightly in her arms.

"All right." Martha nodded, laying a hand on Danny's shoulder. "Take Neal's horse to the barn. The rest of this hay can wait."

"Sure." He reached for the reins and Neal handed them over.

Martha propped her hands on her hips. "What possessed you to ride over here when you could have driven?"

He didn't like driving. It was difficult to judge distances and make turns. Cars coming at him from his blind side seemed to jump into his field of vision, but he wasn't ready to admit that to anyone.

"I need to get in shape for my return to the rodeo. Riding is good exercise. Don't unsaddle him, Danny. I can't stay long."

"You'll stay long enough to have supper with us. I don't want to hear another word about it," Martha declared. She turned and marched after her daughter.

"Sometimes she makes you want to salute and shout, 'Sir! Yes, sir!' doesn't she?" the white-haired man beside him said with a twinkle in his gray eyes. He held out his hand. "I'm Edward Morgan."

"Neal Bryant," he replied as he shook the hand of the man who had to be Robyn's father-in-law.

Edward glanced toward the house. "Neal. I believe I've heard of you."

"Nothing good, I'll bet," Neal observed drily.

"I prefer to form my own opinions. So far, I'd be hard-pressed to believe anything bad about you. Thank you again for saving my grandson. He's all we have left. I don't know what I would do if anything happened to him," he said quietly.

ROBYN SAT DOWN on the edge of Chance's bed and willed her arms to release her son. Slowly, the terror that had gripped her when she'd glanced out the kitchen window and seen her son almost under the wheels of the tractor began to fade. She closed her eyes and took a deep breath. Thank God Neal had been there. His quick action had saved Chance. She hadn't even thanked him.

Chance patted her cheek and she opened her eyes. He signed, "I'm sorry, Mom." His face was the picture of remorse.

She nodded as she tried to smile and reassure him. "I know."

She spoke aloud as she signed, "You scared me. You could have been hurt. You have to be more careful."

"Who's that man? Why does he cover his eye? Is he a pirate? Pirates don't ride horses. Do you think he has a treasure chest and a sword?" The questions flew from his fingers. Robyn had to laugh as she caught hold of his hands and pressed a kiss on one grubby knuckle.

"No, he's not a pirate. He's a cowboy. His name is Neal Bryant."

*And he is your father.* Would she ever be able to say those words to him?

"He is Mrs. Bryant's son, and he's an old friend of mine," she signed.

"He saved me," Chance signed slowly.

"Yes, he did." Pulling her son close, she pressed his head to her breast. She now owed Neal a debt of gratitude she didn't want and could never repay.

Why was he here? To meet Chance in spite of her objections? She should have known he'd come. Now that he'd met Chance, would he go away and stay away?

The only thing worse than keeping a secret from Neal was sharing one with him. What if he blabbed? What if he insisted she tell everyone the truth?

She hid out in the bedroom with Chance until her mother poked her head in the door to tell them supper was almost ready. Chance was playing with a farm set on the rug beside the bed.

"Are you okay?" Martha asked.

Robyn nodded. "Yes, but I aged ten years in two seconds flat."

Martha stepped into the room and laid a hand on Robyn's shoulder. "It was a close call."

"Too close." Robyn looked up at her. "How am I going to live through the next twenty years?"

"Do you think it gets easier when they're grown?"

"Please, Mom, tell me it gets better."

"I'm sorry, honey. I can't lie to you. You will worry about him your whole life. I still worry about you. Maybe more than when you were little."

"I wish I could change him back into a baby. It was so much easier then."

"But you can't. You have to let him grow up."

"I know." She sighed. "Has Neal gone?"

"I insisted he stay for supper."

Robyn frowned at her mother. "I wish you hadn't done that."

Martha raised both eyebrows. "I should think you would be grateful, more than grateful, for what he did."

"I am."

"Well, you've got a funny way of showing it."

Robyn looked away. "I just wish you hadn't asked him to stay, that's all."

"This is still my house, young lady. I can invite anyone to supper that I want to. What is it between you two anyway?"

"I told you."

Martha sat on the bed beside her. "You told me you both drifted apart. After watching you moon over him from the time you were six years old, I have to admit I was surprised to hear it. But your father was ill then. Maybe I wasn't paying as much attention as I should have. When your father was moved to a nursing home, I was glad to have you nearby. But when you married Colin so quickly, I thought you were making a big mistake. I thought you were on the rebound from Neal and that you'd regret your decision."

"It wasn't a mistake." Robyn looked into her mother's eyes. "Colin needed me and I…" She glanced at her son playing quietly on the rug near their feet. "I needed Colin."

"But you didn't love him."

Robyn's brows snapped into a scowl. "What makes you say that?"

Martha tilted her head. "A mother's intuition. Did you?"

Robyn dropped her gaze to her hands clenched in her lap. "Maybe not as much as I should have, but I know I would have grown to love him if he had lived."

"I never asked you this before, but—did you know he was ill when you married him?"

"Yes."

"Oh, Robyn."

"It wasn't pity, if that's what you're thinking. Colin loved me, and I truly cared for him. We were friends, and there were never any secrets between us. He was so brave and selfless. He was always thinking of others." She grew pensive for a long moment until her mother touched her hands.

Tears stung the back of her eyes, but Robyn blinked them away. "He only asked me for one thing."

"And what was that?" her mother inquired gently.

"He wanted a child. He knew how ill his mother was. He wanted to give her something to hold on to after he was gone. Even in the end, he was thinking of someone else. He was thrilled when he learned we were having a baby."

Martha patted her grandson's head as he galloped a toy horse over her shoe. "So was your father. I wish he could have lived to meet Chance."

"I wish so, too." Her father passed away from a second massive stroke when she was eight months pregnant. She'd buried her father less than three weeks after she'd buried Colin. It had been a terrible time for everyone. Oddly, it was Neal that she'd missed the most at her father's funeral.

"Was it wrong of me to bring Chance into the world and let him grow up never knowing his father?" She was thinking of Neal, not of Colin, but her mother didn't know that.

"I can't tell you what's right and what's wrong, honey, but I can tell you that I am mighty glad to have a grandson. I know Colin's parents feel the same. No matter what circumstances prompted his arrival, I am very, very glad to have Chance in my life."

"Thanks, Mom." She threw her arms around her mother and gave her a quick hug.

"Come down to supper now, and be civil to Neal. It's good to have him home, isn't it? I've missed that boy. Things just haven't felt right since the two of you split up."

"He's not back to stay."

Her mother gave her a sly grin. "You never know. He might find he likes it back on the ranch and give up that foolish bull riding."

"I doubt it."

"You could give him a little encouragement. Would that kill you?"

Robyn couldn't believe what she was hearing. "It's not going to happen."

"Oh, whatever. You were always too stubborn for your own good." She tapped Chance's shoulder and signed that supper was ready.

Chance jumped up, grabbed his grandmother's hand and tried with all his might to pull her off the bed.

Robyn couldn't help but smile. "I think that means he's hungry, Mom. What do you think?"

"I think maybe I didn't make a big enough roast," Martha answered.

"You two go on. I'll be down in a minute. I have to make a phone call."

Robyn picked up the phone. If Neal was going to spend the evening with them, she needed some way to show him, and her mother, that he couldn't come waltzing back into her life. She knew someone who might help her with that.

## CHAPTER NINE

NEAL SAT IN the O'Connor living room feeling ill at ease in what had been a second home for him in his youth. So much had changed, not with the furniture or the walls but with the people inside.

Robyn hadn't come down yet. He wasn't sure what to say when he did face her. He had so many questions about Chance and about his needs. Was there anything that could be done for his deafness? What had caused it?

Edward came into the room pushing a frail, white-haired woman in a wheelchair. Neal rose to his feet.

"This is my wife. Clara, dear, this is Neal Bryant."

"How do you do, ma'am." Neal nodded in her direction.

"How do you do." She glanced up at her husband. "Edward, do I know him?"

"No, dear."

"Have you come to tune the piano?" she inquired.

"Ah, no," Neal answered slowly.

"It's very out of tune."

"We sold the piano a long time ago, Clara," Edward said gently.

She flushed with embarrassment. "That's right. I forgot."

"Mr. Bryant is a rodeo cowboy," Edward explained.

"How nice." She began to smooth the front of the pale yellow-and-white patchwork quilt that covered her legs.

Neal felt a pat on his side and looked down to see Chance standing beside him. The boy began to sign. Neal shook his head. "I'm sorry. I don't understand."

"He says thank you for saving his life today. I want to thank you, too," Robyn said from the doorway. She looked composed now and somehow more remote than ever.

What chance did he have at repairing their relationship if she could barely look at him? "It was nothing. Tell him he's welcome."

She made a quick gesture to the boy, and he nodded.

"Supper is on the table," she said.

"I know I'm ready to eat." Edward wheeled his wife past Neal. "Martha makes a man work for his food around here."

"Do you want a ride, Chance?" Clara held out her arms, and the boy climbed into her lap. "I think it will snow, don't you?" Clara asked Neal as she rolled past him.

He stood in the center of the room for a moment as the others left and gave a small shake of his head. "Wouldn't surprise me a bit."

The kitchen was the same one he'd sat in a thousand times as a boy, but he couldn't remember a more uncomfortable meal. Everyone signed as they spoke. Sometimes they forgot to speak. Edward and Martha were kind enough to interpret the things he said for Chance and vice versa, but Robyn was cool and ignored all but his direct questions.

"It was nice of you to stop in for a visit," Martha said, passing him a heaping dish of golden-brown cornbread muffins.

He glanced at Robyn, but she was helping her son cut up his meat. "I didn't just come to visit. Mom said you were looking for a temporary hand. She insisted I apply for the job. I think she's tired of having me underfoot."

"We have all the help we need," Robyn said quickly.

Martha glanced from her daughter's set face back to Neal. "Actually, I was hoping to take on one more man. Are you fit enough to work?"

"Yes, ma'am. I don't think my ribs could take bucking bales yet, but I can ride fence, doctor calves, fix machinery, whatever you need."

"I need all that and more." Martha rubbed her chin, considering his offer.

"Doesn't your family need you to help out on their ranch?" Robyn asked.

Neal shook his head. "With the drought as bad as it's been, Mom has sold off a lot of the cattle. She had to let one ranch hand go already. I'm not needed there."

He glanced at Robyn and back to Martha. "She was pretty insistent that I come and help you, but if you don't need me—"

Martha reached out and gripped his arm. "Bless your mother's heart. I unloaded on her this morning about how much work there was to do around here. Of course I can use you for a few weeks. I'll need someone to check all the fences, make sure all the windmills are in working order and move some of the cattle."

"Mom, I was planning to do that," Robyn said.

"Good, now I won't have to worry about you out on the range all by yourself. You and Neal can do the work together." She sat back with a self-satisfied grin.

Neal tried to hide the smile that sprang to his lips as he watched Robyn bite back whatever reply she wanted to make. He sensed more to Martha's request than needing an extra ranch hand. She and his mother weren't very subtle, but he was glad to have someone on his side.

It got him where he wanted to be. Close to Robyn. Close to his son. Now it was up to him to make the most of it.

When the meal was finished, Martha stood and announced, "You kids can do the dishes. Come on, Chance," she signed. "Grandma will give you your bath tonight."

Edward pulled his wife's chair away from the table. "I'll be back to help once I get Clara into bed."

Neal stood and began to roll up his sleeves. "Don't bother—we can manage."

Robyn shot him a frosty look, but she nodded. "Well, if you're sure. I think I'll turn in myself. I am tired. I haven't worked this hard in years."

"Good night, Edward." Robyn kissed his cheek and leaned down to drop a kiss on Clara's, as well. "Good night, Clara."

Clara smiled vaguely. "Have your young man look at that piano," she called back as Edward pushed her out of the room.

Neal held back a chuckle. He finally had Robyn alone.

ROBYN WATCHED EVERYONE leave as she chewed her lower lip. Her mother was meddling again. They did need another ranch hand, but she never expected Neal to apply for the job. Somehow her mother had set this up. Robyn didn't dare create a scene about it. That might lead to unwanted speculation.

She began to clear the table. The last thing she wanted to do was spend time alone with Neal. He made her too aware of what her life had been missing, too aware that she was a woman with needs and desires, feelings that she had thrust aside as she'd concentrated on raising her son.

"Wash or dry?"

"What?" She turned to face him, and he tossed a dish towel at her.

"I asked if you want to wash or dry."

She threw the towel back, and he snatched it out of the air. "I'll wash," she answered sharply.

They cleared the table together. Robyn began to wash the stacked plates. Neal patiently waited for her to rinse and hand him each wet plate.

"I like your father-in-law," he said at last.

She glanced at him from the corner of her eye. "Yes, Edward is a very kind and likable man. He's a lot like his son was in that respect."

They continued in silence as she tried to ignore his unsettling presence, but it was like trying to ignore a wasp in the kitchen. Not possible. She handed him plate after plate, trying not to touch him and feeling jumpier by the minute. As she handed him her mother's favorite antique china gravy boat, it slipped from her wet fingers. They both made a grab for it, catching it together as his hand closed over hers.

Their eyes met and held for a long moment. He gently pulled the dish from her fingers and began to dry it. Robyn willed her wildly beating heart to slow down and plunged her tingling hand back into the soapy water.

"I'm sorry about that crack I made out in the yard," he said softly, glancing in her direction. "I didn't know about Chance's disability."

"I gathered that. Thanks again for what you did today. My son means everything to me. I can't imagine what I would do if anything happened to him." She looked at Neal then. His eye patch made it hard to read his expression.

He shrugged off her thanks. "I was in the right place at the right time, that's all. Do you mind if I ask what caused his deafness?"

She pushed a lock of hair off her face with the back of her hand. "We don't know why Chance was born that way. All newborn babies have their hearing tested before they leave the hospital in the state of Kansas. That's how we discovered it."

"It must have been rough for you."

"Yes. It was a blow. Especially for Colin's parents so soon after his death, but they were great. They insisted on learning to sign with me and paying for all the extra testing Chance needed. When Chance was eighteen months old, he underwent surgery for cochlear implants. They didn't work for him, and they had to be removed. He'll be deaf all his life."

She stopped washing and turned to face him. "What are you doing here, Neal?"

"I'm waiting for you to hand me another dish."

"I'm serious."

"Okay, I'm sorry. It's been a weird day for me. I'm here because I needed to meet him. I know you don't want me here, but you dropped a bomb on me when you told me about Chance. I'm still finding my way out of the rubble. I have a right to meet my son."

She scowled and shot a quick glance at the doorway to the living room. She lowered her voice. "Not as far as I'm concerned."

"Fair enough. Then let's just say I'm here because my mother made me come. If I can help you and your mother get a better price for this place, then I'm doing something for Chance, too. Why didn't you tell me he was deaf?"

"Because it doesn't matter. He's just Chance."

"He's cute. Is he ornery?"

She relaxed a little and started on the pots and pans. "You have no idea. Oh, the things that kid can get into."

He nodded, and she watched as a small grin tugged at the corner of his mouth. "If he takes after you, I can believe it. How long has your mother-in-law been, ah, wanting to get the piano tuned?"

She smothered a laugh and tried to glare at him, but the smirk on his face did her in. A grin tugged at her lips. She stared at the mounds of white foam in the sink. Dear Lord, how she had missed his smile. She chuckled, and his grin widened.

"It's not funny," she insisted, but she didn't know if she was scolding herself or him.

"You're right, and I'm sorry." He tried to maintain a straight face but couldn't. He leaned forward and pulled aside the curtain as he looked out the window. "I wonder how deep the snow will get?" he choked out.

They burst into laughter and tried to smother it like a pair of guilty schoolkids.

"And what are you two guffawing about?" Martha's voice came from behind them. Robyn straightened.

"Nothing, Mom," she said, trying not to look at Neal, knowing if she did she would start laughing all over again.

"Nothing, Martha," he added innocently.

"Oh, and how many times have I heard that fib from the two of you?"

"Now, Martha, love," Neal coaxed. "When did we ever tell you a fib?"

"A hundred times. You were thick as thieves and just as much trouble."

"For instance?" He crossed his arms and leaned against the counter.

Martha walked up to him and poked a finger at his shirt. "I'll give you for instance. How about the time you made that diving bell?"

Robyn clapped a hand to her mouth. "Oh, heavens! I'd forgotten all about that bit of lunacy."

"Lunacy?" Neal straightened. "It was a perfectly good diving helmet."

Robyn snorted. "It was a plastic bucket, a garden hose and a bicycle pump."

"It worked. Until you tried to drown me."

She planted her hands on her hips. "My arms got tired. I couldn't pump the blasted thing anymore. Besides, you were only going to stay underwater for a minute. I must have pumped on that dang thing for almost twenty. How was I supposed to know you had decided to walk across the bottom of the pond?"

Martha interrupted them. "You both should have known better. You scared the wits out of my best milk cow. She didn't give milk for a week after that."

Neal chuckled as he apologized. "I didn't know she was there getting a drink, Martha. I only wanted to get some air."

Giggling helplessly, Robyn collapsed onto a kitchen chair. "You should have seen her when you shot up out of the water. You still had that stupid bucket on your head, and it was covered with pondweed, like an alien, a slimy green wig. I thought that old cow's eyes were going to pop out of her head."

Her giggling became infectious. In a minute, they were all holding their sides as they rocked with laugher.

A knock sounded at the door. Robyn wiped the tears from her eyes. "I'll get it," she said between chuckles.

She opened the door, and her laughter faded away. Her knight in shining armor had arrived to rescue her. Did she really want to be saved?

"Adam, how nice to see you."

## CHAPTER TEN

"MAY I COME IN?"

"Of course." Robyn stepped back from the door. Neal watched with interest as a tall, blond man stepped into the room. He was vaguely familiar, but Neal couldn't place him.

"Sounds like I'm interrupting a party," the guy said with a smile meant for Robyn alone.

"No, nothing like that. I'm sorry you couldn't make it for supper. I was about to make coffee. Would you like some?"

"Please, don't go to any trouble on my account."

"Oh, it's no trouble," Robyn assured him.

"Well, if you're sure, then I'd love some."

Robyn turned to Neal. "I don't think you have been formally introduced. This is Dr. Adam Cain. The man who saved your life."

She didn't make it sound like the good doctor had done her any favors. Neal didn't understand the challenge in the look she gave him. He held out his hand and the young physician took it with a firm grip. "Pleased to meet you, Dr. Cain. I'm grateful for what you did for me."

"It was a team effort, believe me. I couldn't have done it without the help of many others, especially Robyn."

A faint blush stained her cheeks at his praise, and Neal felt a prickle of resentment. Just what was their relationship?

Martha spoke up. "Robyn, Chance is waiting for you to tuck him in."

Smoothing back her hair with one hand, Robyn said, "If you will excuse me a moment, I have to say good night to my son. Make yourself comfortable, Adam. I'll be right back."

Neal's vague sense of resentment grew as he watched the young doctor's gaze follow Robyn as she left the room. He recognized the look of a man interested in a woman. Very interested.

Martha turned around and reached into the cupboard. "Can I offer you a piece of apple pie to go with your coffee, Dr. Cain?"

"Yes, thank you, but please call me Adam. You have a very nice home, Mrs. O'Connor. Robyn has told me you're putting the place up for sale."

"Yes. It's too much for me to run." She set the pie on the counter and began to slice it. "Now that my husband is gone, there doesn't seem to be much point in holding on to the place."

Neal knew how hard it had to be on everyone in the family. "Robyn loves this ranch. I know she doesn't want to give it up."

"Her career doesn't leave her much time to gather cattle," Adam said with a laugh.

"Herd," Neal stated in a flat voice. "The term is *herd cattle*."

Adam's smile faded and he changed the subject. "Mrs. O'Connor, has Robyn told you about the nurse-practitioner program scholarship she's eligible for?"

"No, she hasn't."

"I thought as much. Robyn is an excellent candidate. The school is in Denver, but the program is only two years. I wish you would urge her to take advantage of this opportunity."

Martha turned back to her pie. "We don't have the money for Robyn to go back to school. We're already wondering how we'll be able to afford the special schooling Chance will need. The sale of this ranch will cover our debts and what's left of my husband's medical bills and that's about all."

"I understand that, but this is a privately funded scholarship program that would cover about eighty percent of her expenses. With her experience, she'd have no trouble finding a part-time job while she went to school. Denver has a fine school for the deaf, too. It would be a terrific opportunity for both of them."

Martha glanced at him over her shoulder. "What does Robyn say about this?"

"She's thinking it over. I know she's very committed to this community. I'm afraid that commitment will keep her from making a wise choice. I want you to help me persuade her to make the right one."

Neal gave a short bark of laughter, and they both turned to stare at him. "You don't know Robyn very well. Nobody can *persuade* her to do anything she doesn't want to do."

Adam's eyes narrowed. "Maybe not, but she deserves the chance to be more than an underpaid nurse in a one-horse town."

Neal crossed his arms and leaned a hip against the counter.

"What's it to you if she stays here?"

"Nothing. I mean, I know she has the potential to be a fine clinician. I don't want to see that skill go to waste."

"You'll be leaving soon yourself, won't you, Dr. Cain?" Martha asked, sliding a large slice of pie onto a thick white plate.

"Yes, my contract with the hospital is up in a month, and my residency is finished in October."

"What will you do then?" she asked.

"I'll be joining my father and my grandfather in their practice."

Neal stood away from the counter. "In Denver, I'll bet."

Adam's head snapped up. "That's right. What of it?"

"I can guess where the privately funded scholarship is coming from. Smooth but a little underhanded."

Martha stepped between the two men and handed Adam the plate of pie. She laid a hand on Neal's arm. "Chance wanted to say good night to you, too. Why don't you go up now?"

Forcing himself to relax, Neal said, "Sure. Thanks, Martha."

"Don't mention it." A grin twitched at the corner of her lips, but she stifled it. Taking Adam by the arm, she led him to the table. "I make a mean apple pie, even if I do say so myself, Dr. Cain."

"Please call me, Adam, Mrs. O'Connor."

"If you'll call me Martha."

"All right. I can assure you, Martha, there are no strings attached to this scholarship offer."

"I believe you. Please, sit down and enjoy the pie."

Neal climbed the stairs and tried to cool his temper. He wasn't even quite sure what it was about Dr. Adam Cain that irked him. Maybe it was because Neal realized he wasn't in a position to influence Robyn's life and Dr. Cain was. Or maybe he was just plain jealous.

Neal shook his head in disgust. First he was jealous of a dead man and now the good doctor, a man she worked with. The list was getting longer by the minute. Oh, he had it bad. He couldn't get Robyn out of his blood.

He stared down the long hall, wondering which room belonged to the boy. The closest door stood open slightly, and he glanced in.

The light from the hall threw a rectangle of brightness across the floor into the dark room. It illuminated the child where he knelt beside a low bed. He was signing as he looked at the ceiling. Neal realized Chance was saying his prayers with his strangely graceful gestures.

The boy's blond hair caught the light and held it around his upturned face like a halo. Robyn sat on the edge of the bed, watching her son. She clutched a ragged brown teddy bear to her chest.

When he finished his prayers, Chance scrambled into bed, and his mother pulled the covers up to his chin. She laid the bear on the edge of the bed beside him, but it slipped to the floor unnoticed as she leaned forward and placed a kiss on her son's brow. Her face came down into the light. Neal's breath caught in his throat at the love shining in her eyes. Gently, she smoothed a hand over her child's tangled curls and smiled at him.

Neal had known her since she was a child as young as Chance. He had seen her face bright with happiness and streaked with tears. He'd seen her eyes snapping with anger and sparkling with laughter. Until this moment, he'd never realized how much love she was capable of giving to another human being. It hit him in the gut like the kick of a mean bull.

He wanted her to look at him with love like that in her eyes. Was he crazy? To do that, he would need to earn back her trust. He wasn't sure that was possible, but he had to try.

She'd said her son was the most important thing in the world to her. Neal saw the truth of that now. If he wanted Robyn back, it meant he would have to accept this child, too.

Could he do it? Could he learn to love a child with a serious handicap, a child he couldn't communicate with? Feeling vaguely ashamed, he faced the fact that he honestly didn't know the answer.

He wanted—needed—Robyn in his life, but he had no idea what she wanted. Was it enough for her to be a nurse in a small town, or did she want more? Did she want what the good doctor had to offer, strings or no strings? Neal owed it to her to find out before he tried to become part of her life again.

He'd return to the rodeo circuit soon. He had to. His fear gnawed at him like the sharp teeth of a rat whenever he thought about lowering himself down onto the twitching back of another bull. It haunted his dreams and brought him jerking awake at night drenched in sweat. The longer he stayed away, the larger his fears seemed to grow. Soon he would have to prove he was still man enough to ride.

But the grueling pace of the pro rodeo circuit was no place to raise a child. Would Robyn be willing to wait for him to come home at the end of each season? Was it fair to ask her to do that? Didn't she deserve a full-time husband? Didn't his son deserve a full-time father?

He faced the unkind truth. He had some prize money safely invested. His brother, Jake, had a head for business, and he had seen to that. But what else did Neal Bryant have to offer? Certainly not a face as handsome as the man downstairs, or a future as secure.

All he had was his ability to ride the twisting, bucking bulls. A national title would bring him a measure of long-term security. Some cowboys could make more from the promotional deals than from riding, and they didn't have to break any bones to do it.

But the top-selling brands didn't want a runner-up to promote their sportswear and boots. They only wanted the winner. And Neal Bryant was still a two-time loser.

Chance caught sight of him in the doorway and waved. Robyn looked over and straightened. The glow faded from her face as Neal walked into the room.

"Your mother said Chance wanted me to come and say good night," he said quietly.

Chance frowned at him, glanced at his mother and signed.

Neal saw Robyn's faint smile before she looked away, and he asked, "What did he say?"

"He wants to know why you can't talk?"

"Why I can't what?" he asked in confusion.

"Why you can't sign."

"Oh. Tell him no one ever taught me." He watched her sign his answer and saw Chance's quick response. She signed to her son again, and a mulish frown sprang to the boy's face. She didn't elaborate until Neal asked, "What did he say now?"

She stood and started for the door. "He said he could teach you, but I told him you weren't going to be around long enough to learn."

Neal glanced at Robyn's retreating back and then to the boy's frowning face. She was right. He wouldn't be around long enough to learn sign language. But looking at Chance, Neal saw himself at the same age when his mother had just told him he couldn't do something he wanted. His own mother must have seen that same mulish expression more than once. In this instance, he had an advantage over Robyn. He understood what it was to be a boy.

Sticking his thumbs in his ears, Neal wiggled

his fingers at Robyn's back and stuck out his tongue. Chance grinned and clapped his hands over his mouth. Some sign language was universal.

Pressing his palms together, Neal laid his cheek on the back of his hand in a gesture of sleep. Chance nodded and flashed him an impish grin as he settled under the covers. Stepping up to the bed, Neal picked up the teddy bear and tucked it in with the child.

He stared at the boy for a long moment. This was his son, the child of the woman he loved. Did it matter that people thought someone else was his father? Neal wanted Robyn to be part of his life again. To do that, he had to find a way to include this child.

Staring down at the face beside the ragged bear, Neal wondered if that would be so hard after all.

ROBYN HELD THE door open and watched as Neal gave Chance his bear. Bear had slept with her son since the day he'd been born. It had been a gift from Colin, something he'd bought on a whim one afternoon when they had been shopping for a crib.

Colin had picked up the homely little bear and declared he looked lonely and no one was allowed to feel lonely when he was feeling so happy.

She had smiled and indulged him and secretly hoped the ugly stuffed toy would sit on the back of her closet shelf and be forgotten. Two weeks later, Colin had taken a turn for the worse.

Together, they'd listened to the news that he was no longer in remission. His doctors had wanted to try a new and experimental treatment. Colin had squeezed her hand and consented. He had packed Bear in his suitcase and kept the toy beside his bed in the hospital, but he'd never come home again.

He'd wanted so badly to live until after the baby was born, but in the end, the cancer had won out. Chance had been born a month later. She'd given her son the two gifts Colin wanted him to have. One was Bear, and the other was his name.

Neal crossed the room, and Robyn stepped aside. He gently closed the door behind him. "You have a beautiful son, Robyn."

"Thank you."

His gaze roved over her face. Her cheeks grew warm under his close scrutiny. "I think he has your nose and your eyebrows."

He leaned toward her as if to study those features more closely. The old hallway suddenly seemed too narrow as he loomed over her. Had he always been so broad and so tall? The scent of him, like leather and musk, surrounded her and filled her mind with a dozen memories of their nights together—wonderful passionate nights, tender loving nights.

A fierce longing grew in her, a longing to step

into his arms and rest her head against his strong chest the way she used to. She swayed toward him, remembering the sweet way he'd made her feel when he held her, the way his chin rested on her head and how sometimes he had kissed the top of it. She had been so happy, until—

Abruptly, she stepped away from him. Until he had come home smelling of stale beer and covered with the scent of another woman.

She hadn't wanted to believe it, not that night, not even when Meredith had admitted it with open gloating. Robyn's father's illness had given her the perfect excuse to get away, to think things over, but it had given her more than that. Her time away from Neal had showed her the bitter truth. He didn't love her, and he didn't want her back.

He hadn't followed her and begged her to forgive him. He'd never said he couldn't live without her, that breathing was hard to do if she wasn't near him. None of the scenes she'd played out in her head had happened. Robyn couldn't bring herself to confront him with the painful incident. When he didn't call for a month, she admitted the truth. It was over between them.

It *was* over between them. She chided herself for this weakness she felt when he was near. Things could never be the same again. He had to understand that.

She pushed past him and hurried down the

stairs. Adam was sitting at the table. Her mother offered him another piece of pie. He held up his hand. "One's enough for me."

"I'm sorry I took so long and that we didn't get to have dinner together," Robyn said brightly.

"So am I. Your mother is a great cook."

Neal came and stood in the doorway. She ignored him and gave Adam a dazzling smile. "I'd love to go for a drive. Do you mind?"

Adam jumped to his feet. "Of course not. That would be great. Thanks for the pie, Martha. It was delicious."

"You're quite welcome, Adam. Robyn, don't stay out too late. We have a lot to do tomorrow."

Martha glanced from Robyn to Neal, who followed her into the kitchen and stood with his arms crossed and one hip leaning against the counter.

Robyn kissed her cheek. "I won't, but don't wait up." She threw a defiant look at Neal and walked out the door as Adam hurried to catch up with her.

NEAL STROLLED TO the coatrack beside the door and took his hat down. Disappointment cut deep, but he wasn't ready to throw in the towel.

"If you had even a lick of sense, you'd go after her," Martha said with sharp disapproval, her hands firmly planted on her hips.

At least he had one person rooting for him. Neal leaned around her, scooped up the last piece of pie and bit into its flaky crust. The tart-sweet taste of apples and cinnamon burst into his mouth. He licked his lips free of the crumbs and planted a kiss on Martha's plump cheek. "You make the best pie in the whole world."

Her reply was a huff of disgust. "Don't try to sweet-talk me. I'm not the one you need to impress."

He settled his hat on his head. "Martha, if I had a lick of sense, I wouldn't ride bulls for a living, and I'd be chasing after you, instead of your stubborn, willful daughter."

She snorted and shook her head. "I can tell you one thing, Neal Bryant, I'd be a whole lot easier to catch."

ADAM HELD OPEN the door of his black Mustang convertible for Robyn to get in. "I can put the top up if you would rather?"

"No, a drive with the top down sounds wonderful." The leather upholstery was soft and supple as she slid onto the seat. She leaned back with a soft sigh. It was such a relief to be away from Neal.

Adam got in and sat behind the wheel, but he didn't start the car. "Is it okay to admit your invitation took me by surprise? Not that I wasn't delighted."

"Thanks for coming on such short notice. I needed rescuing tonight."

He studied her intently. "It's my pleasure to offer you my assistance wherever and whenever you need it. I hope you believe that."

Robyn looked down, feeling flattered and guilty. She was using him to avoid Neal. She wanted to show Neal there wasn't any room for him in her life. Adam deserved better from her. He was a sweet man with a good heart. "I do believe that, and I appreciate it, but I'm just using you, Adam. I hope you can forgive me."

"Is your mother pushing your cowboy down your throat again?"

"How did you know?"

"I think it was the wild panic in your eyes that gave you away."

"If you ever need me to rescue you from Crabby Gabby, just say the word. I'll be there with bells on."

"Thanks. Where shall we go?" He turned on the engine.

"We could catch the late show in town," she offered.

"I've seen it. Twice. There really isn't much to do in Bluff Springs after dark."

"Today is August 10, right?"

"Yes."

"In that case, I know where there's a great show playing. Go to the end of the lane and turn left."

"Okay. Hang on." He flashed a bright grin,

revved the engine and shoved the gearshift into
First. Gravel sprayed from beneath the tires as the
car shot into motion.

Once they hit the highway, he really sped up.
The low sports car hugged the curves like a dream.
The headlights cut a narrow swath of light down
the dark road as they wound their way through the
rugged hills. The wind whipped her hair, and she
laughed in delight at the sense of sheer freedom it
gave her. After a couple of miles, she leaned toward Adam and pointed ahead. "Slow down and
turn left up there."

He slowed the car and glanced at her in disbelief. "That's a cow pasture."

"Just do it."

"All right, but this car isn't made for off-road
travel."

He turned where she pointed. The metal cattle
guard rattled as he drove over it. "If we get stuck,
it'll be a long walk back to town."

"We won't get stuck. It hasn't rained in weeks.
Stay on the track until we get to the top of that
hill."

"And then what?"

"You'll see."

He drove slowly along the rough trail as they
climbed a steep hill. He braked sharply when the
headlights suddenly illuminated three cows bed-
ded down in front of them. He honked the horn.

One cow rose to her feet and ambled a few steps away, but the other two stayed put, chewing their cud and watching the car.

Adam threw his hands up. "Now what?"

"Drive around them, silly."

"I don't believe this," he muttered as he backed up a few feet and pulled around them. Dry grass and brush swept the bottom of the car with a harsh rattle. "Why would they want to sleep in the middle of the road?" he demanded, steering back onto the faint track.

"Because they're cows." She chuckled at his obvious annoyance. "It's not much farther."

A few minutes later, they reached the crest of the hill. "Stop here," she said.

He stopped the car and turned to face her. "Now what?"

"Turn the lights off." He did. Instantly, inky darkness pressed in around them.

"Dare I hope you have brought me out here to 'neck in the woods,' as they say?"

"Men! You only think about one thing."

"That's not true," he said defensively.

"Close your eyes and recline your seat back as far as it will go. And, yes, it is true." She leaned back until she was almost lying flat.

"Sometimes we think about food."

"Hush now, and listen."

The sounds of the night swelled around them.

Insects chirped and trilled in a droning serenade. The wind combed playful fingers through the tall prairie grass and set it to rustling and sighing. Far in the distance, a cow bellowed, then closer, one of its own kind answered the lonesome call. A coyote yipped in the valley below them. Suddenly, a chorus of eerie howling swelled until the sound filled the night, then it ceased abruptly.

"Open your eyes," Robyn said in a hushed whisper.

The night sky spread above them like a black velvet mantle strewn with a million sparkling pinpoints of light. The pale glow of the Milky Way stretched from north to south across the face of the heavens like a tattered ribbon of gauze. The stars seemed close enough to reach out and touch.

"Oh, man," he said quietly, as if the sound of his voice might disturb the magnificent display.

Robyn smiled, pleased by the awe in his voice. "Isn't it perfect?"

"Yes. Hey, there's a falling star." He turned toward her and she could see the light of the stars reflected in his eyes. "Make a wish and it'll come true," he said softly.

"Really?" Her smile widened. She turned her face back to the sky. "Then I hope you have a lot of wishes to make."

Another shooting star and then another flashed across the face of the night.

"Wow, did you see that? Look, another one. What is this?"

"This is the Perseid meteor shower."

"The what?"

She turned toward him. "Do you know the constellations?"

"I can find the Big Dipper, but med school didn't leave a lot of time for stargazing."

She extended her arm and pointed toward the northeastern sky. "That is the constellation Perseus. If you watch closely, all of the meteors seem to be coming from the same place."

Another bright light streaked across the sky and winked out. "They aren't really coming from the constellation. They're from dust debris left by the comet Swift-Tuttle. We cross its orbit every summer in July and August, but tonight is the night you can see the most meteors. Sometimes as many as a hundred in one hour. Look, two more. That makes six."

"You amaze me. When do you find the time to study astronomy?"

"It was a childhood passion. There isn't a lot to do at night when you grow up on a ranch. Stargazing seemed to be a natural choice."

How many countless hours had she spent poring over star charts and books about the constellations by flashlight as she lay on a blanket spread out in the backyard? Sometimes she had been alone, but often Neal had been with her. Together, they'd read about Greek gods and mythological heroes and tried to find their stars in the immense sky.

She pushed those memories from her mind. She had as many memories of Neal as there were stars in the Milky Way, but he wasn't part of her life anymore. She needed to let go of him. She needed to let go of the anger and the passion.

For the next hour, she tried to count all the shooting stars, but somewhere around thirty-five, Adam closed his fingers over her pointing hand and didn't let go, and she lost count.

It was pleasant holding hands with him in the darkness. Unlike Neal, Adam's touch didn't confuse and unnerve her. It was nice, comforting. It didn't carry with it a wealth of memories. Turning slightly, she studied his face in the dim light. Yes, he was nice to be with. Was he the man who could make her forget what it was like to love Neal?

Maybe.

Was she willing to find out? It would mean letting down her guard and letting someone new into her life. Into Chance's life. Could she do that? The thought was as scary as it was exciting.

She heard the clip-clop of hooves approaching. An instant later, a white shape loomed out of the darkness beside her. A long white nose came over her side of the car.

"What the hell? Look out!" Adam's shout startled her. He jerked her out of her seat and across his chest.

The horse outside her door tossed his head and snorted loudly. Robyn laughed. "It's all right. It's only Babe."

"Jeez!" The word came out with a rush of breath. "It scared the wits out of me."

The white gelding reached his long neck across the seat and nibbled at Robyn's hip pocket.

"He thinks I have some sugar for him. I usually do."

She pushed the horse's head aside. "Go on, I didn't bring anything tonight." He snorted once as if in disgust and ambled away.

Robyn realized she was still sprawled across Adam's chest. She smiled at him. "Thanks for trying to save me."

"You're welcome." The tone of his voice had changed. She tried to push herself up, but his hold on her tightened. She gazed into his eyes and saw the passion growing there. She licked her lips.

"I've wanted to do this since the first day I met you, Robyn." He pulled her gently toward him. She didn't resist as his lips closed over hers.

Maybe he was the man who could make her forget Neal Bryant.

## CHAPTER ELEVEN

NEAL OPENED THE green-painted screen door of the O'Connor home the next morning and raised his hand to knock on the front door. It flew open before he touched it. He stepped back quickly as Martha led Edward out of the house with a blood-soaked towel pressed to his head. Chance, still dressed in pajamas, clung to her pant leg.

"Neal, thank God you're here," she said breathlessly.

"What happened?"

"I was trying to help Martha cut back some of those overgrown limbs at the side of the house. The hatchet slipped out of her hand and came down on my head. It's not as bad as it looks," Edward mumbled from beneath the towel.

"Oh, yes it is, you old fool. I darn near scalped you. I'm so sorry." Her voice trembled. She was on the verge of tears.

He peeked at Neal and winked. "It was an accident. I've cut myself worse shaving. I told her to put a couple of butterfly bandages on it, but she's positive I need stitches."

"You aren't making me feel any better, if that's what you're trying to do. You do need stitches and a tetanus shot." She turned to Neal and asked desperately, "Can you keep an eye on Chance and Clara?"

"Sure, I guess. Where's Robyn?"

"It's payday. She went into town to pick up her check. She'll be back any minute."

Leading Edward down the steps, she headed toward her pickup, and Neal hurried to open the door for her.

She paused long enough to sign to Chance. "Stay with Neal, sweetheart. Your mother will be home soon."

"Clara is resting in bed," Edward said as Neal helped him into the truck. "She shouldn't need anything. Martha, I'm going to get blood all over your truck."

"As if I care about that. Just don't bleed to death before I get you to the hospital." She slammed his door closed and rushed to the driver's side.

Neal stepped back as she started the engine, and he bumped into Chance standing behind him. What on earth was he thinking? He couldn't take care of a deaf kid and an old woman.

He hurried toward the truck and called out, "Martha, wait! Wouldn't it make more sense if I—" He leaped back when she gunned the truck and sped out of the yard.

"If I drove him to the hospital and you stayed here?" he finished lamely as the dust cloud began to settle.

He glanced at Chance. The boy stared at him with wide, wary eyes. Martha had said Robyn would be back any minute. Neal could only hope she was right. He motioned with his head toward the house, but the boy only stared at him.

"Okay, I can do this," Neal said as much to bolster his own confidence as anything else. He held out his hand and Chance took it. Relieved, Neal walked into the house and stopped in the kitchen. The boy climbed onto a chair, propped his chin on his hands and stared.

An unnatural silence filled the air. Neal sat at the table opposite the boy and watched the hands on the rooster-shaped wall clock move slowly around.

"Edward?" The frail call came from the back of the house.

*Great.* Neal glanced toward the hall and back to the clock. Martha and Edward had been gone for half an hour and there was still no sign of Robyn.

"Edward? I need you."

He couldn't ignore the impatience in the call. Shaking his head, he stood up. What had he gotten himself into?

With Chance following close behind him, Neal made his way to the bedroom at the back of the house. He knocked and pushed the door open slowly. Clara lay in a big four-poster bed with several pillows stacked behind her.

"Ma'am, Edward isn't here right now. Is there something I can do for you?" Besides tune the piano, he wondered.

"Who are you?"

"I'm Neal Bryant, ma'am. We met last night. I'm a neighbor."

"Where is Edward?"

Neal stepped into the room and rubbed his palms on his jeans. It would be better not to upset her with the details of her husband's accident. "Edward and Martha had to run into town for a moment. They asked me to keep an eye on things."

"Oh." She frowned at him, and then she gestured toward the corner of the room. "Can you get me up in my chair?"

"Yes, ma'am." At least the little woman seemed to have it all together this morning. He unfolded the wheelchair, set it beside the bed and lifted her into it. She smoothed the front of her dressing gown and smiled up at him. "Who are you?"

Neal sighed. So much for having it all together. "My name is Neal Bryant," he began slowly.

"You don't look like a Bryant to me."

"Well, I am."

A faint frown creased her brow. "My cousin Sarah married a Bryant from Junction City in seventy-nine. The whole lot of them were blond as could be."

Neal had to smile as he knelt in front of her and placed her feet on the chrome footrests. "You're right—that side of my family is blond. I take after my mother's side."

She pointed past him. "Now, he looks like a Bryant."

Neal turned to see Chance standing in the doorway. Was it obvious that Chance was his son? Did she know? Had she guessed the truth?

"That's your grandson, Mrs. Morgan," he said gently.

She scowled at Neal and then beckoned to Chance. He darted to her side. "I know who he is. I'm not crazy, you know."

Neal stood beside the chair. As far as he was concerned, the jury was still out on that one.

Chance tugged on Neal's pant leg and signed. Neal shook his head. "I'm sorry. I don't understand."

"He says he's hungry, and so am I," Clara declared. "What's for breakfast?"

"I have no idea." He could manage to grill a steak, but other than that, he rarely cooked. Most of his meals were ordered at fast-food drive-throughs and eaten on the road.

Clara held out her arms, and Chance climbed onto her lap. "This child is hungry. Aren't you going to feed him?"

He tried to explain. "Ma'am, I don't cook."

"Well, I do! Take me to the kitchen."

"I'm not sure that's a good idea." He raked a hand through his hair. Where the hell was Robyn?

"What nonsense," she said with indignation. "I've been cooking since before you were born, young man."

She began to push her chair toward the door. "If you won't help, we'll manage by ourselves."

"All right, I'll help." She couldn't burn the house down if he was there with her, could she? Stepping behind her chair, he wheeled her into the kitchen and up to the table. Robyn had better have a real good excuse for taking so long.

"I believe I would like some pancakes." She patted the chair beside her. Chance slid off her lap and sat on it.

"That sounds fine. I guess you can just tell me what you need," Neal said.

She looked around the kitchen. "Where is Edward?"

Neal said slowly and distinctly, "Edward has gone into town."

Chance reached over and patted his grandmother's hands. She looked at him as he signed. She nodded and smiled. "How silly of me. I was going to make pancakes, wasn't I? I'm so forgetful these days. See if there is pancake mix anywhere, young man," she instructed Neal in a firm voice.

"Yes, ma'am." He opened the cupboard doors one after another until he located a red box with a smiling Aunt Jemima on the front. He set it on the table in front of her. "Found some."

"Good. Now, I'll need a large bowl, milk and some eggs. Fresh ones, mind you."

He found a gallon of milk and a carton of eggs in the refrigerator. He opened it to stare at the identical white shells. How could a body tell if they were fresh or not?

With a shrug, he carried them to the table along with a large blue plastic bowl. He set them in front of Clara and watched her with a wary eye. The trouble was, one minute she seemed fine, and the next minute she was lost in space. Could she manage pancakes? His glance flew to the yard beyond the screen door. Still no sign of Robyn. She was going to owe him big-time for this.

Clara cracked an egg and dropped its contents into the bowl. "Now, you need to find a griddle and heat it."

"A griddle." He glanced around the kitchen. Where was Martha likely to keep a griddle? He had already opened all the upper cabinets, so he started on the bottom ones. He found a griddle in the last one beside the stove. As he straightened, he realized he'd heard the sound of more than a few eggs being cracked.

He turned around to see Clara dropping the last of a dozen eggs into the bowl, shells and all. Chance stood at the table beside her, tipping the bowl precariously as he tried to fish out the shells.

"No!" Neal made a lunge for the bowl, but Chance tipped it too far. It flipped over and landed on the kid's head as the contents splattered across the floor.

Neal's boots hit the slimy stuff, and his feet flew out from under him. Momentum carried him sliding into the boy. He mowed Chance down like a weed.

Neal came to rest flat on his back with Chance clutched to his chest, both of them lying half-under the kitchen table.

Chance lifted the bowl from his head and grinned at Neal. Thick globs of egg whites and yellow yolks streaked his face and dripped from his hair. A large piece of shell slid off his shoulder and plunked onto Neal's shirt.

"What on earth are you doing?" Clara demanded, moving her chair back. She jarred the table and the box of pancake mix fell onto its side, pouring creamy white powder on the pair on the floor.

"Yes, Neal, what are you doing?"

He shook the powder from his face and tilted his head back. Robyn stood outside the screen door, her eyes wide with shock.

Neal lifted Chance and set him carefully on his feet, and then he crawled out from under the table and stood beside the grinning kid. Chance shook his head like a dog coming out of the water. Pancake powder and drops of egg flew everywhere.

Neal's boots slipped again, but he kept his balance by grabbing the table edge. He could feel the cold egg oozing down his chest. "We were— Ah, that is, I was helping Clara make pancakes."

ROBYN OPENED THE screen door and stepped in. She couldn't believe her eyes. What a mess. "This is helping?"

Egg yolk dripped down the front of Neal's shirt. Wiping at it with one hand, he only succeeded in smearing it into a paste with the powder that dusted him. Chance looked like a slimy apparition from a horror movie as goo dripped from his hair and down his chin. He started toward her, but she held up one hand. "Oh, no you don't— stop right there," she signed. "Look at you. Look at my kitchen."

"Don't worry. I'll have it cleaned up in a jiffy." Neal obviously thought that would reassure her.

"Darn right you will."

"What's for breakfast?" Clara piped up. "I'm hungry."

"You had breakfast before I left this morning, Clara."

"I did?"

"She did?" Neal squeaked.

"Yes, she did." Suddenly, Robyn had to look away from his stunned expression to keep from laughing.

"Him, too?" He pointed at the boy beside him.

"Yes, Chance, too."

Neal moved close enough to whisper, "She told me he was hungry and wanted pancakes."

She whispered back, "She also wants her piano tuned."

Robyn stepped behind Clara's chair and pulled her away from the table, being careful not to roll into any of the egg yolks on the floor. "Come and watch TV, Clara. Your favorite soap is on."

"Where is Edward?"

Robyn looked to Neal for an explanation.

"Edward and Martha had to run into town for a little bit. They left me to look after these two."

"And as usual, you couldn't even manage to do that."

He flushed at the sarcasm in her voice.

"What was so important that my mother and Edward had to leave before I got back?"

"I'll explain later," he said with a pointed glance toward Clara.

"All right. You two stand still until I get something to clean up this mess." She pushed Clara's wheelchair quickly out of the room and returned in a few moments with two large white towels. Neal was trying to get Chance out of his pajamas without making more of a mess.

"I don't think a little more egg on either of your faces is going to matter now," Robyn said, fighting back a smile.

"I guess you're right," Neal conceded and pulled Chance's top off over his head.

After tossing Neal a towel, she wrapped the other one around her son, then picked him up and headed for the stairs. "You can use the shower in Edward and Clara's room. I'll bring you something to wear as soon as I'm done with Chance."

Robyn sat Chance on the rim of the old claw-footed tub and turned on the water. His hands quickly shot out of the towel, and he began to sign. "I like Neal. He's lots of fun. Grandma put all the eggshells in the bowl, but I got them out. She poured flour on us. Didn't we look silly?"

A smile crept across her lips, and she nodded. "Yes, you looked very silly." *And so much like your father.* She pulled a tiny piece of shell from his curls. "You like Neal, do you?"

He nodded and signed, "He likes me."

She turned off the water and helped him into the tub. She picked up a large sponge and began to wash his face, but he took the sponge from her and began to do it himself. Leaning back, she marveled at how fast he was growing up. It seemed all the things she had once done for him he was now determined to do by himself.

He dropped his sponge and signed, "Why don't you like Neal?"

Startled, she replied, "I never said I didn't like him."

"You frown at him a lot. Did he do something bad?" He stared at her, waiting for an answer, and Robyn found herself at a loss for words. How like a four-year-old to hit the nail on the head.

"Yes, a long time ago he did something bad."

"Did he say he was sorry?"

"Yes, he did, but that isn't always enough."

Chance's hands moved slowly, as if he wasn't quite sure what he wanted to say. "When I do something bad, I say I'm sorry. Then you kiss me, and you aren't mad anymore."

"I guess that's true."

"Kiss Neal and don't be mad at him anymore."

"Oh, honey, I wish it were that easy," she whispered, knowing he couldn't understand.

## CHAPTER TWELVE

ROBYN FINISHED HER son's bath, dried him off, dressed him and left him in front of the TV with Clara before taking a pair of her father's pants and a shirt into the guest bedroom. The jeans would be short on Neal and big at the waist, but it would have to do until his own clothes could be washed and dried.

She heard the shower still running. The mere thought of Neal standing naked just beyond the closed door caused the heat to pool in her feminine core. She left the clothes on the foot of the bed and beat a hasty retreat.

The kitchen was spotless and smelled of pine cleaner. She heard the washing machine running in the utility room, and she realized he'd already put his clothes in to wash. Sometime in the past few years, he'd learned to clean up after himself.

She set about fixing a pot of coffee and thought about what Chance had said. If it was obvious to a child she was upset with Neal, then it would be obvious to everyone else. Did they wonder what caused her animosity? Were they the objects of speculation by Edward and Martha? The thought was an uncomfortable one.

Perhaps her son was simply more perceptive than she gave him credit for, and she was worrying about nothing. She poured herself a cup of black coffee and sipped it slowly.

If Neal said he was sorry, then she should kiss him and not be mad at him anymore. How simple Chance made it sound. She had used her anger with Neal like a shield to block out the loneliness of the nights without him. Her anger had carried her through the worst days of her life, letting her face tough choices. Maybe she'd let it drive her into making the wrong choices.

No, she wouldn't accept that. She had made the right decision and helped some wonderful people. She had to be satisfied with that knowledge. She had to be.

She didn't hear his barefoot tread, and she didn't know he was behind her until he spoke. "That smells good. Mind if I fix myself a cup?"

She jumped and sloshed hot coffee on her hand.

"Sorry, I didn't mean to startle you. Get some cold water on that." He took her hand. She tried to pull away. He held on and drew her to the sink.

He turned on the faucet and held her hand under it. The sting of the hot coffee didn't begin to compare to the burn of her flesh where his hand was wrapped around her wrist. She could only hope he didn't notice how quickly her pulse began to pound.

As he concentrated on her hand, Robyn found herself studying him. His hair curled in tight, wet ringlets from his shower. A few traces of gray were beginning to appear at his temples. It was a sure sign that this man was older than the boy she had first fallen in love with. Crow's feet fanned out from the corner of his eyes, and laugh lines cut deep creases in his lean cheeks. A faint frown puckered his brow where the black band of his eye patch crossed it. She wanted to reach out and smooth those lines away. Quickly, she looked out the window and tried to regain some self-control.

"I can manage now." She wished her voice didn't sound so weak and breathless. She tried to pull her hand away, but he wouldn't let go.

"I know you can. Why is it that I seem to hurt you without even trying?"

"It's nothing." She pulled her hand free and turned away to blot it dry with a towel. "No harm done."

"I wish I could believe that."

She chose to ignore his comment. "Where did Mom and Edward have to go in such a hurry?"

"Edward got cut with an ax."

She whirled to face him. "What?"

"He said it wasn't serious, but it was bleeding quite a bit. Your mom thought it needed stitches. She took him to the hospital."

"Why didn't you tell me?" she demanded.

"I just did." He seemed amazed at her anger.

"You should have told me right away."

"I didn't want to say anything in front of Clara."

"I hope Adam is on duty." She pulled out her cell phone and dialed the hospital's number.

NEAL WATCHED HER worried face as she spoke into the phone and realized he had done it again. It didn't matter that he felt the injury wasn't serious or that he thought not frightening Clara was the best move. Robyn wouldn't give him a break. He was always the one in the wrong. He turned and left the room.

Chance got off the sofa and came to take Neal's hand when he paused in the doorway of the living room. At least someone wanted his company. Neal followed the boy to the sofa and sat beside him. Chance handed him a book and Neal frowned. A poignant stab of regret filled him. Shaking his head sadly, he said, "I'm sorry, I can't even read to you."

How many hours had his mother spent reading stories and making up tall tales to the delight of Neal and Jake when they were young? Their father had featured heavily in the stories their mother had created. On their father's rare visits home, he'd never measured up to the hero their mother made him out to be.

Had his dad regretted those lost opportunities? The pursuit of a world-championship title was lonely work, no matter how many people watched from the stands.

Chance opened his book to a page with a picture of a horse. He cupped one hand by his forehead and tipped it down twice.

Neal stared at him with a puzzled frown for a moment, and then he smiled. Repeating the sign, he pointed to the picture in the book.

Chance's face broke into a wide grin as he nodded. Turning to the next page, he pointed to a picture of a woman holding a small boy by the hand. Beneath the picture was the word *mother*. Chance held his hand upright with his fingers splayed and touched his thumb to his chin.

Neal repeated the gesture and pointed to the picture and then to a photograph of Robyn holding Chance that sat on the mantel. Chance nodded quickly.

Neal pointed to Clara dozing in her chair in front of the TV. Chance used the same gesture only he lowered his hand slightly twice. Neal repeated it, and Chance patted his cheek. Neal knew the sign meant grandmother. This wasn't so hard. And Chance was a good teacher.

Soon they had covered all the pictures in the small book and all the furniture in the room. Pulling Neal by the hand, Chance led him out the back door.

Neal hesitated. Should he let the boy go outside without telling Robyn? He could still hear her talking on the phone in the kitchen. She was probably making another date with her doctor friend. A burst of resentment hit Neal hard. Chance tugged at his hand again.

Neal gave in and allowed the boy to lead him outside. With Robyn in a mood today, it might be better to ask for forgiveness than permission.

It was amazing how many of the signs made perfect sense once he understood what Chance was doing. Neal didn't expect to remember all the ones the boy showed him, but it was a start. They made their way around the ranch building with Neal pointing at something and Chance showing him the sign. Sometimes Neal got it wrong and Chance laughed. He opened his mouth wide, and his eyes crinkled like he was laughing, but he didn't make a sound. It was strange but cute.

They were lying side by side on the soft hay in the barn, peering under an old wooden crate and watching a gray tabby cat nurse her four black-and-white kittens when Robyn found them.

"What do you think you are doing?" she demanded.

Neal looked up at her scowling face. "Learning sign language."

Raising his hand, he touched his thumb and forefinger together at his upper lip and pulled on imaginary whiskers. "This means cat."

"I know what it means." She knelt and touched Chance to get his attention. "I have been looking everywhere for you," she scolded. "You know you are never, never to leave the house without telling me."

He signed in return.

Shaking her head, she answered, "I don't care if you are teaching Neal to sign. This is our most important rule, and you broke it. You go to your room. Now."

His bottom lip trembled as he stood up. He gave Neal a small wave and walked toward the house with lagging steps.

"Look, I didn't mean to get the kid in trouble. He just wanted to show me the kittens. We didn't hear you calling."

"I wasn't calling. My son is deaf, remember? He isn't like other children who can go out to play and then come running when their mother calls. He can't hear the tractor backing up or a car coming into the yard or a horse galloping toward him. I have to know where he is every minute."

"You knew he was with me."

She stood and brushed her hands together. "Truthfully, that didn't make me feel better." She stalked out of the barn and left him lying on the floor.

"So, wrong again, cowboy," Neal muttered, watching her walk away. At this rate, she'd learn to trust him about when hell froze over. Damn, she made him mad.

He jumped to his feet and yelled, "Your son may be deaf, but I'm not. All you had to do was call for me. Why is that so hard for you to do?"

She stopped walking, and his hopes rose.

He took a step closer. "I will keep your secret. I respect your decision even if I don't agree with it."

If she would just talk to him... But she didn't turn around. She marched on, leaving him fuming and sorry all at the same time.

ROBYN DID HER best to avoid Neal for the next several days, but every time she turned around, he was there. If she was cleaning out a stall, he grabbed a pitchfork and started on the one beside her. If she was painting the picket fence, he found a brush and started on the other side of the same picket. He rarely spoke. She had to admit he worked hard.

She soon ran out of excuses to disappear each time he began to help. She couldn't ignore the speculative glances that Edward and her mother cast whenever she stomped away from Neal. For some reason, she couldn't bring herself to tell them Neal had cheated on her when they were together. She could hold that against him, but it didn't seem fair to malign him to others. Her behavior afterward wasn't beyond reproach, either.

The real trouble was that every time she did manage to get away from Neal, he was all she could think about.

Her mother took her to task for her rude behavior the fourth day after Neal showed up. Planting her hands on her ample hips, Martha glared at Robyn.

"Young lady, what is the matter with you? You're acting like that boy has the plague or something."

Sweeping the porch steps with quick, short strokes, Robyn said, "I don't know what you're talking about."

Martha stepped on the bristles of the broom, halting Robyn's progress and forcing her to look up.

"Can you see the amount of work he's gotten done in just three days?" Martha demanded.

Robyn's chin came up. "It's nothing I couldn't have done by myself."

Pointing toward the corral, Martha said, "He's been digging post holes all morning in the hot sun. Are you eager to do that?"

"No," she admitted reluctantly.

"Neither am I, but it has to get done. You know we need a good price for this place. If we get what I'm hoping for at the auction, there'll be enough money to pay our debts and maybe, just maybe, enough to send you to that school in Colorado."

Startled, Robyn stared at her mother in astonishment. "How did you know about that?"

"Dr. Cain told me."

The application lay in Robyn's desk drawer. Sometimes she took it out and studied it, trying to figure out a way she could afford to go, but it was no use. Short of winning the lottery, they simply wouldn't have enough money to live on while she went to school, and the deadline for the scholarship application was only a month away. Adam had offered to loan her the money. While she knew he meant well, she simply couldn't accept the money from him.

"Don't you see, Robyn?" her mother went on. "To get top dollar for this place, it's going to have to be in top shape. We can't do that without Neal's help."

Her mother was right. The place needed more fixing up than the two women could manage.

She'd have to put up with Neal's presence. For a little while.

That evening her mother insisted Neal stay for supper again, and Robyn spent an uncomfortable hour seated across from him, feeling his eye on her the whole time.

Chance, on the other hand, couldn't get enough of Neal's company. Her son was turning into Neal's constant shadow. To her surprise, Neal made an effort to include the boy at every turn.

He never made the mistake of taking Chance without asking her permission again. He made sure she knew where they would be. She tried not to worry about Chance while he was out of her sight, but she couldn't help it.

Today, Neal and Chance were fixing some of the dozen broken boards on the corral fence. Instead of making an inventory of all the tack in the barn like she was supposed to be doing, she found herself watching the pair through the open barn door.

Neal pried the broken and rotted boards loose from the fence posts and showed Chance how to measure the length of boards they would need. He was more patient than she would have believed as he showed the boy how to mark and cut the wood. His large hand curled around her son's small one as they drew the saw back and forth.

The sight filled her with a painful longing. Was

this the way things might have been if she had told him the truth?

Neal gave Chance the heavy wood to hold in place while he drove in the first nail. She had to force herself not to run out and help her son. His little arms strained to hold the board still, but his happy grin when Neal patted his head made her realize he wouldn't have appreciated her interference.

"He's really good with Chance, isn't he?"

Robyn turned to find her father-in-law behind her. His forehead sported a nasty bruise and a bandage over his stitches.

"I guess." She began sorting the various bridles, bits and cinches into piles on the long workbench.

"I hadn't realized that Chance was so starved for male companionship."

"What do you mean?" She looked at Edward sharply, then out the door toward her son.

"Look how quickly he's warmed up to Neal. It's as if they've known each other for years. Neal's lack of sign language doesn't seem to be much of a problem, although he's picking it up fast. I guess every boy needs a man he can look up to. Someone to show him how to do things. Someone he can imitate and learn from."

"I hardly think a rodeo bum is someone I want him to imitate." She studied the gold band on her left hand. "It should be Colin showing him those things, or you."

Edward laid a hand on her shoulder and gave a gentle squeeze. "I miss him, too. But, honey, the truth is that Colin was just like me. Give him a microscope or a textbook and he was as happy as a lark, but if you gave him a hammer, he wouldn't have known which end was which."

She chuckled. "That's true. I was the one who changed the oil in the car and fixed the squeaky hinge on the bathroom door."

"Chance must take after his mother, then," he said with a smile. As he watched the pair through the open door, his smile became tinged with sadness. "Sometimes I wish I could see more of Colin in him."

Turning back to her, he said, "I know that isn't fair. Chance is his own person. I love him more than life itself."

"I know you do." Guilt ate at her until she thought it would burn a hole in her chest. How could she have been so naive as to think she could live with this lie? She thought it would get easier, but it wasn't. It weighed on her soul like a millstone.

Edward smiled and hugged her. "If Chance gets his father's courage and strength of character, then I guess it is okay for him to have the mailman's good looks."

Robyn couldn't answer him. She stared out the barn door. Neal was letting Chance hammer a nail. She watched as Chance tackled the task with fierce determination. He clutched the hammer with both hands as he tried again and again to hit his target. Neal leaned down and helped him steady the hammer. The smile on her son's face was suddenly painful to see. Why hadn't she noticed how much like Neal's it was?

If Neal continued to spend time with Chance, Edward was sure to notice it, as well. Her heart began to thud painfully. She couldn't let that happen.

She tried to sound nonchalant. "Maybe it isn't such a good idea for Neal to spend so much time with Chance. Chance is going to be brokenhearted when he leaves."

Edward patted her shoulder softly. "I don't think he'll be the only one."

He turned and left before she could think of a comeback. Was Edward suggesting that she would miss Neal? That was preposterous. She was thinking of her son. He was the one who would be hurt when Neal left. She had to make Neal understand that his continued presence would only make things worse in the long run.

The next morning, she was waiting on the porch steps when Neal drove in. She stood and started toward two horses saddled and waiting beside the barn. "We need to check the fences in the east pasture and to see how many of the windmills need repairs. Are you up to an all-day ride?"

"Sure." He grabbed a pair of gloves from the front seat of his truck and followed her. If he was surprised she was planning to spend the day in his company instead of avoiding him, he didn't show it.

The horses were frisky, nipping at each other playfully, tossing their heads and sidestepping like circus performers. She and Neal covered the first four miles of fence without finding any problems and in total silence.

"You'd better get it off your chest," Neal said suddenly.

She shot him a startled glance and then stared between her horse's ears. "I don't know what you mean."

He reined his horse in front of hers, forcing her to stop.

"You've got something on your mind. So just say it."

Taking a deep breath, she faced him squarely. "I want you to stop spending so much time with Chance."

He stared at her for a long moment. "No."

He turned his horse away and rode on.

Stunned, she stared at his back. Anger surged

through her. She kicked her horse into a trot and caught up with him. "What do you mean, no?"

He stared straight ahead. "No means no. I like the kid, and he likes me."

"I want you to stay away from him."

Pulling his horse to a sudden stop, he turned in the saddle to face her. "Give me one good reason why."

"He'll be hurt when you leave."

"He doesn't expect me to stay," he countered.

"Look, I'm his mother, and what I say goes."

"Not good enough. You're still trying to tell me how to live my life, aren't you? Don't ride bulls. Don't go drinking with your friends. Don't waste your prize money helping some down-and-out old cowboy. And now, don't make friends with Chance. He's my son. If he ever finds out, I'd like him to have a few good memories of me."

"Why are you making this so hard?"

"Did you ever once think that a big part of the trouble between us was your constant harping about how *I* needed to change?"

She drew back, offended. "Are you trying to say your affair was my fault?"

He stared at the ground and shook his head. "No, it wasn't your fault."

"Thank you for admitting that."

He looked up. "And it wasn't an affair, either.

I had sex with her once. Most of that I was too drunk to even remember."

"Once? Ha! She told me you'd been seeing her for months."

"She lied," he stated calmly.

Her eyes narrowed with suspicion. "Why would she?"

"I don't know, but it doesn't really matter now, does it? Maybe she wanted to drive a bigger wedge between you and me. She left Ned and made a big play for me when you were gone."

"I'm glad you weren't lonely."

"I couldn't bear the sight of her. She reminded me of what an ass I'd been, as if I needed a reminder. I was lonely, but I never wanted anyone but you. I know you don't believe that, but it's the truth."

Robyn couldn't quite catch her breath. "When I left, I thought you'd been cheating on me for months."

"Well, you thought wrong. You should have hit me over the head with a frying pan or something and demanded the truth. But no, off you went, and I never knew why. I waited for the phone to ring, too, you know. I wanted to call you and tell you everything and beg your forgiveness, but I was a coward. I made myself believe you wanted a different life, and I didn't want to stand in your way."

She couldn't process what he was saying. Was she partly to blame for the way things had turned out?

He said, "We should take a break and sit in the shade. What do you say? There's so much we need to talk about."

Nudging his horse forward, he rode toward a grove of trees on the other side of the creek.

A horrible sensation began to churn in the pit of Robyn's stomach. What if he was telling the truth?

# CHAPTER THIRTEEN

ROBYN FOLLOWED NEAL slowly as the implication of what he'd said sank in. Once. He had betrayed her once. Did it make any difference how often?

No, of course not. And yet it did. It wasn't the calculated, deceptive affair she had been led to believe. And if what he said was true, it was nothing like the deception she had carried out.

The horses splashed into a shallow creek. She jerked hers to a halt as Neal's horse scrambled up the opposite bank. When he realized she wasn't following, he stopped and gave her a puzzled look. She stared at him for a long moment.

He sat on his horse with the grace of a man born to the saddle. If his ribs still pained him, it didn't show. The scar on his face was fading. Soon it would be only a faint white line. The eye patch had become a familiar feature, and she hardly noticed it anymore. She had been right that day by the spring. Underneath it, he was still the same man, a man she had loved with all her heart.

Why hadn't she had the courage to confront him all those years ago and learn the truth? What a mess she had made of her life. Of both their lives. What was there to talk about? She couldn't undo what she had done.

She had promised Colin on his deathbed that she would never reveal Chance wasn't his child. She had already broken that promise by telling Neal the truth. Edward and Clara doted on Chance. How could she tell them another man had fathered their only grandchild, their only link to their beloved son? She couldn't do it. It would crush them.

She'd had no way of knowing Neal would come back into her life when she had made that promise. She'd never dreamed Neal would want to be part of Chance's life. How had it become so complicated?

A slow grin spread across Neal's face, deepening the crease in his cheeks. He leaned an arm on the saddle horn. "I think his hooves are clean now."

She flushed as she realized her horse was still standing in the water.

Neal pushed his hat back on his head and smiled at her. Her heart flipped over. In that instant, she knew where taking a break in the shade would lead. Back to the same thing that had happened at Little Bowl Springs. She'd be in his arms again in no time. This craving to be with him had to stop.

"I have to go back." She needed to think, and

she couldn't do it with Neal only a few feet away. She pulled her horse's head around and rode out of the creek.

Neal straightened in the saddle. "Are you okay?"

"I'm fine. I just need to go back now. You go on."

"I'll ride back with you." He nudged his horse back down to the water.

"No! I said I'm fine." Panic filled her. She had to get away and get her emotions under control. "Finish checking the fence in this pasture. It's what my mother is paying you for."

He jerked his horse to a stop at the edge of the creek and glared at her. Okay, that was a low blow, but she couldn't think of any other way to make him leave her alone. After whirling her horse around, she headed for the ranch house.

"You're running away again, Tweety," he shouted. She didn't answer him as she rode toward the ranch.

NEAL SMOTHERED A curse as Robyn rode away. He pulled his mount's head around. He had been a fool to hope they could patch things up. Every time they came close to having a conversation about their past, she took off at a run.

She couldn't forgive him. She couldn't admit he had made a stupid mistake, couldn't admit he was only human and not the perfect hero of her adolescent fantasies. Maybe if he had tried sooner.

Hell, who was he trying to kid, he thought with disgust. He hadn't just been human. He'd been a flashing-neon jerk. There wasn't any way to undo what he'd done. He turned his horse away from the creek and rode on beside the seemingly endless stretch of barbed wire and steel posts, looking for loose wires. He could mend a fence, but he couldn't mend Robyn's heart.

His horse stumbled in a gopher hole, snapping him out of his gray cloud of self-loathing. He patted the black's glossy neck as he reined to a stop and studied the sweeping vista that spread out around him.

The rugged hills rolled away to the horizon in every direction. A flawless blue sky arched overhead, promising another hot afternoon. A stiff wind lifted the horse's mane and set the long bluestem grass bowing in undulating waves of green and brown. Pulling off his hat, he let the breeze dry the sweat on his brow.

He'd passed his thirtieth birthday last spring. He was smart enough to know his days on the rodeo circuit were numbered. He fingered the patch on his face. That was if he could find the nerve to climb on a bull again. If he couldn't... No, he wouldn't accept that. He would ride again.

But a winning rider needed more than nerve.

He needed lightning reflexes, exceptional balance and the agility of a cat to evade the danger once he dismounted. And luck, a powerful lot of luck.

He kicked his horse into a walk. His luck had damn sure run out on his last ride. He was a long way from over the hill, but already he could tell his reflexes were a shade slower. His years of experience made up for it somewhat, but the bruises and the sprains took longer to heal. There was always some pimple-faced kid telling him what a great ride he'd made while scoring only a few points less. A kid with a fire in his belly to be the best. Neal knew it wouldn't be long before he'd be the one a few points behind. He was losing his edge. What he really needed was his youth back.

Pulling his horse to an abrupt halt, he turned over an unsettling question in his mind. Was that why he was so determined to win Robyn back? Because he wanted to recapture that part of his past, that feeling of being able to conquer the world because she believed he could?

If that was all he wanted from her, then he was a shallow bastard.

Slowly his tight-lipped frown faded as he pictured Robyn's face. He could see the way her eyes sparkled when she laughed, the way she swept her dark curls back with both hands when she was annoyed, the way her lips looked so soft and inviting, as if they were begging for his kisses.

No, he wanted more than to recapture the past. He wanted Robyn back in his life because his life wasn't complete without her.

He had loved her with a carelessness born of familiarity and youth. He had pretended to himself, and to others, that her leaving hadn't broken his heart. He'd done a pretty convincing job of it. But that moment in the emergency room when he'd realized it was Robyn gripping his hand, whispering he would be all right, when he'd looked up and saw her beautiful eyes filled with tenderness and compassion, he'd known losing her had been the worst thing that had ever happened to him.

Week after week, year after year, he'd gone out and made the best ride he could. He hadn't looked beyond his goal of winning a championship because all he had to look forward to was a future without her.

He wanted to change all that. He wanted to build a future for them together. A future that included his son.

The thought was a scary one. He liked Chance, and he knew the kid liked him. He might not be the best dad ever born, but he couldn't be worse than his old man had been. With Robyn for a mother, Chance would be okay.

It might sound like a plan, but it was full of holes big enough to run a steer through.

Problem number one: What if Robyn wouldn't

take him back? It was a real possibility. Unless he could break through the walls she had built around her heart, the point was moot.

If by some miracle they could work things out, would he be able to pretend Chance wasn't his son? He wasn't sure he could agree to that. The boy deserved to know the truth, too.

"Maybe I should give it up and ride out with what little is left of my pride." His horse's ears twitched at the sound of his voice. "I'd do it, too, if only I hadn't kissed her."

The kiss by the spring had changed everything. He'd known then that he wasn't over her. He was crazier about her now than he'd been when he was eighteen. When she was in his arms, the world felt right. Without her, the world was…empty.

She still desired him, too. He'd felt it at the spring and he had seen it in her eyes a dozen times since, though she tried hard to hide it. How was he going to get her to quit listening to her wounded pride and start listening to her heart?

He gave a snort of disgust. If Robyn was anything, she was hardheaded. He couldn't get her alone for three minutes most days. This morning his hopes had soared, but she had bolted the moment they had an opportunity for a real conversation.

Granted, he hadn't used the most tact in bringing up the subject, but she'd made him angry when she had demanded he stop spending time with Chance. She was wrong about that.

Chance was a great kid, but it was easy to see he was lonely and isolated. Robyn was doing her best to keep him safe, but if she continued to keep the boy tucked so tightly under her wing, he was never going to be able to find out what he could do for himself. Neal knew he was no expert, and he'd bet money Robyn wouldn't take his advice if he gave it, but Chance needed to be around kids of his own age more. He needed to learn to play and fight and make up the way kids did, instead of being such a little adult. He needed a friend.

He mulled over the problem as the horse dropped his head to snatch a mouthful of grass. He pulled the animal's head up. "I guess we'd better quit lollygagging. We've got twenty miles of fence to check yet."

That would give him plenty of time to think of a way to help Chance without antagonizing Robyn.

WHEN SHE KNEW she was out of Neal's sight, Robyn drew her horse to a stop. She didn't intend to go back to the ranch. Her mother would start asking questions Robyn didn't want to hear. Turning her horse north, she headed for an old, familiar childhood haunt.

Half an hour later, she dismounted beside a creaking wooden windmill and tied her reins to a weathered crosspiece. The ruins of a small stone house and a few dozen yards of stone fence were all that remained of the original O'Connor homestead. After walking over to the wide stone fence, she sat down in the shade of a towering elm tree. It was a good place to sit and think—it always had been.

Her horse let out a shrill whinny that was instantly answered from the hilltop. She sat up and shaded her eyes. Had Neal followed her? She relaxed when she saw it was only old Babe ambling down the long hill. He spent a moment nose to nose with her mount, and then he trotted over and began a hopeful investigation of her pockets.

"You shameless mooch." She stood and ran a hand down the gelding's sleek neck, pulling a cocklebur free from his mane.

"I'm sorry I haven't been out to visit lately." Genuine regret swept over her.

She scratched her old friend behind the ear. "I just can't seem to find the time. That's a poor excuse, isn't it, after all the adventures you carried me on?"

Tears welled up in her eyes and she struggled to hold them back. Wrapping her arms around Babe's sturdy neck, she buried her face in his mane and poured out her troubles along with her tears.

"We're going to sell the ranch, and I hate it! I

just hate it! I have to pretend it doesn't matter so I won't upset Mom. And Neal has come back."

Drawing a deep, shaky breath, she pulled away and scrubbed at her face. "Oh, God, I've made such a mess of my life."

She sniffed and wiped her cheeks. The horse's big eyes seemed to hold compassion and understanding as he softly nuzzled her cheek.

"I've tried not to love him anymore. God knows I've tried. He's so wrong for me. He's a rodeo bum. That's all he's ever cared about. He'll go back to it even if it kills him, which it almost did. Why would I want to tie myself to someone like that? I don't, but I can't get him out of my head.

"I'm not sure he'll ever forgive me for not telling him about Chance. I robbed him of something precious even though I've told him now. I was so hurt and so angry back then. What do I do if I can't stay angry at him anymore?"

She glanced up at the flawless blue sky. "Oh, Colin, why did you ever ask me to make such a stupid promise? And why did I ever agree to it?"

The horse dropped his head and began to crop at the long grass beside the stone fence. Robyn gave him a sad smile. "Bored with my problems already? I was just getting started."

She stood and ran a hand down the horse's back and over his rump. "Easy, boy," she crooned. She bent and tapped his hind leg. He picked up his foot, and she made a quick check of his hoof and shoe.

"Anyway, it's not like Neal's going to stick around. He's going to go back to riding those stupid bulls." She dropped Babe's hind leg and moved to his front one.

"I have to think about what's best for Chance. That's not having a father who is always riding off into the sunset. Adam Cain is such a good man. I think I could really care for him, but I don't want to use him as a shield to keep Neal at bay. That's not fair to any of us."

She moved to Babe's other hind leg. He raised it obediently. She noticed his shoe was loose. She straightened and patted his rump. "I'll get the farrier out to put a new one on right away. I can at least fix your problem if I can't fix my own."

Moving up to his head, she stroked his cheek. "Thanks for listening. But, as usual, you don't have a bit of advice to offer, do you?"

He shook his head, then lowered it and nudged her boot.

"Heavens, I almost forgot."

Amazed that Babe remembered their long-ago routine, she turned around and held up each of her feet. He touched first one then the other with his nose as if inspecting her shoes. She'd taught him a wide array of tricks. This one had amused her family, schoolmates and every farrier that had ever shod the little white horse. Did he remember the whole trick? It had been years since they'd done it.

With her back to him, she planted her hands firmly on her hips and demanded, "Are you done yet?"

On cue, he flipped her hat off her head.

"Hey!" She bent to retrieve it and he gave her rump a quick push with his nose. In her youth, she would have sprawled in the dirt and laughed herself silly. Now she simply snatched her hat up, slapped it on her head and turned to applaud. Babe lowered his head in a bow.

"Good boy." Smiling, she patted his neck, but her grin faded as the weight of her troubles pressed in again.

"Playing games with you won't help me, Babe. What should I do?"

The answer was nothing.

She would have to leave things as they were. Neal would go his own way when he was ready. She couldn't follow him even if she wanted to. She had too many responsibilities in her life. And then there was Adam.

She was meeting him for dinner tonight. She enjoyed his company, and she knew Adam enjoyed hers. He didn't pressure her or leave her feeling mixed up or angry. He made her feel safe.

But with Neal, she had always felt wild and free.

She shook her head. That was the past. What she had to do was make a future for herself and for Chance.

Babe walked away from her and stopped at the tank beside the windmill. He stuck his head in, way in. The tank shouldn't be that low.

Frowning, she walked up beside him. Only a few inches of water covered the bottom. Glancing up, she saw the rusty metal vanes of the windmill were turning, but no water poured out of the long pipe that ran to the tank.

"Dang, fella, looks like it was a good thing I came this way." There were cattle and horses depending on this water source. She stepped up onto the wooden platform to check the pump and pipes at the base of it. With a sudden sharp crack, the old boards gave way, and she plunged into darkness.

NEAL CLIMBED THE steps of the porch at the O'Connor ranch with weary relief. A full day in the saddle had been a little more than he was ready for, but he'd managed it. He was nearly healed. Now all he had to do was find the courage to try eight seconds on a bull.

He paused outside Martha's screen door and looked down at himself with a grimace of distaste. He pulled off his hat and slapped it against his clothes in an attempt to remove some of the dust. It didn't do much good.

Martha pushed open the door. "My word, don't you look hot and dusty. Don't stand out here all day. Come in and have some lemonade."

Chance squeezed by her to wrap his arms around Neal's leg and grin at him. Neal signed, "Hello."

"Lemonade sounds great." He dropped his hat on Chance's head and swung the boy up to his shoulders. Chance held on to the oversize hat with one hand and wrapped an arm across Neal's face.

"Hey, I've only got one eye that I can see out of." Neal moved the boy's hand. Chance couldn't hear his comment, but Martha could. It was getting a little easier to joke about his injury. Maybe one day he'd become used to his scarred face and each little reminder of what he'd lost wouldn't hurt as much.

Did Chance feel the same way about his hearing? Would he learn to make jokes about his handicap to keep others from laughing at him? Maybe the two of them had more in common than he had thought.

"Come on—you're lettin' flies in the house," Martha scolded, but the twinkle in her eyes belied her stern tone.

Neal ducked through the doorway. The cowboy hat toppled off Chance's head, landing at Martha's feet as she stood holding the door open.

"Men! All I ever do is pick up after 'em," she grumbled, snatching it up.

Neal somersaulted the boy off his neck and set him on the floor with a thump. Chance staggered a few steps with his arms outstretched and rolled his eyes, and then he signed the same word several times.

Neal looked at Martha. "What's he saying?"

Martha grinned as she handed him his hat. "He says, 'Again! Again!'"

Neal laughed as he hung his hat on a peg by the door. "Nope, I'm too thirsty. How do I sign that?"

Martha demonstrated and he repeated it. Chance pouted a moment but brightened when Neal drew a piece of candy from the front pocket of his jeans and held it out. Chance quickly tore off the wrapper and popped the Life Saver gummy into his mouth.

Martha opened the refrigerator and pulled out a tall glass pitcher filled to the brim with lemonade and slices of fresh lemons. She filled two glasses and handed one to each of them. Neal downed his in one long drink.

"That hits the spot." He held out the glass and she filled it again.

"Now that you've cut the dust, try tasting it this time."

He gave her a sheepish grin and nodded.

Pouring another glass, she glanced out the door

and asked, "Is Robyn coming soon? She's going to be late for her date if she doesn't hurry."

Neal froze with the glass halfway to his lips. "She's not here?" he asked sharply.

# CHAPTER FOURTEEN

"I THOUGHT ROBYN was with you." Martha's startled gaze met Neal's.

A spiral of worry formed in the pit of Neal's gut. "She was with me until about four hours ago. We split up at the creek. She said she was going home."

"She hasn't been back." Martha set the pitcher on the table carefully and clasped her hands together. "Where could she be?"

"She probably found some work to do and forgot the time." He was trying to reassure himself as well as Martha.

"I don't think so. She's meeting that young doctor in town for dinner tonight. She wouldn't forget about that." Martha moved to the doorway and scanned the yard before she turned back to Neal.

Another date with the handsome Dr. Cain? No, Robyn wouldn't forget that. That explained a lot. She wouldn't admit she cared for him because she cared for someone else. Maybe he'd waited too long to come back, or maybe it just wasn't meant to be.

None of that mattered now. She was long over-due, and a dozen unpleasant reasons for it crowded into his mind. After setting his glass on the table, he grabbed his hat and started out the door. "I'll saddle a fresh horse and go look for her."

Martha followed him onto the porch. "Thank you, Neal. Do you have your cell phone?"

"I do."

"I'll call if she comes in before you get back. You can call when you find her."

He reached for her hand and gave a gentle squeeze. "Try not to worry. I'll find her."

"I know you will."

"If she's not back by dark, get a search party started. Call Jake—he'll know what to do. Tell them to spread out from Hunter's Creek where the south fence line crosses it. That was the last place I saw her."

"All right."

Within minutes, he was urging a chestnut geld-ing into a ground-eating lope across the dry prai-rie. He pressed the big horse hard, knowing he might need every minute of daylight he had left. The picture of her lying injured and alone some-where out in the vast grassland ate at his soul.

If they hadn't quarreled, if he hadn't kept insist-ing they talk about the past, she would have been safe at home by now. He wasn't much for praying, but he sent a quick plea heavenward now. *Please, God. Let me find her and let her be okay.*

At the top of the hill above Hunter's Creek, he pulled the blowing horse to a halt and studied the ground. Riding in slowly widening circles, he searched for a clue to which way she'd gone. The hard, dry ground held little sign, but at the base of the hill, he found a clear print where she'd crossed a shallow draw, heading due north.

He scanned the rough, broken country ahead. Why would she go that way? There wasn't anything out there except the ruins of an old homestead. He urged the lathered horse on and kept scanning the ground for more signs. He didn't see anything. Half an hour later, he crested a rise and stared at the crumbling stone buildings and old wooden windmill below.

He blew out a sigh of relief as he recognized the horses standing beside it. One was the bay Robyn had been riding and the other was her old gelding, Babe. His relief was short-lived, however, as he scanned the area and failed to see any sign of Robyn. He urged his tired horse down the hill.

Pulling to a halt beside the two horses, he noticed the bay's reins were tied to the windmill. At least the horse hadn't just wandered there after losing his rider. Neal stood in the stirrups and opened his mouth to call her name when a sudden string of swearwords erupted from the ground in front of him. His horse shied in fright as a rock came flying out of a big hole in the windmill's platform, missing his head by inches.

Relief poured through his veins, making his knees weak as he dismounted. If she was swearing and throwing things, she couldn't be hurt too badly.

ROBYN PACED AROUND the bottom of the old well for what seemed like the thousandth time as she searched for a handhold she might have overlooked. The well had been dug by hand, probably a hundred years ago. She judged it to be over fifteen feet deep and at least eight feet wide. The sides were rocked up with tightly fitted stones. The fact it had lasted this long without caving in was proof of how well it had been constructed.

She had tried to climb out using the pipe that led to the pump above, but the ancient cast iron had been too brittle with age and rust. It had snapped off ten feet above her head and now leaned uselessly against the wall.

At least she had the answer as to why the tank was almost empty. The shallow well had dried up in the long drought. It hadn't been dry long, because the ground under her boots was still soft and damp and the smell of wet moss was almost overpowering from where it still clung to a few bottom stones.

On the walls above her, the moss had dried out completely and disintegrated into a fine gray powder whenever she touched it. The stuff coated the front of her shirt and jeans from her attempts to climb out.

At last, her eyes found a small crack, and she wedged her sore fingers into it. Pulling herself up, she found a toehold for first one foot and then the other. She found another hold on a jagged stone and tried pulling herself higher, but the corner of the stone broke away and she fell, landing on her backside in an undignified heap. Again.

She threw the broken piece of stone against the wall in disgust, but it bounced back and rolled to a stop beside her. A check of her smarting fingers showed another torn nail. She had been at it for hours now, and she was still no closer to getting out.

"Damn, damn and double damn!" she shouted louder this time as her frustration grew. She picked up the piece of broken rock beside her and threw it toward the opening above her. It sailed straight out the hole just like the one before it. Her aim was spot-on.

"Great," she muttered. "I just need to find some way to throw myself out."

"From the sounds of it, I'd say you aren't dead, at least."

"Neal!" She looked up and her heart thudded

with relief when she saw his head and shoulders framed in the opening above her. "Oh, thank God!"

"Are you okay?" he called down. "Are you hurt?"

"No, I'm fine." She stood and used both hands to brush the damp dirt off her rump. "Nothing damaged except my pride."

"Are you sure?"

"Yes, I'm sure. Man, am I glad to see you."

His eyebrow shot up. "Now that's a switch. Here I've been thinking you couldn't wait to see the last of me. Was I wrong?"

She didn't answer his gibe, and he began to move some of the splintered wood, widening the opening at the top of the well. "Yessiree, you got yourself in a pickle this time, Tweety."

She closed her eyes and tried to ignore the obvious amusement in his voice. "Just get me out of here and gloat later, okay?"

"You forgot to say please."

Clenching her jaw, she took a deep breath and said, "Please."

"There, that wasn't so hard, was it?" He leaned over to peer in. "What are you doing down there, anyway?"

"Looking for a shortcut to China, you idiot!" She stamped her foot. "Get me out of here!"

He patted the air with both hands. "Temper, temper. I'll get a rope."

He tipped his hat back with one finger. "In a little bit."

"Neal Alexander Bryant, if you don't get me out of here in the next five minutes, I swear you'll live to regret it."

"You're in a pretty poor position to threaten anyone, Robyn Louise O'Connor." His face disappeared from the opening.

"It's Morgan," she yelled, but he didn't answer. Crossing her arms over her chest, she muttered, "God, I hate that man."

His head popped back into the opening. "I heard that," he said and disappeared again.

Clamping her lips closed, she refrained from uttering any further comments and waited. She could hear him talking, but she couldn't make out his words as she waited impatiently. What was he doing? Having a conversation with the horses?

After an eternity, the end of a rope snaked its way down into the well. She reached for it, but it was jerked away from her hand. Biting her lip to keep from screaming, she fumed. Let him have his little bit of fun.

The rope came down again, very slowly. This time she waited until it dangled in front of her face to reach for it. It was snatched away before she could touch it.

"Ha-ha, Neal. Very funny."

His head and shoulders appeared in the opening. "I think it is."

Babe's long head loomed beside Neal's. Pushing the horse aside, Neal said, "Get out of here before you wind up in the well, too."

"You get me out of here, right this minute," she yelled. "*Right this minute! Do you hear me?*"

Neal planted both hands on his hips and waited for her tirade to end. Then he asked, "Are you finished yet?"

Babe promptly knocked his hat off. With a muttered curse, Neal bent to catch it as it landed on the rim of the well and teetered.

"Babe, no!" she screamed, but it was too late. The horse's boost sent Neal tumbling into the opening. He managed to grab on to what was left of the wooden platform. For an instant, he dangled above her. Then the sound of splintering wood rent the air. She pressed against the wall as he fell into the well beside her.

## CHAPTER FIFTEEN

ROBYN STARED IN disbelief at her would-be rescuer lying in the dirt at her feet. She looked up to see Babe nodding his head in a bow. He stretched his long neck down as if he expected her to toss him a treat. "Oh, Babe, how could you?"

Neal groaned, and she dropped to her knees beside him. "Are you hurt?"

He rolled over and sat up with a dazed expression on his face. "I don't think so."

He looked to the opening above them. "Did your damn horse just push me in?"

"Yes, it's an old trick I taught him. Are you sure you're all right?"

"A trick?" His tone was incredulous. Grimacing, he rolled to one side and pulled a flattened mass out from under himself. He stared at it for a long moment. "Dang, this was a new hat."

Her sorely tried temper began to boil. He was worried about his stupid hat? She pounded a fist into his shoulder. "You moron, look what you've done!"

"What I've done?" He pulled away from her and rubbed his arm.

"Once again, your juvenile behavior has landed us in trouble."

"Oh, no. You can't blame this on me. You got in this hole all by yourself, honey, and your old piece of buzzard bait up there pushed me in."

She couldn't argue with his logic, much as she wanted to, but she didn't dare let go of her anger. As long as she stayed angry with him, she could ignore how he made her feel when he was near. He made her feel like she needed to be closer still, as if she needed the warmth of him against her heart to thaw it and bring it to life again. And he made her feel guilty.

She stood and wrapped her arms across her chest. "I am not your honey."

Pushing to his feet, he surveyed the walls. "Believe me, I've noticed."

He reached out and touched the dry gray stuff on the stones, then glanced at her clothes. She brushed at them quickly, but the effort was futile. He turned back to the wall. All her efforts to climb out were clearly marked where the moss was crushed and smeared.

She was startled when he reached out and brushed lightly at her cheek. "Hold still," he said softly.

The feel of his hand on her face was almost

more than she could bear. Against her will, her eyes closed and she leaned into his touch. His hand stilled and she covered it with her own.

"Holy moly! Look at your hand!"

Her eyes flew open at his outburst. After grabbing her other hand, he held them both in front of him. Her nails were broken, some of her fingers had bled from small cuts and her palms were scraped raw. She curled her fingers closed and tried to pull away from him, but he pulled her resisting body into a tight embrace.

"Oh, baby, I'm so sorry. All I ever seem to do is hurt you."

Robyn found herself pressed to the hard wall of Neal's chest as his arms tightened around her. The familiar feel of his strong body against her weary one overwhelmed her. She heard the deep regret in his voice, and her hard-won defenses began to crumble.

"You didn't do this. It's not your fault," she whispered. Slowly, she uncurled her hands and pressed them flat against his shirt. She closed her eyes and relaxed in his embrace. It felt so right to be held like this. It had been a long, long time, and she had missed it more than she cared to admit. If only she could rest a little while longer. She was so very tired.

He drew away and held her at arm's length. She missed his warmth instantly. "It is my fault. If I hadn't badgered you about our past, if I hadn't made you mad, if I had just agreed not to spend time with Chance, we would have finished checking the fences together and you'd be safe at home by now."

His hands dropped away from her shoulders. He rubbed them up and down on his jeans a moment, and then slipped them into his pockets as he stared at the ground between them. "You were running away from me. I'm pretty dense and a little blind to boot, but even I'm beginning to see you don't need or want anything from me. I'm sorry I've inflicted myself on you these past weeks. I promise I'll get out of your life for good now."

He looked so much like the repentant little boy she had once known, so much like Chance did when he was trying to apologize, that it was a wonder the whole world couldn't see they were father and son. Her heart turned over with a queer little somersault, and a smile began to tug at the corners of her lips.

She folded her arms across her chest. "You'll get out of my life now. Right now?"

"Yes. Right now. If that's what you want."

The smile twitched harder, and she couldn't quite keep it out of her voice. "Right now?" she asked again.

He must have heard her amusement because he looked at her with a puzzled expression. She saw the light dawn as his gaze traveled from her face to the steep sides of the well and up to the opening above them.

He nodded once as a sheepish grin appeared. "Okay. Maybe not right now, but soon."

"Soon? You know this for sure. We could be trapped in here for days."

He glanced around the bottom of the well and then settled himself on the dirt floor. Leaning back against the wall, he crossed his long booted legs in front of her. "It won't be more than a few hours."

"How do you know that? Do you have a crystal ball?"

"No, something better. I have a cell phone."

"You've got a phone?" Joy leaped in her chest like a startled doe. She couldn't believe their good luck. "Let me have it."

"Can't. It's in my saddlebag."

She kicked the sole of his boot as disappointment sent her hopes crashing. "A lot of good it will do us there."

She plopped down opposite him and battled back a sudden rush of tears. She was so tired of being in this hole. The last thing she wanted was to break down and cry in front of Neal. That wouldn't solve anything. She wiped at her eyes and blinked back the moisture.

"Hey, I called your mom as soon as I found you, and I told her where you were. If we aren't back in a few hours, they'll come straight here looking for us."

She raised her eyes to meet his. "You really called her? You aren't just saying that to make me feel better?"

"I did. You may have to put up with me for a few more hours, but that's all. Can you do that?"

"I guess I can." She studied his face in the dim light. That was what she wanted, wasn't it? For him to drift out of her life again and leave her and Chance alone?

*Alone.* It was such an ugly word once a person felt the true meaning of it. She had carried her secret alone for years. Her anger against Neal had helped her bear it, made it seem worthwhile, but now her anger was gone. He knew the truth. He respected her decision even if he didn't agree with it. He would keep her secret. She had to trust him.

What choice did she have?

A shudder raced through her body, and she leaned away from the cool stones behind her.

"What's the matter? Are you cold?" Concern filled his eyes.

"A little. Mostly I'm tired." That was the truth. She was tired of trying to climb out of this stupid hole, tired of always being careful not to let the truth slip out, tired of working long hours and still being unable to save the ranch she loved. And she was tired of being alone.

She was still a young woman with needs and desires, but she had pushed them aside as she cared for everyone else. Neal made her all too aware those feelings still simmered below the surface. She stood and crossed her arms.

"Come here," he coaxed.

She shot him a wary glance. "What for?"

He pushed one hand into the front pocket of his jeans, and she heard a faint crackle as he pulled something out and extended it toward her. "Have some," he offered.

She eyed him with suspicion. "What is it?"

"Nectar of the gods."

"Yeah, right," she sneered.

"Almost. Butter Rum Life Savers gummies." He held his hand higher. "Want one?"

"Yes!" Dropping to her knees beside him, she snatched them from his palm before he could change his mind. She tore open one of the individually wrapped pieces and popped it into her mouth. The burst of sweetness was almost indescribable. "Oh, God, that's good. I'm starving." She sat back on her heels. "I love these things."

"I know. I remember." A look of tenderness

flashed across his face. "Chance likes them, too. I've taken to keeping a few in my pocket for him."

She was surprised by his admission. "That's nice of you."

He shrugged. "My granddad always had a piece of candy in his pocket for me, and I loved that about him. They were lemon drops or those pink mints that looked like Pepto-Bismol tablets. Usually, they had lint or grain stuck to them, but I didn't care. They tasted wonderful because I knew he kept them just for me."

Robyn tore the wrapper off the second piece with her teeth and popped it in her mouth. "I remember your granddad. He had the most bowed legs I have ever seen."

Neal laughed. "He did at that. I think the man was born on a horse."

"A lot like someone else I know." She shot him a pointed look.

"Hey! My legs aren't bowed."

"No, they aren't." She looked down in confusion. They were long and straight, and she remembered the heavy feel of them as they tangled with hers late in the night. A shiver coursed down her body again, but it had nothing to do with the coolness of the well.

"You are cold."

She was startled when his hand closed over her

wrist and pulled her toward him. "No, I'm fine," she protested.

"Liar." He grasped her arms and settled her on his lap with her back to his chest. He folded his arms around her.

His warm breath brushed against her ear. Her own breath began to come in short bursts. She tried to get up, but he held her still.

"I know you're cold—I can feel you trembling. Relax."

"I don't think this is such a good idea. Please let me up." She tried to make her quivering voice sound prim.

She felt the rumble of his chuckle start deep in his chest where her back pressed against him. "Tweety, you slay me."

Instantly, she grew defensive. "What's so funny?"

He settled his arms more tightly around her. "You are, girl. I'll admit I've enjoyed my share of fantasies about us, but not once, in my wildest dreams, did that include making love at the bottom of a dark, dank, smelly, abandoned well. I'm being a gentleman and offering a bit of comfort to a friend, that's all. Now shut up and relax."

*Relax? Oh, right.* Of course he didn't realize how the simple touch of his body stirred her suppressed longings. She would have to pretend it didn't matter that he held her close. She could do it. She was good at hiding the truth, even from herself.

NEAL KNEW IF he burned in hell for telling a lie it would be for telling this one. He wanted her so badly he could make love to her on a bed of nails or on a sinking ship. In five minutes, he'd have them both forgetting where they were, but she didn't need sex now. What she needed was warmth and comfort. In spite of what she'd said, he knew he was the reason she'd spent hours trying to climb out of this hellhole. Slowly, her tense body began to relax.

"I'm sorry—you're right," she said at last. "I guess I've gotten out of the habit of accepting help."

She wiggled into a more comfortable position, and he had to grit his teeth. Any more of this and she would be able to tell he was lying. He had to get his mind off the enticing package he held, but it was hard to do with her hair brushing his neck and his arms crossed just below her full breasts.

He began trying to count the rows of stone that circled the well. Twenty-eight rows. *Okay, cowboy, think about something else, anything else. Like the fact she has a date with the good doctor.*

"Have you got any more candy?"

"No, that was the last of it."

"Drat!"

"Sorry." He had to smile. She wasn't thinking about sex; she was thinking about food. "How long have you been down here?"

She slipped her arm out from under his and peered at the dial of her watch. "About four hours, I think."

She slid her arm back under his. "I guess I was getting cold. This feels good."

Yes, it did. In fact, it felt wonderful to hold her again. And it would be the last time. He intended to make good on his promise and get out of her life before he wound up hurting her yet again. He cleared his throat. "The temperature this far in the ground is near fifty-five degrees."

"How do you know that?"

"I read it somewhere."

"We're lucky there isn't water in this thing. We'd be suffering from hypothermia in no time."

"We're lucky it wasn't any deeper. Some of these old wells go down fifty to a hundred feet. A fall like that would kill you."

"I had no idea it was even here. I thought it was a bored well, just a pipe going into the ground like the one under the windmill at home. I'd have been more cautious before I stepped on that old platform if I'd known it was covering empty space."

"What were you doing, anyway?"

"Checking to see if the pump was working. The tank is almost empty. Now I know why. We are going to have to fill this in before we sell the place. It's a hazard the way it is. I can't believe we haven't lost a calf or a horse down it before now."

"I plan to see if Babe will fit as soon as I get out of here," he said drily.

"Don't say that," she chided. "He didn't mean any harm."

She began to giggle, and he tried to peer around at her face. "What's so funny?"

"I was picturing you with your shoulder under his tail trying to push him in."

He began to laugh, too. "Like the time we tried to get him loaded into that boxcar at the old railroad station."

She nodded. "We were going to run away from home and head out to the Wild, Wild West just like your great-uncle Lawrence had done when he was a kid, remember?"

"He was a great storyteller, all right. He made hopping a boxcar and riding it West sound like a piece of cake."

"It almost was."

"Yeah, until you said you weren't going without your horse."

She giggled again. "I was pulling on his lead rope and pleading with him, trying to get him up your makeshift ramp. You were trying to push him from behind, and that's how Mr. Cradock, the stationmaster, found us."

"I've never seen anyone laugh as hard as that man did when you told him what we were doing. It still rankles a bit when I think about it."

"How were we supposed to know the boxcars were only being stored on the side track until the next wheat harvest?" she asked defensively. "I was only eight. Besides, he did think my Babe was pretty smart."

Neal gave a snort of disgust. "He didn't say your horse was smart. He said out of the three of us, the horse was the only one with any sense."

"He was right." She chuckled.

"Yeah, he was." He tipped his head back and stared at the light fading from the piece of sky above them. The vanes of the windmill turned slowly in the wind as the setting sun colored them a bloodred. It would be dark soon. Her mother would come looking for them. And when they were found, he would have to let this wonderful, maddening, enchanting woman out of his arms, and he would never hold her like this again.

The ground under him was cold and damp, and a rock poked his left hip. The moss on the stones behind his head was flaking off. It drifted inside his collar and itched like the devil. By rights, he should feel miserable, but he knew he would endure far worse tortures to keep her in his arms a little longer. She sighed and grew silent, and he wondered what she was thinking.

"We had a lot of wonderful adventures when we were kids, didn't we?" she asked softly.

"Yeah, we did. The two of us must have turned our parents gray before their time."

"I worry sometimes that Chance won't have a childhood like the one we had."

"You mean into trouble six days a week?" he asked with a laugh.

"No, I mean he doesn't have anyone to share his adventures with."

"He's young yet. He'll make friends in school."

"Maybe."

"He will. I could always have Jake send the twins over," he offered. "If you need someone to turn your hair gray, those two can do it."

She laughed. "They are a handful, aren't they?"

"They've settled down a little since Gabriel was born. For a while there, I thought my reputation as the hell-raiser of the family was in jeopardy."

"How is Connie getting along with the new baby? I'm ashamed to say I haven't been over since his christening."

"She's getting along fine. Jake is the one with the stupid grin on his face all the time."

"Jake's a great father."

"Yeah, I envy him that," he admitted wistfully.

"You always said you didn't want kids."

"I know, but I guess time has a way of changing what's important to a man. I look at Jake with

Gabe and you with Chance, and I see I've missed something important." He'd missed a lot.

"When I learned I was pregnant, I thought you wouldn't be happy about it. A kid would just tie us down. Wasn't that what you used to say?"

"Sure, that was the way I felt back then. I didn't want to turn out like my old man. He ended up hating the responsibility of a family. After I was born, he gave up the rodeo and came back to the ranch. Mom couldn't manage it alone with two kids. I knew how much he hated never winning a national championship. He resented me for forcing him to give up that dream."

"I think you're wrong about that. He loved your mother and both his sons. He might have regretted giving up bull riding before he captured his dream, but he knew what he had at home was more valuable."

"You never saw the look in his eyes when I talked about winning this event or that one. He resented the fact that I could do what he couldn't."

"I never knew how estranged you felt from your dad. It explains a lot."

He wasn't sure he wanted to know what she meant by that remark. Silence stretched out between them. The light faded as they sat together in the darkness.

"Do you mind if I ask you a question?" he asked quietly.

"No."

"Why haven't you remarried? Did you love him that much?"

She paused a long moment before answering. "I did love Colin, but I haven't sworn off men because I'm still grieving for him, if that's what you're asking."

"I would have thought some guy would have snapped you up by now. You're still a good-looking woman."

"Yeah, and I still have all my own teeth," she added drily.

"You know what I mean."

"I know. I've dated a few men, but as soon as they learn that my son is deaf, they disappear as fast as a plate of chocolate-chip cookies at a Boy Scout meeting."

"I can't believe that. Chance is a great kid."

"Thanks, I think so."

"Your doctor friend has met Chance, and he hasn't lost interest."

"Adam?" she asked in surprise.

"Yeah, him. Your mom said you two had a date for tonight. I guess you're going to stand him up. I'm sorry about that."

"Yes, it looks like I am."

"He seems like a good man," Neal offered, although he wanted to bite his tongue rather than admit it.

"Yes, he is. He's a fine doctor, and I admire him very much."

Hearing her say it hurt like hell, but if Adam was who she wanted, then he would be happy for her. "Are you going to take him up on his offer to help with your schooling?"

"How'd you know about that?"

"Your mother blabbed."

"She would."

"Are you?"

"I don't know. Would I like to go to a nurse-practitioner program? You bet I would. I didn't expect to have the money, or the time, to further my career until Chance was grown, but…"

"But what?"

"It doesn't seem right, somehow."

"Is he pressuring you?" he asked sharply.

"No, nothing like that. It feels like charity, although I know Adam means well."

"Are you any good?"

"As a nurse?" She considered the question for a moment. "Yes, I am. In fact, I'm a damn fine nurse," she added with conviction. It made him smile.

"Would you make a good practitioner, whatever that is?"

"Yes, I think I would."

"Then it wouldn't be charity if you did a good job. I think you should do what makes you happy."

She gave a small shake of her head. "I'll have to think about it. I have a lot on my plate right now. You never did that before."

"Did what?"

"Ask me about my plans, what I wanted for my future. I used to think what I wanted wasn't important to you."

"Ouch. Sadly, you were right. I was a cocksure pain in the butt in those days, wasn't I? I don't know how you put up with me for as long as you did. I guess I have old Dust Devil to thank for making me see things more clearly."

After a moment, he gave her a gentle shake. "That's a one-eyed-man joke. Get it? See things more clearly?"

"I get it. I just didn't think it was something to laugh about."

"A good joke beats crying any day."

"I'm sorry it happened." Her voice was laced with sympathy. He wished he could see her face.

"Yeah, me, too." He lapsed into silence.

"Will you really go back to riding?"

"I have to." His tone had a ring of desperation that he hoped she missed. "Go to sleep if you can," he told her gruffly. "We'll have an hour or two to wait yet, I reckon."

"I don't think I can sleep."

"Close your eyes and try."

She sighed as she snuggled a little lower. If only

they could forget the hurts of the past and hold on to the gentleness of this moment. If only he had the right to hold her for a lifetime.

Neal felt her body slowly relax. After a while, her breathing grew deep and even and he knew she was asleep. Careful not to disturb her, he shifted his weight and moved the offending rock from beneath his hip.

He stared up for a long time at the sliver of sky and the few stars that twinkled above them. Finally, he closed his eye and waited in the darkness for the people who would come and take her away from him.

## CHAPTER SIXTEEN

A LOW MOAN penetrated the edge of Robyn's consciousness, and she lifted her head. It was pitch-black. The moan came again, punctuated with a short sob. She realized it came from Neal. His arms twitched and jerked as he muttered something she couldn't make out. Was he ill?

"Neal, what's wrong?"

"Get me loose, Kent! Get me loose!" he pleaded.

She heard the panic in his mumbled words and realized he was in the grips of a nightmare. Compassion flooded the very fibers of her heart. "Wake up, Neal," she coaxed gently. "It's all right now."

"My eyes! God, not my eyes!" His whole body jerked once, and then his arms pulled away from her. Another sob racked his body. She moved off his lap and knelt beside him.

"Neal, wake up. You're having a nightmare."

"I can't see." His breathing was short and fast, like a winded runner. "Robyn, I can't see! Where are you?"

"I'm right here." She touched his shoulder.

His hand closed over hers in a painful grip. "I'm blind!"

"No, no," she reassured him. "It's just dark, that's all."

"It's just dark?" His voice was uncertain, but his grip loosened slightly. Tremors racked his body.

Calmly, she said, "We're in the well, remember? It's so dark I can't see my hand in front of my face, but I can see a few stars when I look up."

His breathing began to slow. "Yeah, I can see them, too."

"That's right. You're fine."

He took another deep breath and slowly exhaled. "I'm sorry if I scared you. It was just a dream."

"You didn't scare me. Do you have them often?"

"They always come with these god-awful headaches," he answered in a voice that was little more than a whisper.

Aching with the need to help him, she threaded her fingers into his hair and slowly began to massage his temples. "Does this help?"

"Yes, that feels wonderful. Don't stop." His body slowly began to relax under her firm hands.

"I find it helps me if I can talk about my bad dreams. Somehow it makes them less real. You can tell me about it if you want."

NEAL STRUGGLED TO subdue his panic as the blood pounded in his ears. No, he didn't want to talk about it. This was his problem, and he had to deal with it, but her fingers were working magic on the pain in his head. Once upon a time, he had been able to tell her anything. If only he hadn't foolishly given up that right.

"You don't have to talk if you don't want to," she whispered.

Slipping his arm around her, he pulled her down until her head rested on his shoulder. The pain was bearable now, and he wanted to hold her again.

She continued to amaze him. In spite of everything he'd done, she was still willing to offer him comfort. And God help him, he was willing to accept it.

"It's always the same," he found himself saying. Pausing, he took a deep breath. "My hand is tangled in my rigging, and I can't get loose. Kent is trying to help me, but the bull keeps turning toward him, and he can't reach me. Then suddenly I'm free and on my knees. I look for the bull, but I can't see anything. Something's in my eyes—blood, I think—but I know he's coming for me. I hear him getting closer, I can feel his breath on my face and I— Then I wake up."

He couldn't add that sometimes he woke up

screaming, with his heart pounding so hard he thought it might burst.

Taking another deep breath, he felt the fear and panic began to recede. Maybe she was right and talking did help.

"Nightmares aren't unusual after a traumatic accident. They should get better in time."

Neal pulled her closer. "I know they'll get better. I just have to face the thing I'm afraid of."

"What do you mean?"

"I have to ride again."

"Is that why you're so determined to go back?"

"That's part of it."

"What's the rest?"

*Because riding is all I've got if I don't have you.*

He didn't say the words aloud, but that was the honest truth. And it was something he wouldn't burden her with.

Instead, he said, "I want a world-championship title. I've been so close twice, but I've never been the best. That's why I have to ride again, to prove I'm the best."

"And what if you get hurt or killed? You'd risk your life for that? You've already proved you're a great rider, Neal. No one will think less of you if you give it up now."

"I'll think less of me."

"It's only pride, Neal. Don't let your pride ruin your life. Believe me, it can."

There was deep regret in her voice, but then he caught the sound of something else. The faint rumble of a truck engine. His time was up. He gathered her tightly against him because he knew he would never hold her like this again. "Thanks, Robyn."

"For what? I haven't done anything." Her voice trembled in the darkness, and he wished he could see her face.

"Oh, yes, you have. You care." His lips found her cheek, and he was surprised by the taste of salty tears there. "You've been a good friend when I needed one."

"Yes," she whispered faintly. "I know we can't change the past or the mistakes we've made, but we can still be friends. Can't we?"

He stroked her hair softly. "Always and forever, Tweety. For always and forever."

He wouldn't ask for more; he didn't deserve even her friendship, but he would gladly accept it.

After a small pause she asked, "How soon will you be leaving?"

"There's a PRCA rodeo in Topeka in three weeks. If the doctor gives me the okay, I plan on entering it."

"So soon? Are you sure you're fit?"

"I'll be ready by then."

He heard the slam of a truck door and the sound of voices. He wanted to kiss her soft lips one last time, but he didn't. "I think we are about to be rescued."

A light stabbed into the darkness followed by a man's shout. "Robyn! Robyn, where are you?"

They moved apart and shielded their eyes as the light shone down on them.

"Robyn, are you okay?"

Recognition dawned on her. "Adam? Is that you?"

"Yes. Are you hurt?"

"No, I'm fine."

"Thank God."

"Neal, are you okay?" The voice belonged to his brother, Jake.

"I will be as soon as you get us out of here," Neal answered.

"We'll have you out of there in two shakes."

WITHIN MINUTES, ROBYN was being hoisted up in a makeshift rope sling. Adam reached for her hand as she cleared the top of the well and pulled her to solid ground. She could see her mother holding on to Chance beside the bright lights of the pickup.

She stepped out of the rope, and the two men quickly pulled Neal to the surface.

"How did you manage this one, little brother?" Jake's voice was laced with humor.

"It wasn't easy. I had some help." Neal slipped the rope off as he stood beside the well.

Jake dusted off the back of Neal's shirt. "Are you sure you're okay? You didn't injure those ribs again, did you?"

"I'm fine. Robyn, where is that nag of yours?" He shot a quick glance at her.

She smothered a laugh. "Staying out of sight, if he knows what's good for him."

"I'm glad you two find this so funny," her mother said. She let go of Chance's hand, and he raced past Robyn to wrap his arms around Neal's leg.

Neal ruffled his hair and smiled at him as he signed. "Hey, buddy, I'm fine."

A lump pushed itself into Robyn's throat. She could barely breathe. It was the first time Chance had showed such affection for someone besides his mother or his grandparents. His world had expanded to include someone new. It was a painful, yet wonderful, thing to see. Her eyes met Neal's. He gave a small shrug as if to say he was sorry, but she realized she wasn't.

Adam grasped her shoulders and turned her toward him. "Are you sure you're okay?"

She nodded. "Yes. What are you doing here?"

"When you didn't show, I knew something must be wrong. I called, and your mother said you were missing."

"I'm sorry she worried you."

"I'm not. She told me Neal was out looking for

you, but of course I came right over. Then we got
the call that Neal had found you."

He frowned at Martha as she moved to stand
beside them. "I must admit, no one seemed very
worried when the two of you didn't show in a rea-
sonable period of time. I had the devil of a time
convincing anyone to come out here."

"Did you?" Robyn gave her mother a hard look.

Martha shrugged. "You and Neal used to spend
a lot of time out riding at night. I wasn't worried."
She winked at Neal, and he grinned.

Robyn smiled at Adam. "Then it seems I have
you to thank for keeping me from spending a very
uncomfortable night in that hole."

Adam scrutinized her face, then Neal's. "You
didn't look all that uncomfortable."

Robyn felt herself blushing.

"Now, Doc, you should know looks can be deceiving." Neal lifted Chance's chin and nodded
toward Robyn, then gave him a small push in
her direction. She knelt and wrapped her arms
around her son.

Adam stared at Neal for a long moment, then
turned to Robyn. "We'd better get you home."

She stood with Chance in her arms and nodded. "I need a long soak in a hot bath."

Adam took her elbow and led her to her mother's pickup. He opened the door, lifted Chance
from her and set him down on the seat. Her

mother climbed in behind the wheel. Looking back, Robyn saw Neal watching her. He touched the brim of his hat in a brief salute, then turned away and began to help Jake tie a rope around the legs of the windmill to form a temporary fence that would keep any cattle away from the open pit.

He had promised to get out of her life, and, strangely enough, she believed he would do just that. She might never see him again after tonight. Until this moment, she'd thought that was what she wanted.

Chance tugged on her arm and signed, "Isn't Neal coming?"

She shook her head. Frowning, Chance drew up his knees, propped his elbows on them and cupped his face with his hands. Plainly, he was disappointed. He'd grown more than fond of Neal. It was surprising since Neal had mastered only a few words of sign language.

Was Edward right? Did Chance need a man in his life? Was that the reason he'd become attached to Neal so quickly? As much as she loved Chance, maybe he needed more than she could give him. Glancing back at Neal, she bit her lip as she struggled with her decision.

Again she faced a difficult choice. She could only pray she was making the right one.

*Friends, for always and forever.*

Well, then she wouldn't try to stop Chance from

being friends with the man who should have been much more to him. Neal would be leaving soon, but maybe he'd come home more often now and visit Chance. The idea didn't upset her as it once had.

Perhaps now that all the anger and guilt was behind them, she and Neal really could be friends again. She didn't kid herself. He still sparked a deep passion in her. Maybe he always would, but that didn't mean they were right for each other.

She smiled at Adam standing beside her. "I'm glad you're here."

"Anytime you need rescuing, give me a shout. I'll be here in a flash."

Turning back to Chance, she signed, "You can see Neal tomorrow." His pout disappeared like magic.

She called out, "Hey, Neal."

His hands stilled on the rope he held. "What?"

"I expect you to be at our place by seven tomorrow."

"What for?"

"There's forty head of cattle in this pasture that will have to be moved now that this well is dry. You don't expect me to do it by myself, do you?"

A slow grin spread over his face. "No, I guess I don't. Seven it is."

"Good."

She climbed into the truck and lifted Chance

onto her lap as Adam got in beside her. She ignored her mother's wide grin as Martha started the truck and turned toward home.

Robyn's shoulder was wedged against Adam's as the truck bounced over the rough pasture track, and they bumped against each other. After a few minutes, he slipped his arm around her and held her steady. It was comforting, but it didn't set her insides to churning the way Neal's touch did.

Sometimes comfort was what she needed, even if it wasn't what she craved.

"I'm sorry we missed dinner, but I'm glad you're okay," he said.

"I'm sorry we missed dinner, too."

"I have to be back in Kansas City tomorrow. Looks like I'll have to wait until the next time I'm in town to take you out."

Her glance slid to her mother, who was obviously trying to listen to their conversation. Martha had made every attempt to throw Neal and her together. It would serve her right to hear her matchmaking efforts had failed.

Robyn smiled at Adam. "I don't mind waiting. Any idea when you'll be back?"

"I go on call at six o'clock in the evening next Saturday, but I could be in town as early as two. I could pick you up then for a late lunch."

"Great. Two o'clock it is."

"Robyn, you're forgetting something," her mother said sharply.

"I am?"

"Saturday is Chance's birthday."

"Oh, that's right. Well, we can have his cake and ice cream in the evening."

"No, we can't."

She looked at her mother in annoyance. "Why not?"

"Because—because I've got to be at the church by five. I'm working a booth at the bazaar, you know."

Robyn flashed a skeptical look at her. "I didn't know. When did you decide to do that?"

"A while back. Of course, you could go ahead and have Chance's party without me," Martha offered in a martyred voice.

"I guess we can this year." Robyn waited to hear her mother get out of this one.

Adam spoke up first. "No, Martha, I wouldn't have you miss your grandson's birthday party."

"Thank you, Adam. I'm glad you understand. Well, that's settled," Martha said in a rush.

"Adam, why don't you come to Chance's party?" Robyn suggested. "We can make it cake and ice cream instead of lunch."

"I'm sure Dr. Cain wouldn't enjoy a child's party," Martha interjected.

"Nonsense. I'd love to come."

"Good," Robyn declared, and flashed a smug smile in her mother's direction. "Now it's settled."

TRUE TO HIS word, Neal showed up the next morning, and they spent the day rounding up and moving cattle. The work was hot, dusty and frustrating, in more ways than one. Determined to keep her feelings for Neal under control, Robyn was still unprepared for the impact he had on her as they worked side by side.

He rode with a relaxed, fluid movement that matched the rhythm of his horse exactly. The thick muscles of his thighs bulged beneath the faded denim of his jeans as he gripped his cow pony and turned the pinto with an imperceptible shift of his weight. It was hard to tell he'd been away from ranching for years.

He knew how to work cattle, never pushing them too fast or too hard as he helped her gather the scattered herd. He was quick to spot the obstinate Angus who resented being forced to stay with the herd, and he moved to block the big black steer each time it tried to make a break. In a low, mellow, singsong voice, he urged the cattle along, and Robyn rode beside him, enthralled.

Moving to close the corral gate after the last reluctant steer trotted through, she marveled at how much she had enjoyed the day. And Neal was the reason.

Leaning on his saddle horn, he waited for her to fasten the gate. "I've forgotten how much work ranching is," he said, lifting his hat to run his fingers through his hair.

"That's the truth," she answered.

"Will you miss it?"

Looking up, she nodded and smiled sadly. "Yes, I will."

"Do you mind if I ask why you're selling?"

"The ranch belongs to Mom. It's her decision."

"Still, it doesn't seem right. You love this place. You grew up here."

"Sure I love it, but I love my work as a nurse, too. I can't do both. The ranch is a full-time job."

They both looked toward the house as the screen door slammed. Chance and Edward headed toward them across the yard.

"What does Chance think about moving away?" Neal asked.

"He isn't happy about it, but I told him there would be other kids to play with if we lived in town, and he likes that idea."

"He's a special kid, Robyn. You're lucky to have him."

"Yeah, I know. Thank you for keeping quiet about being his father. I wasn't sure that you would."

"And now you are?"

"Yes. Now I am."

He gazed at the boy headed their way. "Maybe someday things will change, and he can know the truth."

"Maybe so. I hope so."

Chance raced up to them, reached his arms up to Neal and began to jump up and down. He signed quickly, and Neal grinned at Robyn. "Let me guess. That means he wants a ride."

"You got it," she said with a laugh.

"This sign language thing isn't so hard." He reached down, lifted the boy into the saddle in front of him then turned the horse. The two of them trotted around the yard.

Edward walked up to Robyn and smiled. "You look beat."

"Beat, hot and dusty enough to plant a garden on."

"Go on up to the house. I'll put your horse up for you."

"Are you sure?"

"I may not be much of a rider, but I can unsaddle a horse. Go on."

She kissed his cheek and handed him the reins. "Thanks, I owe you one."

NEAL DREW HIS horse to a stop beside Edward.

Chance turned around and signed, "Again."

Neal shook his head and handed the boy down to Edward. "He wouldn't think it was such fun if he'd spent the past six hours up here," Neal said, dismounting stiffly.

"I imagine you're right, but I think you would have a hard time convincing him of that."

Chance skipped along in front of them as the two men walked side by side and led the horses toward the barn.

"You and Robyn seem to be getting along better," Edward commented as he opened the stall door.

Chance climbed the boards to the top of the stall and looked on. Neal led his horse into the adjacent stall and glanced over at Edward. "I'm not sure I know what you mean."

"There for a while I wasn't sure if she was going to just plain ignore you or get a gun and shoot you."

Neal chuckled. "I wouldn't put it past her."

"You two have quite a history together, if half of what Martha tells me is true."

Neal hefted the saddle onto the boards between the stalls. "Martha doesn't know *half* of what we did as kids, and I hope to God she never finds out."

"I didn't mean your childhood."

Neal stared at him for a long minute. "Yeah, we had quite a history, but that was before she met your son."

He turned away, picked up a brush and began to rub down his horse.

Edward began to brush his horse, as well. "I didn't mean to pry. It's pretty obvious Martha thinks you two belong back together."

"Martha's about as subtle as a thunderstorm," Neal said.

"You can tell me to mind my own business if you want, but I care about Robyn, and not just because she was married to my son. I think of her as a daughter, and I want to see her happy."

Neal stopped brushing and stared over the horse's back at Edward. "What's this leading up to?"

"She's had a rough time since my son died."

"And?"

"And I don't want to see her get hurt again."

"What makes you think I would hurt her?"

"The way she looks at you when she thinks you don't see."

Neal resumed the long strokes with his brush. "You can rest easy. I don't want to see Robyn hurt any more than you do. I'm almost fit. I'll be headed back on the road soon."

Edward laid down his brush and gave the horse a final pat on the rump as he left the stall. "That's not what I was hoping to hear."

"What were you hoping to hear?"

"I was hoping to hear you wanted to stay, because I think you're in love with her." He turned and left the barn.

Neal watched him walk away and sighed. What the hell was he supposed to do? Love wasn't enough. Robyn and Chance needed more than the rootless existence he lived. Adam Cain could give them all they needed—a home and stability.

Neal had seen her pining for those things during the years he'd dragged her from one town to another, from one state to another, but he'd refused to acknowledge it then. Oh, she had followed him willingly because she loved him, but in the end, he had betrayed that love and left her with nothing.

What good would it do to admit he loved her more now than ever? He still didn't have anything to offer her. He was less of a man now than he'd been a few months ago.

Chance watched him from the top rail. A piece of straw dangled from the corner of his mouth as he pushed his little tan cowboy hat back. Neal had to smile. He could remember leaning on the boards of the stall and watching his father groom the horses. He knew he must have had the same look of longing on his face that Chance wore now—wishing he could help but not wanting to be told he was too little.

He beckoned with a tilt of his head and the boy eagerly climbed into the stall. After swinging him up onto the horse's back, Neal gave him the comb, then showed him how to hold the mane and pull the comb through it carefully.

Movement caught his eye, and he saw Robyn enter the barn. A worried frown marred her face, but she relaxed when she caught sight of Chance. She hated it when she didn't know where the boy was. Pretending not to see her, Neal lifted the boy off the horse. Bending down, he showed Chance how to check the animal's hooves. Either she trusted him with the boy or she didn't. Now was as good a time as any to find out.

## CHAPTER SEVENTEEN

WHEN ROBYN SAW Edward leave the barn without Chance, she suspected she would find her son with Neal, but she couldn't feel easy until she knew for sure where he was. She had been right.

Quietly, she stood and watched Neal show Chance how to care for the horse. She'd never let Chance help with the grooming, he was too small, and it was too easy to see a dozen ways he could be hurt.

Obviously, Neal didn't feel that way. He handed Chance the brush, then picked the boy up and guided his hand in long strokes down the animal's side.

They looked so right together. Both of them wore their hats pushed back and a tangle of curls covered their foreheads. Neal's was dark brown; her son's was still baby blond but growing darker each year. The smile that beamed from Chance's face was identical to the one Neal wore. She watched them until she couldn't bear the pain a moment longer, and then she turned and left them alone.

NEAL TRIED NOT to let his elation go to his head as Robyn walked back to the house. It was a huge step for her and he knew it. He continued to hold the boy until they had finished brushing one side of the horse. He set Chance on his feet and moved to the other side of the animal. Chance decided to walk under the horse's belly to reach the other side.

Neal's heart gave a sickening lurch. He spoke soothingly to the horse and held his breath until the boy was in the clear. He squatted down beside him and took him by the shoulders. How did he make Chance understand that was a dangerous thing to do?

Neal scowled and pointed underneath the horse. What was the sign for bad idea? He shook him slightly and said, "Never do that."

He wasn't sure if Chance understood, but a mutinous pout appeared on his face. He jerked away from Neal's hold and threw the brush in the dirt. It startled the horse, and he shied away. Neal grabbed Chance and carried him out of the stall. "Okay, equine-care class is over."

He set the boy on top of a nearby stack of hay bales so that they could be face-to-face. He pointed at the stall and shook his head.

Chance realized he had done something wrong. A single tear rolled down his cheek. Neal stood in front of him, feeling like a heel. This parenting stuff was a lot harder than it looked.

He gave Chance a hug, hoping to convey to the boy that he wasn't in trouble. He wasn't sure if he got his point across or not. Neal went back into the stall, soothed the horse, picked up the brush and began to finish grooming him.

"I'm not mad at you, kid. I just want you to be careful." He realized the boy couldn't hear his explanation. Signing wasn't yet second nature for him. He glanced over his shoulder. Chance was nowhere in sight.

Neal left the stall and searched for the boy. There was no point in yelling for him. He didn't see him anywhere. How far could he have gotten?

*Great.* The first time Robyn left the boy with him and he lost the kid. Where could he be?

Suddenly Neal remembered the kittens. He went back to the rear of the barn, and, sure enough, Chance was sitting on the crate, holding a kitten in his lap. Neal tapped him on the shoulder and motioned for him to come up to the house.

"Your mother needs to put a bell on you. That might make you easier to locate."

Chance smiled, put the kitten down and ran out of the barn. Neal hurried to catch up with him and keep him in sight.

CLOUDS ROLLED IN the afternoon of Chance's birthday and brought the welcome relief of a rain shower to settle the dust and dispel some of the heat of late August.

Pulling a yellow-print sundress from her closet, Robyn slipped it on and then turned first one way and then the other in front of the rosewood-framed mirror in her room. The yellow-and-white daisy print looked fresh and cool, and the simple flared skirt swirled around her tan legs when she moved. Would Neal like it?

She frowned at her reflection. It didn't matter if he did or not. She had bought the dress for herself, because it made her feel young and carefree, certainly not like the mother of a four-year-old.

Her baby was four. Where had the time gone? She turned away from the mirror, added a bow to the top of Chance's present and glanced at the clock. Adam would be here any minute.

His kiss hadn't put an end to her feelings for Neal. Maybe nothing would. But Adam was a great guy and Neal was going back to the rodeo. She liked Adam. Maybe that liking would grow into something more if she gave it a chance. She slipped on her new white sandals, gave one last glance at herself in the mirror and lifted her chin. No, she certainly hadn't bought a new dress because Neal was coming. He wouldn't notice, but Adam would.

Her mother and Edward had gone all out decorating the screened-in back porch for the occasion.

Balloons and streamers hung from the ceiling and waved gaily in the breeze. The banner with clowns and balloons Robyn had printed on her computer was tacked in place around the front of the table holding the cake, a tall, frosty pitcher of lemonade and the paper plates and cups Chance had insisted on having—the ones decorated with Power Rangers.

Clara sat beside the table and dozed in her wheelchair. Edward and Chance were busy taking turns at the crank of a battered ice-cream freezer and piling ice and salt into its wooden bucket.

Edward looked up as she stepped out of the house. "Wow! You look fabulous," he said. He signed to Chance, "Your mother is beautiful."

Chance signed, "I know. Is that for me?" he asked when he spied the package in her hand.

She nodded, setting it on the table by two others. "Unless you know someone else who has a birthday today?" she signed. "You'd better get to cranking or that ice cream won't be ready before our company arrives."

"Too late," Martha said from the open door. Identical nine-year-old girls dressed in matching pink-and-white-striped tank tops and pink shorts stood beside her, each holding a gift. The twins dashed up to Chance.

"Happy birthday!" they said and signed together.

"We brought you a present—" one started.

"But you can't open it yet," the other finished. Turning to Edward, they asked, "Can we help?"

"Crank away," he offered as he sat back in his chair. The twins immediately moved to take over the cumbersome job.

"Too bad they aren't that quick to do work at home."

Robyn turned as Connie Bryant stepped out onto the porch. The willowy blonde was dressed in a mint-green halter-top sundress. She looked every inch the classical ballerina she was. Her hair was drawn back from her oval face in a thick French braid that swayed as she moved with fluid grace. The only flaw in the image was the gurgling, drooling infant she held on her shoulder. Ellie Bryant followed her out the door.

Robyn laughed. "You don't understand, Connie. It's only work if their mother asks them to do it. Let me see that baby. My goodness, he's grown."

"Where's Jake?" She glanced behind the women. And where was Neal, she wondered, but she couldn't bring herself to ask.

"Jake can't make it," Connie said with regret. "He had to make a fast trip to Oklahoma City this morning to pick up a new stallion."

"Neal is coming," Ellie added. "He said he had to go pick up Chance's present. Leave it to that boy to wait until the last minute for everything," she said with a shake of her head.

"That's a man for you," Connie said, and all the women laughed in agreement.

"Is this where the party is?"

They all turned at the sound of a male voice as Adam walked around the corner of the house. Robyn hurried to the screen door and held it open. "This is the place."

Adam smiled warmly as he climbed the steps. "You look great," he murmured as he moved past her, and she felt a blush bloom in her cheeks.

Quickly, she made the introductions, and Adam took a seat on the porch swing. There was plenty of room to sit beside him, but Robyn found herself reluctant to do so. Instead, she turned to Connie. "May I hold the baby?"

"Sure." Connie handed the infant over. "Be warned though, he drools worse than a Saint Bernard."

Holding the bright-eyed, sweet-smelling infant filled Robyn with a sudden, sharp longing for another baby of her own. Silly thought. It took two to make a baby. She glanced at Adam and wondered at the thoughtful look on his face as he gazed back at her.

Neal still hadn't arrived by the time the ice cream was ready. Chance shifted from one foot to the other in front of his presents, and Robyn took pity on his growing impatience. Signaling her mother to light the candles on the cake, she handed Gabe back to Connie and stood, then led the group in singing and signing "Happy Birthday" to her grinning son.

Chance blew out his candles on the first try and everyone applauded.

The cake and ice cream was devoured in short order, and Chance quickly tore the wrappings off his presents. The present he liked best was the black-and-white soccer ball from Edward. Chance and the twins raced out the screen door and into the backyard and began an impromptu game.

Robyn looked at the torn wrapping paper and colorful paper plates scattered across the gray-painted porch floor and smiled at Adam. "I believe it took me longer to wrap one present than it took him to unwrap them all."

She bent to pick up the largest pieces of paper and the CD case of a computer game Adam had given Chance. Adam moved to help her. She said, "Thank you for the game. I know he'll enjoy playing it."

"Have I missed the party?"

Robyn straightened and spun around at the sound of Neal's voice coming from the door into the house. She couldn't stop the glad leap her heart took, even as she struggled to keep her face blank. She was saved from framing an answer by the shouts of the twins.

"Uncle Neal!" They dashed up the porch steps,

followed closely by Chance. Each girl grabbed his hand and began to pull him toward the yard. "Come play with us."

Chance bounced up and down in front of him and signed.

Neal shook his head and glanced at Robyn to interpret, but the twins supplied the answer to his unspoken question.

"He wants to know—"

"What you brought him."

"And what makes him think I brought him anything?" Neal asked.

"'Cause it's his—"

"Birthday, silly." They giggled.

Neal freed a hand and rubbed it slowly across his jaw. "Then that's why I have a present on the front seat of my truck. I was wondering who it belonged to."

Robyn signed to Chance, and, with a delighted grin, he shot out the screen door and raced around the house.

The twins started to follow him, but Neal stopped them. "Hold it, girls. Chance needs to discover this present by himself." He glanced at Robyn and hoped he hadn't made a mistake.

"But what—"

"Is it?" the girls insisted.

"Wait a minute and you'll see," he told them, but he didn't take his eyes off Robyn's puzzled face.

Just then, the faint sound of jingling bells could be heard coming from the side of the house. Chance burst into view, followed by a fluffy black-and-white puppy dancing at his heels. The jingling came from the brass sleigh bells sewn onto the pup's red-leather collar.

Chance darted up to the screen door and glanced back at the pup, who tried but couldn't quite make it up the first step. The boy hurried back down and scooped the pup into his arms. It promptly began to lick his face in gratitude.

Neal held open the screen door as Chance struggled up the steps with his burden and hurried to his mother. He tried to sign, but finally had to put the wiggling pup down. The twins dropped to their knees in delight as the curious puppy scampered to them.

Beaming with excitement, Chance signed, "Is she really mine? Can I keep her?"

Robyn nodded. "Yes, you can keep her. She's your present."

The bells on the pup's collar jingled as she raced back to the boy. Chance turned and flung himself into Neal's arms for a quick hug. Tenderness filled Neal's heart as he returned the embrace, and then Chance bounded out of his arms, scooped up the puppy and began to show her to each of the adults seated around the porch.

Edward patted the silky black head and looked at Neal. "What kind of dog is it?"

"A border collie."

"A sheepdog?" Adam asked.

"Sheep and cattle." Neal nodded. "I've seen them work huge herds of cattle and sheep guided only by hand signals from their owners."

"A dog that knows sign language. Well, I'll be," Edward muttered.

"She won't find many cattle or sheep to herd in town," Adam said.

Ellie flashed a bright grin at her son as she spoke, "Border collies make very good pets for children. They have that protective instinct. Neal had a dog like this when he was young. Every place he went, Scamp went, too."

Chance moved to show his puppy to Clara. She patted it and asked, "What's its name?"

He shrugged and looked at Neal. He signed the phrase he'd been practicing. "She's your dog. You name her."

"Bell," Chance signed. "I'm going to call her Bell."

Neal ducked his head to hide a smile. "Now, why didn't I think of that?"

Standing, he motioned to the twins. "Come on, girls, I've got some accessories to go with Bell in my truck. Help me bring them in."

Robyn listened to the jingle of the puppy's collar as she followed the group around the house, and she smiled softly.

Adam moved to stand beside her. "I don't know why he thinks the dog needs those bells. The sound is going to get annoying, and it's not like the boy can hear them."

The smile stayed on her lips as she closed her eyes to listen. "The bells aren't for Chance," she said softly. "They're for me. So I can hear where he is because that pup will always be near him."

"I'm thirsty," Clara said suddenly.

"Would you like some more lemonade?" Robyn asked. She crossed the porch, picked up the half-empty pitcher and turned to fill Clara's glass. Clara smiled brightly at her, then frowned as Neal held open the screen door while Chance struggled in with a ten-pound sack of puppy food in his arms.

"Shame on you, young man." Clara scowled at Neal. "Don't let your son lift such a heavy package."

The glass pitcher slipped from Robyn's hand and shattered on the floor.

## CHAPTER EIGHTEEN

MARTHA AND EDWARD rushed to help Robyn clean up the broken glass, ice cubes and lemon slices scattered across the porch floor. Robyn quickly realized her shock at hearing Clara's words had gone unnoticed. Everyone was used to Clara's strange pronouncements and paid them little attention.

Robyn glanced at Neal, but he was staring at Clara with a strange look on his face until Chance and the twins claimed his attention. They were ready for the piñata to be hung from a branch of the tree in the yard.

The party continued without any further incidents until Adam announced he had to leave to start his shift at the hospital. He gave Chance a high five and signed "happy birthday" to him. Robyn was touched that he had learned the gesture. He came over and stood close beside her. "Walk me to my car?"

"Sure."

He took her hand and they strolled together around the side of the house. At the gate, he stopped and cupped her face between his hands. "I had a great time. Thanks for inviting me."

"You're welcome."

"You have a wonderful family."

"Thank you." She was puzzled by his hesitant tone.

"We haven't known each other very long, but I would love to get to know you and your family much better."

"I'd like that, too."

"Before we head down that path, I need to know if you're ready for a serious relationship, Robyn."

Was she? She bit her lower lip. She'd only recently discovered she wasn't over Neal the way she'd thought she was. How could she risk hurting Adam until she was sure where her heart lay?

He smiled gently. "I can see that you need to give that question a little more thought."

"You're a very perceptive man. I like that about you."

"Please don't say you just want to be friends."

She chuckled. "I'm willing to keep all my options open. Let me ask you a question."

"Sure."

"Are you up to the task of taking on a ready-made family?"

"That's a very good question, Nurse Morgan. I'm giving it very serious consideration."

She gazed up into his bright blue eyes. "Then it seems we both have a lot to think about."

"Any reason why we can't think about it over dinner next week?"

"None whatsoever."

"Good." He kissed her cheek and walked away. She stood at the gate and watched until he drove out of the yard.

"He seems like a nice fellow."

She turned around and found Neal watching her from the kitchen door. "Yes, he's a very nice man."

"You should go for it."

She walked toward him, shaking her head. "He's not some prize to be won."

"No, you're the prize. I hope he knows that."

She checked to make sure they were alone and stepped close to him. "How would it make you feel if Adam wanted to raise Chance?"

"I'd try to be happy for all of you. He's a man with compassion, education and the ability to give you and Chance the better things in life. Yeah, I'm happy for you if you love him."

She gazed at his face. "You mean that, don't you?"

"Oh, hell, no. Given half a chance, I'd knock him down, throw you over my shoulder and ride off into the sunset with Chance and Bell tagging along, and maybe your mother on a pack mule, because she's a really good cook."

Giggling, she punched his shoulder. "Are you ever serious?"

"Not if I don't have to be. Come on—there's more party going on. Edward is setting out the horseshoes, and the kids want more lemonade."

"I'll have to fix some." She walked past him and into the house. "I've seen Edward pitch horseshoes. You can take him. He's got terrible aim."

"Maybe, but he's got two good eyes. My depth perception is pretty much shot."

She opened the fridge and pulled out a handful of lemons. Looking over her shoulder, she said, "I'll still put my money on you. You have a seriously wide competitive streak."

"With you in my corner, I can't lose." He walked through the house and out the back door.

As the evening drew to a close, Ellie and Martha tried to convince Edward and Clara to come with them to the church bazaar. "You'll have a great time," Ellie assured him.

Martha rubbed her hands together. "You never know what kind of treasures you'll find. Sometimes you can get great antiques for a song."

Clara looked up at Edward. "I'd like to go."

Martha jumped on that. "See. Clara wants to go."

Edward glanced from his wife to Robyn to the

back porch still strewn with balloons and trash
from the party. "We can't all go and leave Robyn
to clean up alone."

Robyn folded her arms across her middle. "I'm
perfectly happy waiting until tomorrow to tackle
this. You go on. I'm going to bed early. I'm beat."

Connie looked at her tired children. "I'd better
take my brood home. Thanks for a great party."
She waved goodbye, loaded her kids in her mini
van and drove away.

Ellie turned to Neal, who was sitting beside
Chance on the porch swing. "What about you,
son? Do you want to come with us?"

He rose to his feet and patted Chance's head.
"No, I need to go down to the corral and check
on a couple of steers. I noticed earlier that they
were acting sick. If they are, I'll separate them
from the others and put them in the barn to keep
a closer eye on them."

A little later, Robyn and Chance waved goodbye to everyone from the front gate. Robyn saw
the lights in the barn were blazing brightly. Obviously, one or both of the steers required Neal's
attention. Biting her lip, she hoped it wasn't serious. They couldn't afford a big vet bill just now.

She put her exhausted son to bed after a quick
bath. He was asleep almost before his head hit the
pillow. Bell curled up on the rug beside his bed
and seemed content to stay there.

Robyn checked the barn from the kitchen window when she came downstairs, but the lights were off now. Had he gone? Disappointment hit her when she realized he hadn't come to say good-night. She wanted to tell him how wonderful his gift was, and how much she appreciated the thought he'd put into the gesture.

She turned away from the window and leaned against the sink. Neal would be leaving in a week. A month ago, she would have been thrilled by the idea, but now the knowledge produced an intense sadness. Chance was going to miss him. She was going to miss him. It had been so good to have her friend back.

Thankfully, her vacation would be over in a few more days. Going back to work would help. It would make it easier to forget about him.

She pressed her fingers to her temples. Oh, who was she fooling? She'd deluded herself into thinking she was going on with her life. The hard truth was her life had merely been on hold, waiting for Neal to come back. Would it be this way forever?

If she was honest, she would admit he was the reason she had come home after Colin had passed away. She'd settled on the ranch with her mother because she knew Neal would be back to visit his family, maybe even to settle down when he finally gave up the rodeo.

Running both hands through her hair, she gave

a heavy sigh. There was no point in going to bec now. She would only find herself going over anc over the one conversation they wouldn't have. A conversation about a future together.

Neal wouldn't give up the rodeo. She wouldn' live that lifestyle with Chance in tow, traveling fo months at a time to a new town every week. Nor was she willing to sit at home and wait for Neal to make a rare appearance, wondering each time he rode if she would get that devastating phone call So where did that leave them? Nowhere.

She never expected Neal to forgive her for keeping him in the dark about Chance. Her lie hac denied him a son, cheated his mother of a grand-child, but Neal had come to terms with it in a way that surprised her.

He wanted what was best for his son, even i he couldn't be in the picture to provide it. He hac matured a lot in their time apart. He was a better man than the one she had left.

Would he have changed as much for the better if they had stayed together?

Her new sandals had started pinching her little toes. She kicked them off and they flew across the room. What use was it to wonder how things might have been? Nothing was going to change Neal would leave. She had to accept that they would never be together.

She left the kitchen and padded barefoo

through the silent house. She needed something to do. She could start by cleaning up the mess on the porch. After opening the back door, she froze in surprise.

Neal was gathering up the helium-filled balloons and tying their long strings together. He turned at the sound of the door and smiled at her. "I thought Chance might want these in his room for a while. They'll last a few more days before they go flat."

"I'm sure he'd like that." She stepped out into the glow of the porch light and began to gather up discarded paper plates, napkins, wrapping paper and plastic forks. She was acutely aware of him and the fact that they were alone in the house except for her sleeping child.

With all the balloons in one bunch, Neal tied them to the arm of the swing and moved to help her. He picked up a trash bag and held it open. "It was a nice party."

She dropped her handfuls of trash into the bag and glanced at his face. Was he thinking of all the birthday parties he had missed? "Yes, it was. I haven't thanked you yet for Chance's gift."

He shrugged. "I remember how crazy I was about my dog at that age. I think with a little training, she'll turn out to be a good dog. When she'd old enough, you can look into having her trained as a hearing ear dog. It might make things a little easier for you. Chance isn't going to want to stay in the yard much longer, no matter how much you want him to."

"I know." She moved to pull the banner off the table. A sharp pain lanced her instep. She gave a small cry. Neal caught her by the arm as she staggered backward.

"What's wrong?"

"I stepped on something."

He guided her to the swing. "Sit down and let me see."

Dropping onto the swing seat, she held her foot up. "I must have missed a piece of glass after I cleaned up the broken pitcher."

"Clara gave us all a bit of a shock with that. Do you think she knows?"

"That the piano is out of tune or that the forecast is calling for snow? No, I don't think she knows Chance is your son."

Wet warmth oozed down her foot as drops of bright blood splattered on the gray board floor. Neal knelt in front of her and grasped her foot with gentle hands. "Do you honestly believe they would love Chance less if they knew?"

"I don't want to find out."

"Point taken. You should know better than to come out without shoes," he chided.

"They were pinching my toes," she offered in self-defense.

He grabbed a handful of napkins and blotted the bottom of her sole. "And this feels better?"

"No. I think something's still in there," she said, wincing when he touched the wound.

"You're right. Hold still," he ordered and bent closer. A twinge shot through her instep. He leaned back and held up a small shard of bloody glass. He tossed it into the trash bag on the floor beside him.

He pressed the napkin against her sole until he'd made sure the bleeding had stopped. He cupped her heel in one hand and brushed the bottom of her foot to make sure there weren't any more pieces on her skin. Instead of putting her foot down, he continued to hold it. A flush of heat stole through her body.

"Thanks."

He looked up at her. His eyes darkened with desire. "My pleasure."

# CHAPTER NINETEEN

A WEALTH OF sensations swept over Robyn as she stared into Neal's eyes. The intensity of his gaze held her motionless as he knelt in front of her, holding her bare foot in his hands. Gentle, warm hands. Her pulse pounded as the sultry darkness beyond the porch seemed to press in on them.

Tension shimmered between them. His hand moved slightly up the back of her calf. She licked her suddenly dry lips.

Abruptly, he looked away and released her foot. "You should get some disinfectant on that."

Robyn nodded, not trusting her voice. She drew up her foot and tucked it beneath her. The soft, bright material of her dress whispered like silk as she smoothed it over her long, tan legs, hiding them from his view. The warmth of his touch still lingered on her skin.

He glanced around the floor. "There may be other pieces out here. You shouldn't take the chance of walking barefoot."

"No, I shouldn't."

"I'll have to carry you."

"Okay," she said meekly.

*Okay?* What was she thinking? When he had held her foot, she'd almost turned into a puddle of jelly. What would happen if he held her in his arms? She studied his face and saw him hesitate. His lips pressed into a tight line as he suddenly bent, scooped her up and held her against his chest.

Of their own accord, her arms circled his neck. The tenseness of her body slowly ebbed away and a feeling of rightness filled her. This was where she belonged, where she had always belonged. Safe in his arms. She closed her eyes and leaned her face into the crook of his neck.

His scent filled her nostrils, so masculine, so uniquely his own. She drew in a deep breath, as if she could draw his essence into her soul. She yearned to kiss him, to press her lips against his firm jaw and his neck until he turned his mouth to meet hers, but she didn't dare. If his lips touched hers, she would go up in flames.

His heart beat as wildly as hers; she could feel it through the thin fabric of his shirt. For the longest instant he stood motionless, but then he turned and carried her into the house.

He halted inside the back door, and disappointment flooded her when he lowered her feet to the floor. He was going to let her go again. She couldn't bear it. Suddenly she knew this time she wanted to hang on to him for all she was worth.

His arms fell to his sides, but hers remained around his neck.

He cleared his throat and asked, "Can you walk?"

"No," she whispered against the warm flesh of his throat.

His deep groan filled her with hope. "Robyn, do you know what you're doing?"

She leaned back to see his face, and then she cupped it with both hands. "Yes, I do," she answered.

For a timeless moment, he held her with an almost desperate fierceness. His lips touched her forehead, then her eyelids and her cheeks until they settled at last on her lips.

Tentative at first, his kiss deepened slowly, and Robyn lost herself in the surge of pleasure as his mouth moved over hers, slanting first one way and then another, feeding the hunger growing in her. His hands skimmed up her back to cup the nape of her neck as the kiss ended. He leaned his forehead against hers and whispered, "I think we had better stop right here."

Her mind was a riot of jumbled desires. How could she make him understand what she barely understood herself? He lifted her chin until she had to look at him. He said, "We're friends, remember?"

"What if I want to be more than friends?"

Would he understand what she was trying to say? That she was still in love with him? She wanted to whisper those words, no, shout those words, but something stopped her. Gazing up at his face, she was suddenly afraid those words would send him away, and she knew she couldn't bear that.

She wanted to be held by him. She wanted to lie curled against his side all through the night and listen to the sound of his breathing in the darkness. But she didn't want it for one night. She wanted it forever.

He took a step back. "I should be going."

She laid her heart on the line. "What if I don't want you to go?"

"Robyn, honey, I've made my share of mistakes in the past. I don't want to make another one."

Shame filled her. "And staying with me would be a mistake?"

"That's not what I meant. I want to be part of your life, Robyn and part of our son's life. Can you let me do that?"

Was it possible? Could she let him be a father to her son even if they never revealed the truth to anyone else? It had been one thing to live with that kind of lie when Neal hadn't been around, but how could she keep it up day after day?

Suddenly, a rectangle of light swung across the darkened room as a car drove past the window. Her mother was home, along with Edward and

Clara. Robyn moved away from Neal. "I need to think about this."

"Sure." Disappointment filled his voice.

"Can you meet me tomorrow afternoon?" she asked suddenly.

"I can be here anytime you want."

"No, not here. Meet me at the springs?" She heard the slam of a car door and voices outside.

"When?" he asked quietly.

"Late afternoon." She looked toward the front door.

He grasped her face gently and turned it toward him. "If you don't come, I'll understand, okay?"

LATE THE NEXT afternoon, Robyn turned her horse into the mouth of the canyon. After tossing and turning for hours the previous night, she still hadn't decided what she was going to say to Neal. She loved him. Chance adored him. But would that be enough in the end? Could he continue to live the lie she had started? She just didn't know, but she did know one thing—she loved Neal. She always had, no matter how hard she had tried to deny it.

The smell of wood smoke drifted to her. He was already there. He had a small campfire going in the clearing, and he'd spread a quilt in the shade of the cottonwood trees. A towel fluttered from a low branch and his hair glistened with drops of water. He must have been swimming. He looked up as she rode in, and a relieved smile appeared on his face.

"You made it." He stood and caught hold of her horse's bridle when she stopped beside him. Her heart turned over in her chest at the sight of his happiness. After so much heartache, didn't they both deserve a chance at happiness?

"Were you worried I wouldn't come?"

He gestured toward the hamper that sat in the shade. "A little, but I brought enough food for two. Fried chicken, potato salad and chocolate brownies."

"Sounds wonderful. I haven't eaten a thing all day," she said, swinging down from her horse. She'd been too distracted and agitated to eat.

He led her horse away and hobbled it with his own. Robyn sat on a fallen log beside the fire and rummaged through the wooden hamper. In a few minutes, she had spread out the feast. Neal climbed up to the springs and pulled a pair of long-necked beer bottles from the cold water.

Too nervous and uncertain to handle the conversation she knew was coming, Robyn applied herself to the meal with a gusto she didn't really feel. Neal kept up a flow of small talk that didn't require much in the way of replies, and, after a while, she began to relax and enjoy the surroundings and the food.

She licked the last bit of brownie icing from her fingers. "There's no surer way to a woman's heart than chocolate."

"No kidding? I thought it was pancakes."

They looked at each other and burst out laughing.

His smile slowly faded and he said, "I love that sound."

"What sound?"

"Your laughter. It's the sexiest sound on earth. I think I've missed it more than anything else."

Her own smile faded. She wanted him to kiss her again. She reached out and brushed a bit of frosting from the corner of his lip. He caught her hand and held it as he studied her face, and then he pressed a kiss to her palm. When she didn't draw away, he moved his free hand to the back of her head and pulled her close. Gently, he kissed her lips.

After a long moment, she broke away. Staring at him, she asked, "Did you mean it?"

"What?"

"What you said last night. That you wanted to be part of my life and part of Chance's life."

"Yes, I did." Stroking her cheek softly with his knuckle, he said, "I've never wanted anything more."

"More than you want a world championship?"

He studied her silently, then he moved away

from her and sat up. "Is that what you're asking me to do? Give up riding?"

Was she asking for more than he could give? She took a deep breath. "Yes, I am. Chance and I can't follow you on the road. I'm not sure I could stand it, waiting here for you, wondering every time you rode if you were going to get hurt or worse."

He stared down at the quilt for a long time without answering her. Her heart began to pound painfully.

NEAL PICKED AT a loose bit of thread as he avoided looking at Robyn. Could he do as she asked? Could he quit cold turkey, never knowing if he still had the guts to climb down in a chute and straddle a bull again?

Part of him wanted to shout, "Hell, yes, I quit!" Part of him wanted to tell her no. She couldn't ask him to give up the thing he loved. It wasn't fair of her to ask so much.

He rose to his feet and walked several feet away. She watched him but didn't say anything.

Which was the right answer? Which was the answer they could both live with? It seemed so simple, but it wasn't.

He thought of all he had to gain and all he had to lose if he made the wrong choice. He wanted Robyn and Chance to be part of his daily life. But he also wanted to be a man with self-respect. If he didn't have that, what kind of husband and what kind of father could he be?

All the emotional stuff aside, how could he support a family without his rodeo winnings? He had some earnings socked away, but that wouldn't last forever. Robyn had a good job, but he didn't want to live on her salary. Maybe he was old-fashioned, but he believed a man earned a wage and didn't live off his wife's money.

He knew he couldn't ride bulls forever, but he didn't think his career should be over today.

Robyn crossed her arms over her chest as if she was cold. This wasn't easy for her, either. Everything he had worked for was riding on the answer he gave her.

Would love be enough? Or would he come to resent Robyn and his son for making him give up his dream the way his father resented the choice his wife had forced him to make? The last thing Neal wanted was to walk in his father's footsteps.

Robyn bit her lower lip as she waited for him to speak. God, she was so beautiful. How could he deny them both this second chance at love? There was only one answer. He walked back to the quilt and sat beside her.

"All right, I'll quit riding."

She stared at him in disbelief. "Just like that? I honestly didn't believe you would agree."

He stood and held out his hand. "Just like that, Tweety. I'm an ex-rodeo bum."

Grasping her hand, he pulled her to her feet and into his arms. Bracing her hands on his chest, she peered closely at his face. "Neal, are you sure?"

"Yes."

"Maybe you should think it over. I know I'm asking a lot."

"Honey, there's nothing to think about."

"But it's meant so much to you." He silenced her with a finger to her lips.

"You mean more. I want to spend the rest of my life with you and Chance."

"You won't be able to tell anyone he's your son."

"You and I will know it. Someday, we'll tell him. That's good enough for me. I love you, Tweety."

ROBYN'S HEART SOARED with joy. How she had longed to hear him say those words. "Oh, Neal, I love you, too."

She threw her arms around his neck and kissed him with all the passion she had kept hidden, even from herself.

They were both breathless by the time the kiss ended. His smile was soft as he studied her face.

"What do you think Chance will say about my courting his mother?"

"I think he'll like the idea. At least I hope he will. Now, my mother is going to be totally delighted."

He gave a short bark of laughter. "Mine, too. I think they've been planning this all along."

"I think you're right."

He pulled her close again and rested his chin on top of her hair. "You know, the county fair starts tomorrow in Everett City. How about you, me and Chance spending the day together? Just the three of us. Like a family."

She knew the wide grin on her face must look foolish, but she didn't care. Her most secret wish, so long denied, was coming true at last.

"Just the three of us—I like the sound of that. I love the sound of that."

"So do I."

Her smile faded slightly, and she drew away. "Oh, wait. I almost forgot. I volunteered to work at the hospital's health screening booth from three to five on the opening day of the fair."

"No problem. Chance and I can kick around the midway for a couple of hours and then we can all go to the parade after you're done."

"All right," she agreed slowly. "I guess that will work."

He tipped up her chin with one hand and fixed

her with a steady stare. "Letting me have Chance for a few hours can't be that hard, can it? What's the matter—don't you trust me?"

"It's not that. It's just that he's so small, and he can't communicate with anyone who doesn't sign and he doesn't like crowds."

Neal pulled her into a quick hug. "You worry too much. We'll get along fine. After all, it's only for a couple of hours. What could go wrong?"

He kissed her again and drove the last of her worries out of her head.

His lips feathered across her cheek and down the curve of her neck. She leaned back, offering him greater access, but he returned to her mouth. His lips became firm and demanding. A low moan escaped his throat as she responded in kind. The passion she had denied for so long rushed up in an all-consuming wave. She wanted to be closer. She needed every square inch of her body touching his. She wanted his weight pressing her down and bringing her the pleasure she knew he could give her.

By unspoken agreement, they settled side by side on the quilt. She pulled at his shirt, wanting her hands on his skin.

"Not yet," his breathy voice stopped her.

"Why?" She didn't want to wait. She had waited long enough. She reached for his belt buckle.

"Oh, baby, I've dreamed of this moment for so long. I don't want to rush it."

She caught his lower lip between her teeth and pulled gently. When she released him, she asked, "Did you bring protection?"

"It's in my hip pocket." He was breathing hard. The sound fueled her excitement.

"More than one?"

"Yes."

"Good, 'cause we're gonna rush it now. Later, you can take your time."

"Ah, woman, you say the sexiest things."

"Shut up and I'll show you sexy."

And she did, until they were both spent and resting in each other's arms.

Curled against him, basking in the comforting feel of his arm over her waist and his broad chest behind her, Robyn smiled as she let the peace of the place and her utter happiness wash away every last bit of anger and remorse. They were starting over. She couldn't ask for more.

As Robyn rode the long miles home that evening, her euphoria faded as her doubts and fears pressed in again. Was she being fair to Neal? Could he really give up his lifelong dream of a rodeo championship on top of continuing her charade? She was asking a lot.

His quick assertion he would quit the rodeo

troubled her, as well. She couldn't help feeling that something was wrong. After so many years and so many fights about his riding, suddenly he was willing to give it up?

It didn't feel right, but then who was she to say what was right and wrong? Maybe she should just accept that by some miracle she was being given her heart's desire.

And it was her heart's desire.

A life with Neal. Neal being a father to Chance. It was more than she expected or deserved.

She rode into the corral and dismounted. The house was quiet. Leading her horse into the barn, she stopped short at the sight of Edward measuring out grain to feed the other horses.

"You don't have to do my chores," she said, leading her horse into a stall.

"I don't mind. You were gone a long time. What were you doing?"

"I went riding with Neal."

What would Edward think of Neal taking Colin's place in their lives? She braced herself to find out.

## CHAPTER TWENTY

"ROBYN, YOU KNOW I love you like a daughter, don't you?" Edward asked as he poured the feed into the manger. Her horse pulled at the reins, eager for his supper.

"Of course I know that." After slipping the bridle off, she turned the animal loose in the box stall.

Robyn chewed her lower lip as she wondered how to tell Edward that Neal would be taking Colin's place in their lives. She didn't want to hurt his feelings, but he would have to know sooner or later.

Edward leaned on the stall door, watching her. "You really care about Neal, don't you?"

"Yes, I do." She smiled gently.

"I'm glad."

Relief filled her. "You are? Really?"

"Oh, honey, you're much too young to spend your life alone. Neal seems like a fine young man. He likes Chance, and Chance adores him."

"Yes, Chance does adore him. Are you okay with that?"

Stepping up to her, Edward enfolded her in a comforting hug. "I wish my son had lived to raise Chance. He would have made a wonderful father, but it didn't happen."

He held her at arm's length and searched her face. "You don't believe I want Chance to grow up without a father, or for you to spend the rest of your life alone because Colin can't be here, do you?"

"I guess I don't."

He gave her a gentle shake. "Good. Now let's go get some supper, shall we? It's a good thing we're leaving in the morning. I'd have to buy all new clothes if I keep eating your mother's cooking much longer. My pants are already getting tight."

"We'll miss you."

He draped an arm over her shoulder, and she slipped an arm around his waist as they walked out of the barn. "Thanks, kiddo. I'll miss you, too. I'm only a phone call away if you ever need anything."

NEAL DROVE INTO the O'Connor yard the next afternoon and stepped out of his truck. Chance was playing in the front yard with Bell and his new soccer ball. Barking excitedly, Bell raced toward the gate. Chance waved when he saw Neal. Chance ran to the gate and pushed it open, and

Neal dropped to one knee to pet the puppy as she scampered up to him and fawned at his feet.

Chance tucked his ball under one arm as he carefully closed the picket gate, and Neal was struck again by the familiarity of that image. The boy reminded him of someone, but who? He frowned as he tried to pin down the elusive memory. If only he could picture where he'd seen him before.

A picture. That was it. Somewhere he'd seen a photograph of a boy who looked like Chance holding a ball in front of a picket fence. But where?

Robyn stepped out of the house and hurried down the steps, looking fresh and beautiful in jeans and a yellow blouse and sporting a matching yellow bow in her hair. She stopped in front of him. "What are you frowning about? Don't you like my outfit?"

He'd made the right decision, Neal thought as he stared up at the beautiful woman in front of him. She'd forgiven him. She loved him. No belt buckle or championship title could ever make him this happy.

Grinning, he tilted his head to one side. He rose, leaned close and whispered, "The outfit is okay, but I like you better naked."

Blushing furiously, she pushed him toward the truck. "I should have known better than to ask you."

Chance looked at her and signed, "What did he say?"

"Never mind," she signed. She shot Neal a menacing look. "Get in the truck or we'll be late."

Neal turned to Chance and signed slowly, "I said your mother is beautiful."

Neal looked at Robyn. "Did I get that right?"

Her eyes sparkled with happiness as a slow smile curved her lip. "You got it right."

"The twins have been helping me work on my signing," he admitted.

She pressed a quick kiss to his cheek. "Remind me to thank them."

"You won't need this, sport." Neal took the soccer ball from Chance and tossed it over the fence into the yard. He scooped up the puppy, intending to deposit her in the yard as well, but Chance grabbed his arm, then signed quickly. Before Robyn could interpret, Neal said, "Let me guess, he wants to take the dog."

"Yes."

Neal hesitated a second, then nodded, and Chance beamed as he pulled Bell from Neal's arms.

Robyn frowned. "Are you sure you want to take a puppy to the fair?"

He answered honestly, "No, but I think I can handle one pup better than I could handle one pouting boy if I made him leave her at home."

Shaking her head, Robyn muttered, "He sure has you wrapped around his little finger."

She signed to Chance, "Go get her leash."

Chance dashed into the house with Bell close on his heels.

With Chance out of sight, Neal did the one thing he'd wanted to do since they had parted the day before. He pulled Robyn into his arms and kissed her soundly. As her lips parted softly beneath his, he knew he wanted to do this every day for the rest of his life.

"Well, it's about time!"

Neal shot a look to the gate, where Martha stood with her hands planted on her hips and a satisfied smile on her face. Robyn stepped away, and Neal turned to her mother.

Reaching over the fence, he cupped her face in his hands. "Forgive me. It's just a fling, Martha. It's you I really want."

She batted his hands away as she blushed bright red. "Oh, you scamp! Get out of here and take these two with you." Chance brushed past her with Bell on a leash.

"All right," Neal drawled. "But you're breaking my heart, honey."

"I'll break more than that if you don't mind your manners."

Laughing, Neal opened the truck door and helped Chance and Robyn in.

As they drove toward town, Robyn noticed Neal seemed distracted. He frequently glanced at Chance and his puzzled frown reappeared. Chance was sitting between them, holding Bell in his lap. The pup was behaving better in the truck than Robyn had expected. "What's wrong?" she asked Neal at last.

"What? Oh, nothing, I guess."

A smile twitched at the corner of her mouth. "Regretting bringing the dog already?"

"No." He reached over and scratched Bell behind her ear. The pup promptly tried to lick his hand.

"Something's on your mind," she insisted. There would be a rodeo at the fair tonight. Was he regretting that he wouldn't be riding in it?

He shrugged. "It's just something Clara said once."

"When she asked you to tune her piano?"

He laughed and shook his head. "No, Clara told me I didn't look like a Bryant." He glanced at Robyn. "But she said that Chance did."

"What a strange thing for her to say."

"She was right. He does."

Robyn frowned at him. "What do you mean?"

"I take after Mom's side of the family. Most of our cousins from Dad's side are blue-eyed, curly-headed blonds. It makes me wonder if anyone else has noticed the resemblance."

"Like Edward?"

"I was thinking about my mother and Jake."

"Why wouldn't they say something?" She hadn't considered that her secret might not be much of a secret after all.

"I've been wondering that, too."

He slowed the truck and turned into the grassy lot at the edge of town, which was rapidly filling with cars and pickups. "Okay, we're here. Let's enjoy the day and forget about everything else."

She smiled at him and nodded. "Excellent plan."

The county fair was in full swing by the time they reached the fairgrounds.

She turned to Neal. "Don't let him fill up on junk food. Don't let him stuff himself with corn dogs, and make sure you know where he is at all times. Do you know the sign for bathroom?"

"I've got this. See you later."

Neal and Chance left Robyn at the hospital booth and set off to explore the varied delights the fair had to offer.

Robyn stepped under the red-and-white-striped awning and saw that Jane Rawlings was already there. Jane sat behind a folding table lined with pamphlets about the hospital and its programs. Behind her, a lab technician was setting up the simple lab equipment that could be used to run blood tests from finger pricks.

After pulling her stethoscope from her pocket, Robyn looped it over her neck and joined Jane.

"I knew the rumor mill was wrong." Jane sat back and crossed her arms.

"Which rumor and which mill?" Robyn started arranging the consents fairgoers would have to sign before she could draw their blood.

"Mary Beth said you were dating Dr. Cain."

"We did go out."

Jane narrowed her eyes. "But you came to the fair with Neal Bryant?"

"You are very observant."

"Do not tell me that you are letting a gorgeous doctor slip through your fingers for a cowboy. I don't believe it. You've got more sense than that."

"Jane, I had no idea you were so prejudiced against cowboys."

"Don't get me wrong—I like cowboys. Some of my best friends are cowboys. But it makes a whole lot more sense to marry a doctor."

Robyn shook her head. "Only if you are in love with the doctor."

Jane leaned forward eagerly. "So you're telling me that you are in love with the cowboy?"

"Yes." It was exciting to finally admit it out loud. She hadn't felt this giddy in ages.

Jane squealed with delight and threw her arms around Robyn. "I'm so happy for you. Do you have a date set?"

"Hold those horses, girlfriend. We are a long way from the wedding chapel. I have a son to consider. He likes Neal, but I don't know how he would feel about adding him permanently to the family."

"I can understand that."

Robyn stared out the tent toward the midway. "Today is sort of a test to see how well they do together."

"They'll be fine. You'll see."

"I hope you're right. Today I'm not staying one minute later than I agreed. We've got to get good seats along the parade route."

"You don't fool me. You just want to ride the Ferris wheel with your guys."

"You are so right." She looked up and greeted their first customer.

Chance was enchanted with the whirling rides and colorful tents and booths that lined the midway. With Bell's leash clutched tightly in his hand, he dashed ahead of Neal to first one booth and then another. Neal was ready to switch the lead from the dog to the kid. He was pretty sure Bell would stick closer than Chance was inclined to do.

The first ride Chance wanted to go on was the merry-go-round. The calliope music played as families stood in line to put their little ones on mechanical horses. Judging from the number of well-worn cowboy hats in the group, most of the families had real horses at home. Neal wasn't sure what the draw was unless it was the fancifully painted ponies.

When it was their turn, Neal held Bell under one arm and lifted Chance to the back of a shiny black steed with a flaming red-and-yellow mane and tail. Chance was grinning from ear to ear. On the other side of him, another cowboy was holding on to a little girl in a pink shorts set.

Neal struggled with his balance for a few seconds when the ride started, but he managed not to drop the dog or fall off the ride.

The cowboy across the way looked from his excited daughter to Chance. "That's a mighty fine-looking horse you're on, partner."

Chance ignored him and watched the faces of the crowd spinning by. Neal said, "He's deaf. He can't hear you."

Sympathy filled the man's eyes. "That's a tough break for your son."

Neal opened his mouth to deny that Chance was his son, but he couldn't say it. He wasn't sure he would ever be able to say it out loud. Chance was his. No one else's. Although he had agreed to Robyn's stipulation, he hadn't realized how difficult maintaining the lie would be.

How had Robyn managed to do it for so long?

It was something the two of them needed to discuss. He knew she wasn't going to like it.

An hour later, Chance had consumed a cone of cotton candy and three corn dogs, although Neal thought Bell had wound up with the lion's share of those. It was a day he would always remember, Neal decided as he watched Chance ride around in a swing shaped like an airplane.

Would he make a good father for his boy? He was more than willing to try, but how could he be sure he was doing the right thing? Would he know if he was making mistakes? What if he and Robyn disagreed on something more important than cotton candy and maximum corn dog numbers?

When the ride ended, he waited for the teenage operator to steer Chance to the exit. Neal was waiting on the other side. Chance hopped up and down and signed, "Again. Again."

Neal shook his head. "We are all out of tickets. Time to go look at something else. What do you think, the butter sculpture shaped like a giant ear of corn or the 4-H animals?"

Chance tipped his head to the side the same way Bell did when she didn't understand something. Neal's smile slipped a little. "I've got to master sign language, and quick. There are so many things I want to share with you, son."

He'd started out wanting to make amends with

Robyn and had ended up with a family instead. How lucky could one man get?

His nightmares still plagued him, but he hoped they would fade with time. Robyn and Chance were more important now than his riding. He'd always known his bull-riding days were numbered, that the day would come when he'd make his last ride. He wasn't going to wake up when he was fifty and decide which rodeo to go ride in that day.

The only thing was, he'd wanted to go out a winner. His one regret was that the bull had won the last round.

Regrets aside, making a home and having a family were the things he needed to concentrate on now. Tomorrow he'd ask Jake if he could start working for him. Jake had always said there would be a place on the ranch when Neal was ready. Well, he was ready now.

He and Chance left the midway behind and set out to view the livestock hopeful 4-H'ers had fed and groomed to perfection as they vied for that all-important grand champion ribbon. Chance wasn't impressed with the glossy, sleek Angus and Hereford steers, but the lop-eared rabbits were a big hit with him. Neal had trouble conveying to the boy that he couldn't take them out of the cages to meet Bell.

As they passed along the front of the grandstand, Neal paused. There would be a rodeo to-

night. What would it hurt to take a look at the
kind of stock that would be ridden? Motioning to
Chance to follow him, Neal walked to the pens
behind the rodeo arena.

Neal recognized Lance Carpenter, a local stock
contractor, pulling up the gate of the semitrailer
and unloading his string of bucking horses. Lance
caught sight of Neal at the same time. He stepped
down from the truck and walked toward Neal with
a pronounced limp.

"Good to see you're still kickin', Bryant." He
held out his hand.

Neal took it in a firm grip. "Good to see you
too."

"Gee, that bull sure did a job on you."

Neal touched the scar on his face. "Yeah, he
did."

"Aw, you was too pretty anyway." Lance tapped
his right leg, and the artificial limb echoed dully.
"Some of us don't have enough sense to get out
while we're ahead, do we?"

"Guess not."

A second semitrailer backed up to the loading
chutes. The end gate was raised by a cowboy beside the truck. A dozen bulls crowded into each
other as they plunged down the ramp and into
the pens.

Neal staggered back from the fence as they
thundered past him. Mortified at his inability to

control the fear that gripped him, he shot a quick look at Lance. Lance's face was full of understanding. "It's like that, is it?"

"I don't know what you mean."

Lance braced his arms on the fence and looked at the tips of his boot. "I remember how it was at first. How scared I was to get near a bronc."

Slowly, Neal moved back to stand beside him. Chance leaned on the second rail of the fence, obviously awed at the size of the bulls in the pen. Bell barked and strained at her leash, eager to follow her herding instinct and enter the fray.

"How'd you get over it?" Neal asked when the hammering of his heart slowed.

Lance straightened. "I'm not sure I ever did, but rodeo is all I know. I figured if I couldn't ride 'em, maybe I could raise 'em. What about you? Are you goin' back to it?"

Neal shook his head. Taking the leash of the excited Bell away from Chance, he tied it to the fence post and then lifted the boy so he could sit on the top rail. "No. I promised his mother I wouldn't."

"I guess every rodeo cowboy has to face that decision someday. Nobody rides forever. Your son?" Lance asked with a nod in the boy's direction.

Chance's delight with the activity around him

was obvious. Neal smiled. "If I'm real lucky, maybe one day he'll think of me as his dad."

"Well, if you ever find you've got the itch to ride again, come on out to the ranch. I got some watered-down bulls you can try. That brindle and the gray in there are a couple of 'em. I bring 'em in case any of the boys want a practice bull. Something that's not too tough but can give them a decent bucking."

An idea began to form in Neal's mind. He glanced at the empty stands. He had to know if he could do it. He might never find a better time to test his nerve. Lance understood what he was going through. Neal could see it in his eyes.

He throat went dry as he gripped the fence. "How about right now?"

Lance glanced at him sharply. "You want a try now?"

Neal's blood turned to water at the prospect, but he nodded. He couldn't spend the rest of his life wondering if he had quit because he was afraid or because Robyn had asked him to.

"Yes, I want to try now," he said quickly.

Here was his chance to prove he still had the guts it took. Robyn didn't understand what she had asked him to give up. He didn't intend to go back on the circuit, but he needed to prove to himself he was still man enough to ride, that underneath his eye patch he was still the man he used to be. He needed to know he wasn't a coward.

And if he found he couldn't go through with it, well, only Lance would know, and he would understand. Neal's hands clenched into fists. He wouldn't consider that possibility.

Lance laid a hand on Neal's shoulder. "You sure?"

"I'm sure." He wasn't, and he might never be. There was only one way to find out. Climb to the top of the chute and put his legs on either side of a bull.

"You got your glove and bull rope handy?"

"No, but I can find someone who'll lend me theirs."

Lance called to one of the men lounging beside the now-empty truck. "Jerry, have you got your rigging handy?"

The gangly young cowboy nodded. "Sure do."

"Would you mind letting Bryant borrow it for a practice bull?"

"Heck, no, boss. It'd be an honor."

"Thanks. Fetch it over here and run the brindle bull into the chutes. And, Jerry, keep this under your hat, you hear? I don't want any gawkers."

"Okay, boss."

"Put the gray one in," Neal said quietly.

Lance shot a quick glance at him and nodded. "Okay, the gray it is."

Jerry came running back with his bull rope, a glove and a can of rosin. "I hope the glove fits."

Neal pulled the buckskin on. He didn't know if he was relieved or sorry that it fit snugly.

Jerry grinned. "I'll get my horse and ride pickup man for you."

Turning to Chance, Neal lifted him off the fence and signed, "Stay here, okay?"

Chance smiled and nodded.

Neal looked to Lance. "Can you keep an eye on him for me? He's deaf. I don't know how to make him understand what I'm going to do."

He guessed the boy would figure it out in a few minutes. Bell lay quietly chewing on her lead now that the arena was empty.

"Sure, I can watch him," Lance said.

Neal considered sending Chance back to Robyn with Jerry, but he'd need someone in the arena with him when he came off the bull one way or another. Lance wouldn't be agile enough with his bum leg. Jerry seemed eager to lend a hand, and the fewer people who knew about this the better. If Robyn found out what he intended to do, she'd put a stop to it.

Neal's heart thudded in his chest as the big gray bull was driven into the chute beside him. He worked the rope and the rosin until he was satisfied with it. Beads of sweat broke out on his forehead, and he wiped it quickly with his shirtsleeve.

"You don't have to do this, son," Lance said, working the rope around the bull.

"Yes, I do."

"All right, then. Goner here—"

"Goner?" Startled, Neal asked, "What kind of name is that?"

Lance smiled. "He bucks, but he knows where the out gate is, and as soon as he can, he's a goner." His smiled faded. "You ready, Neal?"

"As I'll ever be." Neal took a deep breath and stepped across the chute.

Lance returned to stand beside Chance leaving Jerry to open the gate from horseback.

The big gray shuffled restlessly beneath Neal. Knowing he would rather die than admit to the men beside him he couldn't do it, he slipped his hand into the bull rope.

Years of practice and instinct took over then as he wrapped his hand and pounded his fingers tightly around the rope, then gripped the bull's sides with his legs.

With a barely perceptible nod to Jerry, the gate flew open.

The bull turned out with a high leap and landed hard on all fours. Kicking from side to side, he bucked down the length of the arena. Neal stuck tight. Each kick jarred his newly healed ribs and pulled at his shoulder painfully, but his sense of balance kept him over his hand and in the middle of the bull.

He'd done it. Elation filled him. He'd gotten on, and he was staying on.

With two fingers in his mouth, Lance sent a piercing whistle to signal that eight seconds was up. Neal stayed on board for two more bucks just for good measure. Then, after pulling his hand free of the rope, he made his dismount and wound up getting a face full of dirt.

Scrambling to his knees, he looked for the bull. The big animal had stopped bucking the instant his rider was off. He turned suddenly to face Neal. Giving his head one impatient shake, the bull whirled away and thundered toward the exit gate. Jerry rode up beside Neal. "Nice ride."

Neal stood and blew out his breath as exhilaration filled him. He'd done it. Now that it was over, he wished Robyn had been there to see it.

Suddenly, excited yapping filled the air as Bell slipped her collar and dashed between the running bull and the open exit gate. Before Neal's horrified eyes, Chance scrambled through the fence. Lance made a grab for the boy, but Chance was too quick for him. Everyone shouted, but Chance never heard them. Both the boy and the dog went down under the massive animal's hooves.

## CHAPTER TWENTY-ONE

ROBYN PLANTED HER hands on her hips and surveyed the growing crowds on the midway. After two complete circuits of the rides and shows, she still couldn't locate Neal and Chance. Glancing impatiently at her watch, she frowned. They should have met her at the health screening booth twenty minutes ago. Where could they be?

A hand touched her shoulder. Relieved, she spun around, but it wasn't Neal. A pale and breathless Jane Rawlings faced her.

"Robyn, there's been an accident. You have to go to the rodeo arena, right now."

Cold fear gripped Robyn's heart. Surely Neal wouldn't have gone there. He'd promised. "Why?"

"It's Chance."

"Oh, my God, is he hurt? How bad is it?" Terror pumped through her veins as her heart began to pound painfully.

"I don't know. They just sent someone to the booth to find you."

Whirling away from Jane, Robyn began to run toward the grandstand at the far end of the fairgrounds. The crowd became an obstacle course blocking her way, keeping her from her son. She plowed through them ruthlessly, knocking drinks from hands and pushing between startled couples, oblivious to the indignant shouts behind her.

An ambulance was parked inside the arena, and a group of men clustered beside it.

Her baby! She had to get to her baby. *Please, dear God, let him be all right.*

More people blocked her way. Pushing between them, she battled back the scream rising in her throat.

Suddenly, Neal was in front of her, grasping her arms and halting her progress.

"Let me go." Frantic now, she tried to shove him away. "Where's Chance?"

"They're getting him on the stretcher."

"Is he—" She couldn't say the word. The world receded until only Neal's face filled it.

"Is he dead?" she whispered.

Pulling her into a fierce hug, he said, "No, no."

Relief made her knees weak, and she clung to him, grateful for his strength. The paramedics lifted their stretcher and moved toward the ambulance. Still clutching Neal's arm, Robyn moved to intercept them.

They only paused a moment. Her hand was shaking as she brushed the dirt from Chance's pale, still face and whispered his name. How she wished he would open his eyes, so she could tell him how much she loved him. Quickly, the men carried him to the waiting ambulance. Shaking off Neal's hold, she followed them, but Neal caught her again and held her back as the men loaded the stretcher into ambulance and secured it.

"What happened?" She looked to Neal for an explanation.

"I talked Lance into letting me try a practice bull. Chance was watching, and suddenly Bell got loose and chased after the bull. Chance ran into the arena after her, and the bull ran him down."

Disbelief, then fury surged through her. "You rode a bull? With Chance watching? Who was watching him? He's four years old, damn you! Why weren't you watching him?" She slammed her fists into his chest.

"I'm sorry. I know I messed up. Lance was watching him, but Chance got away from him. I'm so, so sorry." His voice broke on a raw sob. His eyes were filled with shock and pain, but she could only think of her son.

"Your stupid bull riding almost got you killed, but that wasn't enough, was it? You had to let it try to kill our son."

She struck him again. Why didn't he try to stop her? Why was he taking blow after blow?

"I'm sorry. I don't know what else to say."

"You said we would be enough for you, damn you! I trusted you. I trusted you with our son and look what you've done to him. I don't want you anywhere near him again. Do you understand?"

He grabbed her hands and stilled them in a painful grip. "I'm so sorry. It was an accident. I'd never hurt him."

"You already have."

The paramedic closed one door of the ambulance and turned to her. "You can ride in back with him, Robyn."

Nodding, she climbed into the ambulance and gripped Chance's still hand.

Neal stepped up to the back, but the paramedic halted him. "Sorry, only one."

A deep, biting cold filled Robyn as she stared at her son's pale face streaked with dirt. It was a cold that seeped down into her heart. She turned to look at Neal framed in the open door. His face was a mask of pain and confusion, but she couldn't care about him now. Chance needed her.

She wanted to shout, but her voice came out deadly flat. "Leave us alone, Neal. Just leave us alone. We were doing just fine until you showed up."

He didn't answer. The door swung shut, cutting him off from her sight. Leaning down, she placed a kiss on her son's cheek and began to cry.

NEAL WATCHED THE ambulance roll away, and he knew it was over between him and Robyn. She would never forgive him for this. The fragile trust he had painstakingly rebuilt with her had been destroyed in eight heart-stopping seconds.

Lance Carpenter, with Bell in his arms, walked up beside Neal. "I'll get the pup over to the vet's office. Her front leg is broken. I don't think there's anything else wrong with her. You go on to the hospital and be with your boy. I'm sure sorry about this."

"It wasn't your fault. I promised her I would give up riding bulls."

"If you explain to her what happened, she'll understand."

"I don't think she will. Not this time. Thanks for taking care of the pup. Tell the vet that I'll be responsible for the bill."

"Sure thing. You had better get to the hospital."

Neal made his way to the parking lot and climbed in the truck. Robyn wanted him to stay away, but he couldn't do it. He had to know that Chance would be all right.

It took him twenty agonizing minutes to reach Bluff Springs and the parking lot beside the hospital on top of the hill. The ambulance was pulling away as he drove up.

He got out and hurried into the emergency

room. People were rushing back and forth. The nurse behind the reception desk was on the phone. "Prep surgery room one right now and make it fast. Exploratory laparotomy, possible ruptured spleen."

When she slammed down the receiver and began to gather together papers, Neal asked, "Can you tell me how Chance Morgan is? They just brought him in by ambulance."

"Are you a relative?"

"No." It was the hardest word he'd ever spoken.

"I'm sorry—we're only allowed to give information to the parents. If you'll have a seat in the waiting area, I'll let Robyn know that you're here. I'm afraid we're really busy right now. You'll have to excuse me." She rushed away with her papers into a room down the hall.

He knew without being told that they were working on Chance in there. Robyn would be at his side. They wouldn't be able to tear her away. He wanted so much to offer what comfort he could, but he stood rooted to the spot.

A moment later, the door of the room opened and several women in brightly colored hospital scrubs wheeled a cart out into the hallway. He had a glimpse of Chance's blond hair and pale face before they disappeared down the hall.

Dr. Cain came out of the room behind them. He had his arm around Robyn. She was crying as she clung to him. He said, "Dr. Parker is the surgeon on call. He'll be here in a few minutes. We'll do everything we can."

She lifted her tearstained face to gaze at him. "I know you will. There's no one I'd rather have with him than you."

They walked down the hall together and turned the corner. Neal hung his head and walked out the emergency room doors. He wasn't needed there.

THE SURGICAL WAITING room at the hospital was empty except for Robyn. She had called her mother and Martha was on the way. She had called Edward, too. He would return as soon as he could. Alone, she waited and prayed.

Her son was in surgery. Adam had been on duty in the E.R. He had quickly assessed Chance and rushed him into surgery with a suspected ruptured spleen. Her son's life hung in the balance. Why?

Because Neal couldn't give up riding bulls, even after he had promised he would.

She was so glad when her mother rushed in. "How is he?"

"Still in surgery. He has a broken arm, and Adam thinks he has a ruptured spleen."

"That's bad, isn't it?"

It was bad for a young child. If the spleen had to be removed, the risk of deadly infections was frighteningly high. "It can be. Why did I ever bring him to the fair?"

"It was an accident, honey. Don't blame yourself." Martha enfolded Robyn in a comforting hug.

"He's so little. I should have been with him."

"Honey, you can't hold on to his hand forever, no matter how much you want to."

That was exactly what Robyn had been thinking. If only she'd been there, she could have held on to his hand and kept him from running after Bell.

She sat down and stared sightlessly at the TV playing in the corner as her mother went to get a cup of coffee from the half-empty pot beside it. The evening news was on.

A two-car crash near Salina had taken the lives of three people. A house fire in Marion had left a family homeless. The weather would remain hot and dry for the next week. There wasn't a single chance of rain in sight. The Kansas State football team was looking good for the coming season.

Robyn's shock gradually faded. As it did, she realized how brutal she had been to Neal. She had taken her fright and anger out on him, but he wasn't entirely to blame.

She knew how afraid he was that he wouldn't have the courage to ride again. He'd seen the opportunity to lay that fear to rest, and she was glad that he had succeeded. He couldn't have foreseen that Chance would run into danger.

She knew her son's limitations better than anyone, yet a month ago, Chance had darted into the path of a tractor while she looked on. If it hadn't been for Neal's quick action that day, Chance might have been killed. She'd seen the whole thing, but she'd been powerless to stop it.

It wasn't fair to blame Neal because he hadn't been able to save Chance this time.

She closed her eyes and gripped her hands together. *Please, God, let my baby be okay.*

A hand covered hers gently. She looked up and saw Adam. She gripped his hand. "How is he?"

He sat in the chair next to her. Her mother hurried to join them. Adam looked tired, but he was smiling gently. "Chance is out of surgery and in recovery now, but his condition is still serious."

Robyn's grip tightened on Adam's hand. "How serious?"

"He has suffered some internal injuries with considerable blood loss. There was a tear in the spleen capsule, but Dr. Parker repaired that. Chance also has a broken left forearm. I've set it and put him in a splint until the swelling goes down. I'll put a cast on in a few days. Dr. Parker ordered a unit of blood for him. We'll have to see how he responds to that. He may need another."

"Are you going to transfer him to a bigger hospital?" Martha asked.

"I will if you feel it is necessary. I happen to know his mother is a fine nurse. She won't leave his side until he's out of here. I'm sure he'll get the best possible care right where he is."

Robyn squeezed his hand. "Thank you."

"Just doing my job. Any questions?"

"How soon can I see him?"


NEAL HEARD HIS mother's footsteps on the stairs. She stopped outside his bedroom door and knocked. He was across the hall in her bedroom, sitting on the side of her bed and staring at an oval-framed picture in his hands. Bell lay on the bed beside him with a blue splint on her front leg. She whined and snuggled closer to him.

"I'm over here, Mom. How is he?"

"Martha just called. He's out of surgery, but his condition is still guarded. I think you should be there, son."

"Robyn said she didn't want me near him."

"I'm sure she didn't mean that."

"She meant it."

Fixing his mother with a steely stare, Neal held up the old photograph. "You knew he was my son."

She glanced toward the empty space in her collection of framed memories on the wall. After crossing the room, she sat beside him and took the picture from his hand. She ran a finger over the face of a blond, curly-haired boy standing in front of a white picket fence. He held a large ball in his hands as if the camera had caught him in the midst of a game of catch. "I suspected."

Neal lunged to his feet, crossed the room and then spun around to face her. "You should have told me."

"What could I say if Robyn told everyone the child belonged to her dead husband? I could hardly call her a liar. Besides, I had no proof."

Neal let out a sigh of frustration and raked a hand through his hair. "The first time I saw Chance, he was playing with a ball. Something about the whole thing seemed familiar, but it didn't click."

He gestured toward the photograph. "I'd forgotten about this."

"There wasn't any reason you should remember it."

"He was Dad's little brother, wasn't he? The one who died when he was five or six?"

Nodding, she said, "His name was Matthew, and he died of pneumonia when he was five. This was the only picture of him your father had, and he cherished it."

"I understand why Robyn didn't tell me, but if

you suspected something, *you* should have told me. I would have come back for her."

"It was her choice."

"Didn't any of you think I should have a say in the matter?"

"I knew what the rodeo meant to you. I saw how your father resented giving it up because I insisted he come home and help me raise you kids. I was ready to divorce him if he didn't."

"I'm not my dad!"

"No. You're right. I'm sorry. I thought Robyn had made the tough choice that I couldn't make. She gave you the freedom you needed."

Ellie looked at him for a long moment. "There is something else you should know about Matthew. He was born deaf."

Neal stared at his mother in shock as what she said sank in. He closed his eye and bowed his head. "So I'm responsible for his deafness, too. He inherited it from me."

The knowledge cut into his heart like a knife. Chance was his child and deaf because of it. And because of his carelessness, his ego, his need to prove something, Chance had suffered even more. Bell whined, and Neal moved to pick her up and comfort her. She missed Chance, too.

His mother laid a hand on his shoulder. "I'm sure Robyn was frightened and angry when she lashed out and told you to stay away. The two

of you have avoided each other when you really
needed to sit down and talk about what's happened. If your father had been able to do that, we
would have had a happier marriage. I loved him,
but I didn't always understand him. I know it's
not easy for you to see, but Robyn needs you, and
so does Chance."

"I wish I could believe that, but you know what
I see? I see that they were both better off without me."

His mother's face grew hard as she stared at
him. "If that is what you see, then you're more
than half-blind." She left the room, slamming the
door behind her.

Neal stared at the picture in his hand. Did his
mother think it was easy for him to sit idly by and
wait for word about Chance's condition?

Hell, no, it wasn't easy. He'd been calling the
hospital every half hour, but all he got was the
same answer. They would only release information to family members. He wanted to shout that
he was the boy's father, but no one there would
believe him.

Chance could die. It was his fault, all of it. His
need to prove his manhood, to master his fear,
had nearly cost a child his life.

Not just any child—his son.

A son he could never acknowledge because he

had destroyed the love and trust Robyn once had for him.

She had been right to leave him. He wasn't cut out to be a father and a husband. His old man had known the truth all along. Neal was irresponsible, selfish and thoughtless. He was a bull rider and a rodeo junkie. It was all he'd ever be.

Now that he knew he could still ride, he'd go back on the circuit. He would do what Robyn wanted. He'd stay out of their lives for good. Just as soon as he knew Chance was out of danger.

He ran his hand over Bell's soft fur. He would take care of the puppy until Chance was out of the hospital. It was the least he could do for the family he wanted so desperately to call his own.

THE DOOR TO the hospital room opened early the next morning. Robyn glanced toward it as she sat up in the recliner beside Chance's bed. Adam walked in, followed by a young nurse. Robyn struggled to ignore the painful crick in her neck that a night in a chair had produced.

She watched Adam leaf through her son's chart. Apparently, what he saw didn't please him. Edward and her mother walked in. She was thankful once again for their support. Edward had arrived late the previous evening after arranging home care for Clara. He had been at Chance's side all night, too.

Adam closed Chance's chart and looked at everyone. "Chance's tests show his blood pressure and his hematocrit are both lower than I would like, so we need to keep a close eye on that. I've notified the Red Cross in Manhattan to have another unit on standby."

Edward frowned. "Why don't you have blood available at this hospital?"

"We do. It's just that Chance is AB positive, not the rarest type, but close to it. We gave him the single unit we had available in surgery yesterday. I was hoping he wouldn't need more, but it's best to play it safe."

"AB positive. I see." Edward gazed at Chance sleeping quietly in the bed beside them. A great sadness settled over his features. He sighed and looked at Robyn. Her heart sank. Somehow, he knew.

Martha stood up. "I need to get back to the ranch. Robyn, do you need me to bring you anything?"

"A change of clothes, that's all. The staff has given me everything else I need."

Adam opened the door. "I'll walk you out, Martha."

When the door closed behind them, Edward looked at Robyn. "Colin underwent radiation therapy for malignant lymph nodes in his groin when his cancer was first discovered. Did you know that?"

"No."

"The doctors warned us he would most likely become sterile. We were delighted when Colin announced he was getting married, but it came as quite a shock when he told us you were pregnant. My son needed numerous transfusions over the course of his illness, even before he met you. Clara and I both donated for him. We are 0 positive, and so was he. If Chance is AB positive, Colin can't be his father."

Shame burned through her body. "I have wanted to tell you for so long. Colin made me promise I wouldn't. He did it for Clara. To give her something to hang on to when he was gone. It was the only thing Colin ever asked of me. I had to do it for him. Edward, please forgive me for deceiving you. If you suspected, why didn't you say something?"

Edward's eyes filled with tears. "Because of Clara. She needed to believe that some part of Colin lived on. I guess I needed to believe that, too. Later, when her mind began to slip away, I was afraid."

"Afraid of what?"

He turned away. "I was afraid of ending up all alone, and I couldn't face that."

Robyn bolted out of her chair and threw her

arms around him. "You will always be Chance's grandpa. He loves you so much. Nothing will change that. You are part of our family. A strange, broken family, but still a family. A little thing like someone's blood type can't change that."

He patted her back awkwardly and then he held her at arm's length and studied her face. "I couldn't love Chance more if I tried. I'm sorry you've been burdened with this for so long. Neal is Chance's real father, isn't he?"

She nodded mutely. Everything was out in the open now. The burden of her secret had been lifted, and yet she'd never felt more like crying.

Edward frowned. "I can't believe Neal didn't want to be involved in Chance's life. He seems to love the boy."

This admission was the hardest to make. "He didn't know until a few weeks ago."

Edward pulled her back into his arms. "Oh, Robyn. Why hasn't Neal been here to see Chance?"

"Because I told him to go away. What am I going to do now? I've made such a mess of my life," she whispered, wishing and hoping he could tell her how to undo all the pain she had caused.

"I don't know, girl. I just don't know."

Robyn had regained her composure when Adam returned a short time later. Chance was awake by then, and Robyn explained as best she could that he would have to stay in the hospital for a few more days.

Chance's biggest concern was for Bell. He wanted to see her. Robyn assured him Bell was being taken care of. Her mother had told her that the pup had been taken to the vet and was being looked after by Neal. She had a broken leg but would be fine.

Chance, of course, wanted his cast to match the one Bell had. He thought it was cool that they would both be wearing one.

Robyn was surprised and hurt that Neal hadn't come to visit Chance. Obviously, Neal had taken her words to heart and intended to stay away. She owed him an apology. She tried calling his cell phone but got no answer.

When her mother returned, Robyn took the opportunity to step out for a few minutes.

She found Adam waiting for her. "I'm taking you to get something to eat. Don't argue."

"I'm not hungry. Besides, you've done so much already, Adam. I don't know how I would have made it through this past day without you."

"I'm glad I was there for you. I always want to be there for you."

He surprised her by kissing her firmly on the lips. She drew back and looked down at her feet. She was about to hurt someone else.

"What's wrong?" he asked.

"Adam, you have been the best possible friend to Chance and to me. I can't thank you enough for your support and comfort when I dearly needed it."

He took a step back and shoved his hands in his pockets. "I was hoping you saw me as more than a friend. I think I'm falling in love with you, Robyn."

She took a deep breath. "I admire you very much, Adam, but I'm not in love with you."

The happiness and hope faded from his face. He let go of her hand. "He doesn't deserve you."

She didn't pretend to misunderstand him. "It may be that I don't deserve him, but Neal and I will have to work that out for ourselves."

"Are you sure there isn't any hope for us? I can wait if you need more time."

"More time won't change how I feel. I'm sorry. You're a fine doctor and a wonderful man, but—"

"But not the man for you," he finished for her.

"I honestly wish things were different."

"Yes, I do, too. Go get something to eat. You need to keep your strength up. Tell Chance I'll see him in the morning. After that, I'm finished with my contract here."

"Will you be back? You're a fine doctor. If you decided to stay, everyone would be happy about it."

"I have considered it, but I think I'll go into

practice with my father in Denver. I know you won't be able to attend the nurse-practitioner program this year, but next year, there will be another scholarship recommendation waiting for you." He started to say something more, but he seemed to change his mind.

Robyn managed to choke down a sandwich and a soda in the cafeteria. Everyone stopped to talk to her and find out how Chance was doing. It was a small and close-knit hospital. She appreciated all the concern and well wishes. It took longer than she expected to get back to Chance's room.

Her mother was waiting for her with a change of clothes for Robyn lying on the chair beside her. Chance was asleep again. Robyn glanced around the room. "Where is Edward?"

"He said he would be back in the morning. I'm going to go home for a while, too. There's just so much to get done before the auction."

There was one more confession Robyn had to make. She dreaded this one more than any of the others. "Before you go, Mom, there's something I need to tell you."

Robyn sat down and quietly told her mother about the deception she had carried out for nearly five years.

"And Neal knew nothing about this?" Martha

asked when Robyn was through. She stared at Robyn as if she were a stranger.

"Not until a few weeks ago. I was upset, and I let it slip."

"I honestly don't know what to say. I find it hard to believe my own daughter could lie to all of us so easily."

Robyn rubbed her aching forehead. "Believe me, Mom, not one day of it was easy."

"Poor Edward. No wonder he left. I don't how I'm ever going to face him again. And Ellie! Chance is her grandson, and you kept it from her. Oh, Robyn, how could you do this?"

"I'm sorry, Mom. I thought I was doing the best thing for everyone. I know now I was only doing what was best for me. I wanted to hide from the pain Neal caused me. I wanted to hurt him back. He broke my heart. It felt like all our time together had been a waste. That it meant nothing."

She crossed the room to stare out the hospital window. She didn't see anything beyond the glass except the mistakes of her past. "I honestly believed I was helping Colin. He was so kind and understanding. When he proposed the idea, I jumped at the chance to turn those wasted years into something positive. I had no idea what a mess I would make of things."

"What about Neal? What happens now?"

Robyn sighed. "Yes, what about Neal? I'm not sure. He cares about Chance, I know that, but I'm not sure I can trust my heart to him. What if he breaks it all over again?"

"Maybe you should be asking if Neal can trust his heart to you? You've broken mine today. I never would have believed you could do such a thing."

She whirled to face her mother. "I've already said I'm sorry, Mom. What else can I say?"

"Maybe you could tell me the same thing you need to hear from Neal that will restore your love and trust in him."

Robyn wiped at the tears rolling down her cheeks. "I don't know what that would be."

"You're my daughter and I love you, but I've never been so disappointed in you in all my life. I've got to go home. Call me if Chance needs anything." She stormed out of the room.

Robyn sank into the chair by her son's bed and gave in to her tears.

LATE THE NEXT morning, Robyn knocked on Ellie Bryant's front door. She held her head up, but she was quaking inside when the door opened. Ellie stood there staring at her for a full second, and then she threw her arms around Robyn and pulled her into a hug.

The tears Robyn thought were finished spilled down her cheeks. "I'm sorry, I'm so sorry," she muttered.

"Hush, child. I know, I know," Ellie crooned until Robyn was able to gather herself together.

Pulling away, Robyn wiped the tears from her face. "Ellie, I need to see Neal."

"I wish you could," she answered sadly. "But he's gone."

Robyn stared at her in shock. "Gone? Gone where?"

Ellie shook her head. "I don't know where he went. He left this morning, and he took his bull-riding gear with him. I'm afraid he's gone back on the rodeo circuit."

The full import of Ellie's words sank in. Neal was gone. He had taken her cruelly spoken words to heart and left them alone. Now what did she do?

## CHAPTER TWENTY-TWO

CHANCE REMAINED IN the hospital until the day after the ranch was sold. Robyn was glad he wasn't there to watch as his childhood home passed into the hands of strangers. As it turned out, Jake Bryant bought the place for a fair price. Both Robyn and her mother were relieved. They knew he'd manage it well. He stopped by the hospital that day.

"Hey, Robyn, how's your boy?" He held his hat in his hands.

"They are letting him go home tomorrow evening."

"That's good. I wanted you to know that I bought some of the stock. Including your old horse. He can live out his life on his home range. I thought you'd want to know."

"Thanks, Jake. That makes me feel better. Have you heard from Neal?"

"He's okay. Don't worry about him."

"Do you know where he is? Can I see him?"

"He needs some time to get his head on straight. He's devastated by this."

"Is he coming back?"

"I don't know. I honestly don't know."

"When you talk to him, tell him I don't blame him. I was upset and I said some stupid things. 'd take them back if I could. Will you tell him hat for me?"

"I'll tell him."

When Jake left, Robyn sat down to cry, but she ealized she didn't have any more tears to shed.

Adam called the next morning. Their conversation was stilted. Robyn regretted the loss of the :asy friendship she'd shared with the young doc- or. They wished each other well and hung up.

Robyn kept hoping that after her conversation vith Jake that Neal would come or call. He didn't. t was if he had dropped off the face of the earth.

When Chance was finally released, Robyn took him home to the small house in Bluff Springs her mother had rented. It stood on a fenced corner lot across the street from a small park and was only a few blocks from the hospital. It would be con- venient.

Robyn stood on the front steps. Perhaps it would ook more inviting in the daylight. Now, illumi- nated only by a single street lamp and a yellow porch light, it seemed small and sad. But maybe hat was only because she was feeling small and sad. And alone.

A dog barked somewhere in the park. Robyn

thought she heard the jingle of bells. She turned to stare into the darkness, but only shadows met her gaze. She opened her truck door and helped Chance out. His surgery had left him physically drained. He gazed solemnly at the house as Robyn set his feet on the ground and steadied him.

"It doesn't look like home," he signed with difficulty.

"No, not yet, but it will." She tried to reassure him.

The sound of jingling bells came again. Robyn turned to stare at the park once more. This time movement caught her eye. A small black-and-white dog hurried out of the shadows and limped toward them. She touched Chance's shoulder, signed and pointed. "Look. It's Bell."

Chance sank to his knees and wrapped his good arm around the puppy's neck as she proceeded to lick every inch of his face. Her front leg was wrapped in a hard blue splint, but it didn't seem to bother her as she wiggled with excitement. Robyn's heart gave a happy leap. She faced the park and waited with her heart pounding in her chest. It had to be Neal. He had taken the dog with him when he left.

No handsome cowboy with a black eye patch and a wide, roguish grin appeared. Slowly, her smile faded as she waited.

*He doesn't want to see me. He can't forgive me.*

The words echoed inside her head. Her chin quivered and tears threatened to spill from her eyes. Lifting her head, she called out, "Please, Neal. I need to talk to you."

There was no answer.

After a moment, a figure stepped out of the shadows and raised a hand in a salute. It was Jake, not Neal, and her heart plummeted.

The front door opened, and her mother stood silhouetted in the light. "Who are you talking to?"

"No one," Robyn said softly. Lifting Bell, she carried the puppy into the house as Chance followed close behind her.

"You're a fool, little brother." Jake spoke to the deep shadow of an old elm.

Neal stepped out and stood beside Jake. He watched the house for a moment longer. "So I've been told," he replied.

"What are you going to do now?"

"Just what I planned."

Jake grabbed his arm as Neal turned away. "Robyn has been through hell these past few days. You heard her. She wants to talk to you."

"I don't want to talk to her. I've been through hell, too. She kept my son from me, Jake. I've tried to understand her side of it, but it still hurts. She ordered me to stay away when Chance was injured. I wasn't even entitled to information about

his condition. Don't you get it? I'm damned if
do what she wants and I'm damned if I don't. It's
time to cut my losses and get out of Dodge."

"How did this become all about you? You're
wrong, and running away won't fix things. Cowboy up and admit it."

Neal rubbed a weary hand over his face. He
wasn't angry with Robyn, he just wanted Jake
to think he was so he'd let him leave town without having this conversation. He hated admitting
the truth, but his emotions were so raw that he
couldn't hide it anymore. "Don't you get it? Robyn
does. I'm not father material. It nearly cost my
son his life to make me see that clearly. I'm just
like our old man. He knew once I had rodeo in
my blood, I'd never be good for anything else."
Shaking off his brother's hand, Neal walked back
to the truck they had parked on a side street.

It took them less than twenty minutes to reach
Jake's quarter-horse ranch. Neal walked in the
front door and turned toward the hall leading to
the bedrooms. He wasn't in the mood to spend
the evening with Connie and the kids.

Jake said, "I have something you need to see."

"Can't it wait?"

"I don't think so. Step into my office for a minute."

Neal followed his brother to the small room
made smaller by a massive wooden desk and tall

bookshelves along one wall. Photos of Jake's prize stallions and mares covered the remaining walls. He pulled three large leather-bound books from the shelf and handed them to Neal.

"I needed some stud papers from Dad's old office about a month ago. Mom was busy and couldn't find them for me, so I went hunting for them. That's when I found these in the bottom drawer of his desk. It was locked, but Mom had given me the key."

"What are they?"

He opened one and laid it flat on his desk. "They're scrapbooks. This is mine. It starts with my birth announcement and goes all the way to photos of my wedding."

What was so important about a bunch of old mementos? "So our mother likes to scrapbook. So what?"

"They aren't Mom's. Dad put these together."

"Are you serious?" Neal took a closer look.

"I was as surprised as you are. Mom knew that he kept them but never thought to mention it. This one is mine. These two are yours." Jake held out a pair of matching maroon books.

Neal opened the first one. His birth announcement graced the front page. After that came odds and ends of his childhood, including a picture he had drawn of a turkey using his hand as the outline. "Dad compiled all of this?"

"Apparently. Open the other one. I wondered why there were two for you and only one for me."

Neal opened the second scrapbook. On the first page was a yellowed newspaper write-up about his first Little Britches rodeo win. As he leafed through the pages, numerous articles gathered from newspapers and printed from online detailed his rodeo career up until his win at the Wild Bill Hickok Rodeo in Abilene just two days before his father's death.

Neal looked at Jake for some kind of explanation. "He hated the fact that I made a career out of bull riding. Why would he do this?"

"Apparently, he didn't hate what you do. I think he was very proud of what you accomplished. You only have to look at what's in your hand to see that."

"Why not tell me? He never had a single good thing to say about my riding. Nothing I did measured up to his yardstick."

"Dad was a man who didn't believe in coddling his kids or heaping praise on anyone. He kept his emotions locked inside. Was it because of the way he was raised? I doubt we'll ever know."

"I thought he was jealous of my success. I thought he couldn't stand the idea that I was a better rider than he was."

"He may have been, for all I know. Mom believes he resented having to give up the rodeo to take care of the ranch and us. But these books tell a different story."

Neal ran his hand over the carefully placed bits of paper and photos in the book. It made no sense.

Jake returned his book to the shelf and looked at Neal. "Is this what you want Chance to discover after you're gone? Do you want him to have to wait until you're dead to find out how much you loved him and how proud you were of all he accomplished?"

Neal blinked back tears. "No. Do you *know* what I would have given for an inkling of how Dad felt about anything I did? He never encouraged me, never told me to go for my dreams."

"Maybe that was because he didn't want you to resent giving them up the way he had to do when his family needed him more."

"We're guessing. We'll never know for sure."

"I know you always thought he loved me best. Of course, I am the oldest, the best looking and the smartest. However, I have one scrapbook and you have two. You should look through them. He wrote a few notes in the margins you may want to read."

Jake left the room, and Neal spent the next two hours readjusting his entire concept of his father. One note in the margin stuck out more than the others. It said, "Neal's a true chip off the old block."

If there was one thing he didn't want to be, it was a chip off the block that his father had presented to his sons. Neal wanted to be a father who treasured his child's every accomplishment, not in some leather-bound shrine but in words and deeds. In praise and encouragement. That was the way to bring up a son.

Neal closed the books and returned them to Jake's shelf.

What Robyn had done was wrong. He deserved to know his son and Chance deserved to know him. Neal needed to understand what had driven her to make such a choice. He needed to hear her side of the story.

He loved her, but he wasn't sure she would ever trust him again. The only way to find out was to stick around and be the best kind of man and the best kind of father he could be. If it wasn't enough for her, he would accept that, but he wasn't leaving. No champion belt buckle was worth more than his family.

Somehow, he knew his father would agree.

He left the office and found Jake watching TV in the living room. Jake shut the set off as soon as he caught sight of Neal. "It's an amazing collection, isn't it?"

"Eye-opening. Jake, I need a job. Any suggestions?"

Jake grinned. "I was hoping you would say that.

I'm expanding my breeding program to include Appaloosas. I recently bought a nice little ranch nearby. What would you think about managing that part of my operation?"

"For a salary or for shares?"

"Shares? You're getting ahead of yourself, little brother. It's all my capital. Salary for now, but you could live on the place rent-free until the program starts turning a profit, and then we will talk about shares."

"I've seen some really good pickup riders on Appaloosas. They've got heart. Would you let me train some for that?"

"I was thinking more along the lines of raising and training roping and cutting horses, but I'm always open to new ideas. I would need someone with some good inside rodeo contacts for that, wouldn't I?"

Neal smiled. "Yes, you would."

ROBYN WENT THROUGH the motions and managed to get through each day, but she desperately wanted to speak to Neal. When she questioned Ellie about him, Robyn didn't learn anything new. Only that he had been in contact with Jake but not with his mother.

Surprised by the information, she was even more surprised when Ellie explained the reason one evening when she had come to visit Martha.

Ellie had also suspected Chance was Neal's son, and Neal blamed his mother for not telling him.

Jake flatly refused her requests for information about Neal. "He's fine," he said when Robyn called him at his ranch.

"Jake, I need to talk to him. Please, can't you tell me how to get in touch with him? At least let me tell him Chance is doing well now. I know he would want to know that."

"He knows," Jake assured her. "I've told him everything that's happened. He's doing what he needs to do. Don't give up on him."

Encouraged by his words, she asked, "Do you think he can ever forgive me?"

"He's a stubborn man, but I believe he will, in time."

"Thanks, Jake. Tell him for me— Just tell him Chance misses him and asks about him every day."

Ellie became a frequent visitor at their new house, and while Robyn was glad for her mother's sake, she still found it a painful reminder that Neal had chosen to stay away from her and from his son.

"Jake has a renter for your old house. I understand he's already moved in," Ellie announced one afternoon when Chance had been home for a week. She sat with Martha and Robyn on the front porch and watched Chance toss a small ball over and over to an eager Bell. They both still wore their matching blue casts.

"I hope the new renter likes the place," Martha said. "I know it's silly, but I hate the idea of someone changing the wallpaper that Frank and I picked out together."

"You'll have a chance to find out. Jake says the man found a box of photos and papers. They must belong to you."

Martha smiled brightly. "Oh, my goodness, I've been looking everywhere for the box with the photographs that belonged to my mother. I must have left them behind. Everything was such a jumble, what with Chance in the hospital and all. Oh, but I don't think I can bear to go back out there yet. Robyn, do you think you could run out and pick them up?"

"I don't know if I'm ready to go back there yet, either."

"Please," Martha pleaded. "Those photographs mean so much to me. They're all I have left of my mother."

"All right, I'll go out in the morning."

"Good." Ellie stood. "I'll have Jake let the man know you're coming. Martha, walk me to my car, won't you?"

"Of course."

Beside her car, Ellie glanced back at Robyn and Chance still sitting on the porch and waved. She and Martha exchanged a few words and a brief hug; then Ellie drove off.

Robyn pulled into her old driveway the next morning and for a moment she thought she would cry after all. It wasn't because she missed the buildings or the corrals or the flowers along the walk. It was because everything in front of her reminded her of Neal.

The last time he'd kissed her they had been standing in front of the white picket gate before they left to go to the fair. She had been so happy that morning, and yet her life had been turned upside down and nearly destroyed only a few hours later.

It seemed that since the accident, every minute of her life had been devoted to caring for Chance. Now, with Chance on the road to a full recovery, she found herself at a loss. All she could think about was Neal.

Where was he? She'd pored over the rodeo news, but there was never any mention of his name. Was he all right? She could only hope that one day she would have the chance to tell him how sorry she was for the way she had treated him.

Stepping out of the truck, she saw a man down in the corral beside the barn. The cowboy held the front hoof of a small white horse between his knees. He was bent over and his black hat obscured his face as he filed the hoof with a large rasp. Apparently, he hadn't heard her drive in. She looked more closely at the horse. Was that Babe?

Moving toward the corral, Robyn's heart began to hammer painfully in her chest. There was something familiar about the man, too, but she didn't dare hope.

# CHAPTER TWENTY-THREE

BABE WAS BECOMING impatient with the process of getting his hoof filed. Neal felt the little horse shifting his weight from one hind leg to the other, but Neal was determined to finish the job he'd started. Never at a loss to try to gain attention, Babe reached his head around and flipped Neal's hat off.

"You worthless piece of buzzard bait," Neal muttered. "You're not getting off this time. We're going to finish your feet whether you like it or not. Do you want to wind up lame? Robyn will rip me up one side and down the other if I let that happen."

Babe tossed his head and tried to pull away, but Neal held on to his hoof. Babe changed his tactics. After pulling a mouthful of hay from the bale in front of him, the little horse swung his head around and flung it on Neal's bare neck.

Dropping Babe's hoof, Neal stood up as the leaves and stalks of alfalfa trickled down inside his shirt. "You miserable nag."

He threw down his file, yanked off his gloves

and began to unbutton his shirt. "I'm going to make glue out of you yet." He took off his shirt, shook it out then brushed at the back of his neck and his hair with both hands. A sharp indrawn hiss of breath alerted him to the presence of someone else. He looked up and met Robyn's wide eyes across the fence. He wasn't prepared to face her yet.

"Neal, what are you doing here?"

He swallowed hard. "I live here now. How is Chance?"

"He's better. He thinks it's cool that he and Bell have matching casts. You live here?"

"Yes." At least she wasn't shouting at him.

He put his shirt back on and picked up his hat. This was his chance to convince her nothing like that would ever happen again. "Robyn, I need to say how sorry I am for almost getting him killed. It was stupid. There wasn't any reason to prove I was still the big, brave, bull rider. I hope you believe me, and I hope someday you can find it in your heart to forgive me. I will never, ever put my needs in front of his needs again. I swear that to you on my life."

When she didn't say anything, he looked down and kicked the dirt with his boot.

TEARS STUNG ROBYN'S eyes as she saw the pain on his face. She wanted to throw her arms around him and hold him close. She gripped the fence with both hands, struggling to put all her regrets into words. "I'm so sorry for the hurtful things I said to you, for the way I treated you. I'm sorry for so many things. I'm sorry that I tried to make you into something you couldn't be. I'm sorry I ran away instead of facing what was wrong between us, and I am so very, very sorry that I kept your son away from you."

He stood with his head bowed, and she waited for him to speak. He looked at her finally. "You were dead wrong about that."

"I know." A tear trickled down her cheek.

He reached the fence in two long strides and gripped the rail. "Help me understand why you did it. Tell me about Colin."

She drew a ragged breath and faced him squarely. "I was so hurt by your betrayal, but more than that, I was angry with you for not needing me the way I needed you. I couldn't see then what I realize now. We were headstrong kids, both too stubborn to try to change. Too stubborn to admit we were wrong, or even that we needed help."

"I did need you, Robyn. I just didn't know how much until after you were gone."

She studied his face as she asked the question that had haunted her days and nights. "Why didn't you ask me to come back?"

He looked down and scuffed the dirt with the

toe of his boot. "Because I was ashamed. I betrayed you—my best friend. And I betrayed myself. I didn't much care for the man who looked back at me in the mirror for those next few months. I knew you wanted a life away from the rodeo circuit, a home and kids and a husband who wasn't putting his life on the line day after day. When you didn't come back, I figured it was because you'd finally realized I wasn't the man who could give you those things."

"Neal, I did want those things, but I wanted them with you."

"After what I did, I knew you deserved better. Besides, a man has to have some pride. I couldn't find it in me to beg you to come back."

"I thought you didn't want me."

He stared at her face for a long moment and then said quietly, "Tweety, I've wanted you every single day and every single night since the day we first made love when we were seventeen."

She turned away from him. All this time. All this wasted time and heartache because they had been too proud, too hurt and stubborn to face each other. They'd wound up running away from each other instead of trying to save the friendship and love they shared.

She looked at the bright blue sky overhead. A lone hawk rode the air currents in wide lazy circles. She was tired of being alone. She had to find a way back to him. *Please, God, let me make him understand. Let me get this right.*

She began to speak softly. "My father recovered from his first stroke, but I could see he would never be as strong as he had been. He and Mom were going to need me to help take care of him sooner or later. When he was in the hospital, one of his nurses told me about a two-year nursing program at the junior college. I thought it would be a good way to stay close to home and have a job where I could do some good."

She gave a wry laugh. "Nurses are always needed. Anyway, I enrolled and started the program in less than a month. I met Colin my first day of class. He was so pale and thin. My mothering instincts took off full blast. He was someone who really needed me."

She stopped and looked at Neal. "I don't want you to think it was merely pity, because it wasn't. We became good friends. He was so full of life, so determined to beat his illness. He joked about it all the time."

She could picture Colin's infectious grin even now, and she smiled softly.

"What was wrong with him?"

"He had Hodgkin's disease, a form of cancer that often strikes young adults. He never made a secret of it. I think he wanted me to understand right from the start that he might not have a long life. I knew, but I was still terrified when he had an acute attack and was hospitalized."

She gazed at Neal's impassive face. "After all, I had already lost one best friend, or so I thought."

"He was a lucky man to have found you."

"Soon after that, I discovered I was pregnant. I didn't know what to do. I told Colin. He said I should tell you, but I didn't know how. I wrote you a dozen letters, but I couldn't send any of them."

"Why not?"

"Because I was afraid."

"Of what?"

"I was afraid you wouldn't care one way or the other. At least, that's what I told myself."

She tilted her head, studying his tall, lean form. She saw so much in him that reminded her of Chance. His long, sturdy fingers, the shape of his eyebrows and the way his lips tightened when he was angry.

"In reality, I wanted to hurt you as badly as you'd hurt me. Not very noble of me, was it?"

His lips tightened then, but she knew it wasn't anger. It was pain.

"Besides, I was afraid of trapping you. You were always so carefree. That wild Bryant boy, so full of adventure and so eager to see what was over the next hill. I knew what the rodeo meant to you. I didn't want to destroy that. In my own stupid way, I was trying to protect you. You would have insisted we get married, and you would have resented it every single day."

They both fell silent for a long time. Finally, he pushed his hat back and rested one boot on the bottom rail of the fence. "What happened after that?"

She let out a long sigh. At least he was willing to listen to her side of the story without getting angry.

"I told Colin about my decision, and he asked me to marry him. He begged me, really. He said he wanted a child more than anything in the world, my child, and I believed him. I think he knew he wasn't going to beat his cancer."

Robyn bit her lip as the memories of those tragic final days played out in her mind. She gave a quick shake of her head to dispel them and continued, "As enlightened as the world is today, I still didn't relish the idea of telling my parents I was pregnant. Colin, on the other hand, couldn't wait to tell his. Clara had been in frail health for years. Colin needed to give his mother something to live for. He wanted to give her a grandchild, but he knew time was against him. I was the answer he'd been praying for. He needed me, and I needed someone who needed me. So we got married."

"And you let everyone believe my son was the son of another man. It was that easy?"

"Easy?" She took several long strides along the

fence before she stopped. She crossed her arms tightly and turned to face him.

"Easy? No, it wasn't easy. Chance was born a month after Colin died. Every time Edward or Clara saw something about him that reminded them of Colin, I wanted to crawl away and die. What a cruel trick I was playing on them. They tried to help me out with money while I was in school, but I couldn't take it. I know they only wanted to help, but each gift, each savings bond for the baby, each suggestion that Chance was sure to want to follow in his father's footsteps and study science was salt in a wound of guilt that never healed."

"So why didn't you tell them?"

"Because—" Her voice cracked, and she pressed a hand to her trembling lips. "Because Colin made me promise. He was dying. He made me promise I'd never tell. I didn't tell anyone until after I saw you being wheeled into the emergency room. I knew then that I had made a terrible mistake."

NEAL COULD SEE Robyn struggle to control her tears. He wanted to take her in his arms and kiss away all the hurt he'd caused. They'd hurt each other enough. Nothing could bring back those lost years. If he took it, he had the chance now to make amends, but he stood on one side of the fence, and she stood on the other. If they were going to stop hurting each other, they would have to both be on the same side.

She had become a strong and independent woman, and she wouldn't come to him for comfort. She'd followed him around from the time she had learned to walk and begged for his attention, and he had taken her love for granted.

Well, not anymore. Not ever again. The time for talking was past. He turned and walked toward the gate. This time it was up to him.

Robyn saw him walking away. Panic engulfed her. He had to understand. He had to forgive her. She had to make him stay and listen to how sorry she was. How could she?

A coiled lariat hung over a fence post beside her. She grabbed it, shook out a loop, put one foot up on the fence and let fly. She'd once been the best heeler in the county.

Neal never knew what happened until he found himself facedown in the dirt with a rope around his boots. "What the hell?"

Robyn came over the fence and jerked the rope tight before he could loosen it. With purposeful strides, she moved to stand over him.

"What was this for?" he demanded.

She jerked hard on the rope. "You're not going anywhere until I've had my say. You are going to listen to me, and you are going to hear me."

He rested back on his elbows. "All right, Robyn. Have at it."

"I'm sorry!" she shouted. "Do you hear me? I'm sorry for taking Chance away from you."

"I hear you loud and clear."

"Chance loves you. He needs you to be part of his life. He deserves it and so do you."

"All right," he agreed slowly. "I'm living here. I fully intend to see my son as often as I can. I would love to adopt him so there will never be a question in his mind about whether or not his father loves him. Did you have something else you wanted to say, or can I get up now?"

She drew a deep breath. "Yes, I have more to say. I love you, and I need you to be part of my life, too. I don't want to face a future without you in it. You complete me in so many ways that I can't even count them all. That's it. I love you."

"Sounds like you want me to marry you."

"Well, yes."

"Okay."

She stared down at him for a long moment as his reply sank in. "Okay? Just like that?"

"Can I get up now?" A grin tugged at the corner of his mouth.

"Ah, yes. Did you just say okay, you'll marry me?"

He slipped the rope off his boots and stood to face her. "Come here." He held open his arms.

With a glad cry, she flung herself against him "I thought you were going to walk away again. had to make you stay and listen to me."

"I was going to go around to the gate. I didn' think I could leap over the fence. My ribs are stil sore."

She pulled away and stared at him in horror. "Oh, my God, did I hurt you?"

He pulled her back into his embrace. "It only hurts when you aren't kissing me."

Joy welled up in her heart and overflowed. " can fix that. I'm a nurse," she whispered.

Cupping his face, she kissed him with all the pent-up longing of the past lonely years.

He broke off the kiss and held her close. "I love you, Robyn, but there is something you should know."

"I don't care if you want to go back to the rodeo. We'll wait at home for you, or travel with you, if that's what you want."

"No, my riding days are over. I meant it when I said you and Chance were more important. I only rode that last time to prove to myself that I could do it. To conquer my fear."

His hands dropped away from her. "This concerns Chance."

Worry creased her brow. "I'm listening."

"Chance is deaf because of me."

She shook her head. "I don't understand."

"My father had a brother who was born deaf. Chance inherited his deafness through me. So might any other children we have."

The glow of her happiness faded from her face as she stared at him. "Do you mean you don't want more children?"

"No, I don't mean that." He crushed her in a tight embrace. "Of course I want more children with you, Robyn. I don't care if they are deaf or twins like Jake's or green as eggs and ham. I just want you to know what you're facing. I'll understand if you don't want to take the risk."

Could she face having another deaf child? The prospect didn't frighten her as it once had. With Neal beside her, she could face any problem that life dealt her. He was her other half, the piece of her that had been missing for so long.

He held her away and looked into her eyes. "I want another Chance. I want another son or daughter. Hell, I want a dozen Chances, and I want them to grow up on this ranch. My plan is to raise and train horses with Jake and someday buy this spread from him. The place needs a little fixing up, but the thing this ranch needs most is a family. Our family. Call me old-fashioned, but I like to do the asking. Will you marry me, Robyn O'Connor Morgan?"

"Yes," Robyn whispered, her happiness all but

choking her with the emotions that swelled inside her heart.

Neal gazed tenderly at the face of the woman who haunted his dreams, and he marveled at the love that shone in her eyes. Fate had brought him back to her. Now it was up to him to keep her in his arms. Now it would be up to him to show her just how much he needed her. She would never doubt that again.

"I can't live without you, Robyn. I know because I tried. I need you. I need your love now and for always."

"For always?" A beautiful smile trembled on her lips. She arched one eyebrow. "That's a pretty long time, cowboy."

"For always and forever, Tweety. For always and forever."

He bent to kiss her once more. As her soft lips parted beneath his, he knew forever wouldn't be long enough to show her how much he loved her. But it would be a start.

* * * * *

# LARGER-PRINT BOOKS!
## GET 2 FREE LARGER-PRINT NOVELS PLUS
## 2 FREE GIFTS!

**HARLEQUIN**

*super romance*

## More Story...More Romance

**YES!** Please send me 2 FREE LARGER-PRINT Harlequin® Superromance® novels and my 2 FREE gifts (gifts are worth about $10). After receiving them, if I don't wish to receive any more books, I can return the shipping statement marked "cancel." If I don't cancel, I will receive 6 brand-new novels every month and be billed just $5.69 per book in the U.S. or $5.99 per book in Canada. That's a savings of at least 16% off the cover price! It's quite a bargain! Shipping and handling is just 50¢ per book in the U.S. or 75¢ per book in Canada.* I understand that accepting the 2 free books and gifts places me under no obligation to buy anything. I can always return a shipment and cancel at any time. Even if I never buy another book, the two free books and gifts are mine to keep forever.

139/339 HDN F46Y

Name _____ (PLEASE PRINT) _____

Address _____ Apt. # _____

City _____ State/Prov. _____ Zip/Postal Code _____

Signature (if under 18, a parent or guardian must sign) _____

### Mail to the **Harlequin® Reader Service:**
**IN U.S.A.:** P.O. Box 1867, Buffalo, NY 14240-1867
**IN CANADA:** P.O. Box 609, Fort Erie, Ontario L2A 5X3

**Are you a current subscriber to Harlequin Superromance books
and want to receive the larger-print edition?
Call 1-800-873-8635 today or visit www.ReaderService.com.**

\* Terms and prices subject to change without notice. Prices do not include applicable taxes. Sales tax applicable in N.Y. Canadian residents will be charged applicable taxes. Offer not valid in Quebec. This offer is limited to one order per household. Not valid for current subscribers to Harlequin Superromance Larger-Print books. All orders subject to credit approval. Credit or debit balances in a customer's account(s) may be offset by any other outstanding balance owed by or to the customer. Please allow 4 to 6 weeks for delivery. Offer available while quantities last.

**Your Privacy**—The Harlequin® Reader Service is committed to protecting your privacy. Our Privacy Policy is available online at www.ReaderService.com or upon request from the Harlequin Reader Service.

We make a portion of our mailing list available to reputable third parties that offer products we believe may interest you. If you prefer that we not exchange your name with third parties, or if you wish to clarify or modify your communication preferences, please visit us at www.ReaderService.com/consumerschoice or write to us at Harlequin Reader Service Preference Service, P.O. Box 9062, Buffalo, NY 14269. Include your complete name and address.

HSRLP13R

# LARGER-PRINT BOOKS!

## GET 2 FREE LARGER-PRINT NOVELS PLUS

## 2 FREE GIFTS!

### ◆ HARLEQUIN®

*Romance*

### From the Heart, For the Heart

**YES!** Please send me 2 FREE LARGER-PRINT Harlequin® Romance novels and my 2 FREE gifts (gifts are worth about $10). After receiving them, if I don't wish to receive any more books, I can return the shipping statement marked "cancel." If I don't cancel, I will receive 4 brand-new novels every month and be billed just $4.84 per book in the U.S. or $5.24 per book in Canada. That's a savings of at least 19% off the cover price! It's quite a bargain! Shipping and handling is just 50¢ per book in the U.S. and 75¢ per book in Canada.* I understand that accepting the 2 free books and gifts places me under no obligation to buy anything. I can always return a shipment and cancel at any time. Even if I never buy another book, the two free books and gifts are mine to keep forever.

119/319 HDN F43Y

| Name | (PLEASE PRINT) | |
|------|------|------|

| Address | | Apt. # |
|------|------|------|

| City | State/Prov. | Zip/Postal Code |
|------|------|------|

Signature (if under 18, a parent or guardian must sign)

Mail to the **Harlequin® Reader Service:**
**IN U.S.A.:** P.O. Box 1867, Buffalo, NY 14240-1867
**IN CANADA:** P.O. Box 609, Fort Erie, Ontario L2A 5X3
**Want to try two free books from another line?**
**Call 1-800-873-8635 or visit www.ReaderService.com.**

* Terms and prices subject to change without notice. Prices do not include applicable taxes. Sales tax applicable in N.Y. Canadian residents will be charged applicable taxes. Offer not valid in Quebec. This offer is limited to one order per household. Not valid for current subscribers to Harlequin Romance Larger-Print books. All orders subject to credit approval. Credit or debit balances in a customer's account(s) may be offset by any other outstanding balance owed by or to the customer. Please allow 4 to 6 weeks for delivery. Offer available while quantities last.

**Your Privacy**—The Harlequin® Reader Service is committed to protecting your privacy. Our Privacy Policy is available online at www.ReaderService.com or upon request from the Harlequin Reader Service.

We make a portion of our mailing list available to reputable third parties that offer products we believe may interest you. If you prefer that we not exchange your name with third parties, or if you wish to clarify or modify your communication preferences, please visit us at www.ReaderService.com/consumerschoice or write to us at Harlequin Reader Service Preference Service, P.O. Box 9062, Buffalo, NY 14269. Include your complete name and address.

# *Reader Service*.com

## Manage your account online!

- Review your order history
- Manage your payments
- Update your address

---

*We've designed
the Harlequin® Reader Service
website just for you.*

---

## Enjoy all the features!

- Reader excerpts from any series
- Respond to mailings and
  special monthly offers
- Discover new series available to you
- Browse the Bonus Bucks catalog
- Share your feedback

*Visit us at:*
## ReaderService.com